DEATH AMONG THE UNDEAD

SHIJINSO NO SATSUJIN

DEATH AMONG THE UNDEAD

Masahiro Imamura

Introduction by Soji Shimada

Translated by Ho-Ling Wong

Death Among the Undead

SHIJINSO NO SATSUJIN
Copyright © Imamura Masahiro 2017
English translation rights arranged with
TOKYO SOGENSHA CO., LTD
through Japan UNI Agency, Inc, Tokyo

Death Among the Undead
English translation copyright © by John Pugmire 2021

For information, contact: pugmire1@yahoo.com

FIRST AMERICAN EDITION
Library of Congress Cataloguing-in-Publication Data
Imamura, Masahiro
[*SHIJINSO NO SATSUJIN* English]
SHIJINSO NO SATSUJIN / Masahiro Imamura
Translated from the Japanese by Ho-Ling Wong

CONTENTS

Introduction:
Death Among the Undead
Sōji Shimada

Death Among the Undead was first released in Japan in 2017 as the winner of the 27th Ayukawa Tetsuya Award, organised by Tokyo Sogensha. This award is one of Japan's most prestigious for debuting mystery novelists. The book's reception showed that Japanese fans of the mystery genre had been craving a *honkaku* (orthodox) mystery novel of this kind. Upon its release, *Death Among the Undead* won the Honkaku Mystery Award, as well as the number one spot in all the major annual mystery rankings published in Japan. This debut work by an unknown newcomer became a smash hit, with the original publication reaching more than 200,000 copies in print.

Death Among the Undead was, simply put, a social phenomenon. Its unprecedented reception is closely linked to historical reasons unique to Japan and the book is therefore unlikely to have caused the same waves had it first been published in the West. Even the author, Masahiro Imamura, was probably surprised by the enormous impact his book made. I will take a look at the unique factors that made its success possible, in the hope that my analysis will prove to be a great help for people outside Japan to understand Japanese mystery fiction culture.

First, I want to focus on the topic of the newcomer awards for mystery fiction in Japan. You will find countless literary awards for debuting novelists around the world, but for some reason newcomer awards specifically for mystery fiction only exist in Japan. To be strictly precise, they only exist in Japan and Taiwan, but since I am the organiser of the latter, one could consider that award to belong in the same category as the Japanese awards.

In the United Kingdom there are the Dagger Awards, but those awards do not include a publishing contract for winning submissions. China had several newcomer awards in the past that also encompassed mystery fiction, but none of them lasted for long. Russia didn't have one until last year, when a major television station started organising a grand mystery award that included categories for mystery films, television dramas and prose fiction. One of the categories was also a newcomer award for printed material. I was involved with this project as a jury member, but the submissions were not from Russian authors, but were all published books from recently debuted authors from the United States, the United Kingdom and Canada.

In Japan, however, there are several newcomer awards for unpublished mystery fiction. Most of them are for novels and include a publishing contract for the winning submission. The reason why Japanese mystery fiction has flourished so much, and why there's always a steady supply of new talent, is directly connected to the fact there are so many newcomer awards. Locked Room International has in the past published *The Decagon House Murders*, *The Moai Island Puzzle* and *The 8 Mansion Murders*. Like *Death Among the Undead*, these were all works written as submissions for newcomer awards.

However, none of those works even made it to the final selection, which is why it took a relatively long time before they received the appreciation they deserved. *Death Among the Undead,* on the other hand, not only won the Ayukawa Tetsuya Award in 2017, but also managed a clean sweep of all the accolades a debuting mystery author could achieve. The book had the best start possible, becoming an instant best-seller upon release. It is worth studying the historical factors which led to such a success, so allow me to briefly discuss the evolution of Japanese detective fiction.

To do so, we must go back to the nineteenth century, when Edgar Allan Poe and Arthur Conan Doyle created a new genre known as detective fiction, which emphasised deduction and the scientific method. The Japanese, who have always had an exceptionally strong love of mysteries and are always interested in new fads, took a look at this new genre, but it was only the cultural elite who imported the stories. The new genre did not find a foothold amongst the general reading public until the twentieth century.

It was during the democratic society of the Taishō period (1912-1926) that Edogawa Rampo, the father of Japanese detective fiction, made his debut, hoping to secure a place for the new literary genre in his country. Early in his career, Rampo wrote short scientific detective stories in the tradition of Doyle, but the Japanese were not yet ready for the purely scientific method, so he started targeting the masses in a more calculated manner, taking the greatest sources of amusement from the eighteenth century: show tents and *kibyōshi*, yellow-covered picture books reminiscent of comics. Simply put, Rampo combined the horrors of London freak shows like the Elephant Man with elements from popular erotic fiction. The combination served as a basis for Rampo's detective stories about freakish crimes and the investigation into those cases.

The approach worked and the Rampo style became a hit in Japan, ushering in a new era of mystery fiction which was nothing at all like the works of Poe and Doyle. The authors who followed in Rampo's footsteps knew nothing about the past, and mistakenly thought that detective stories were simply a new variation of the popular entertainment with erotic elements they knew from the Edo Period (1603-1867). As a result, detective stories quickly degenerated into the type of stories one couldn't read in the train or out in public. Consequently, people involved with mainstream literature looked down at detective stories with disdain, and there was no place for detective novelists in the literary world.

It was Seichō Matsumoto, winner of the Akutagawa Prize, who saved the detective novel from this desperate situation. He was a lover of classic literature, with an interest in the naturalism of Guy de Maupassant and Émile Zola. Due to straightened circumstances, he needed to take care of several family members, so it became vital that his work would do well commercially. He decided to try his hand at detective fiction.

Seichō Matsumoto's concept of the detective story, however, was radically different from that of Poe, Doyle, and Rampo. Not for him the Sherlock Holmes-esque private detective, or criminals using fancy tricks to commit their crimes. It was only the professional police detective with the proper qualifications who could carry out a criminal investigation, and it was the motive behind the crime, the criminal's personal circumstances, and the realistic depiction of the people involved that were important.

His works were commercially as successful as Rampo's had been, and his naturalist style garnered high praise from a literary point of view. Detective novels were no longer automatically despised, and Seichō Matsumoto became an idolised figure.

Thus the world of detective fiction became entranced by what would later be known as the Spell of Seichō and what became known as the social school. It became taboo to write stories using the horror and erotic elements from the Rampo-style stories. It was those elements that had led detective novelists to their predicament in the past, and could have done the same in the future.

In turning its back on those who had been influenced by Rampo's work, the publishing industry committed a grave error, however.

There were already some authors writing *honkaku*-style mysteries, even though the term had not yet been coined and was not clearly defined. But, because *honkaku* elements and the Holmes-type character had been featured in the Rampo-style detective stories, *honkaku* and the great detective were also foolishly seen as part of the Rampo tradition and rejected as well, even though they were completely unrelated.

Writing in the naturalist Seichō style became virtually the law, and no newcomers were allowed to debut unless they followed the social school. The strong hunger for true *honkaku* mystery fiction, particularly amongst the youngsters belonging to university mystery clubs, was only fuelled by this suppression, however.

It was under these circumstances that I, quite recklessly, made my debut with *The Tokyo Zodiac Murders* and *Murder in the Crooked House*. To borrow the words of Yukito Ayatsuji: 'It was a shock that mystery novels like those were still allowed to be written in a time like this.'

Ayatsuji had approached me and asked for my help, as he wanted to become a published novelist, too. Luckily, there was also an editor at the publisher Kodansha who also understood *honkaku* well, and together we helped Ayatsuji make his debut with *The Decagon House Murders*. This is how the *shin honkaku* boom started in Japan. I myself had expected that the Seichō-style social school and the *shin honkaku* school would compete with each other, but by then the Seichō trend had passed and the public was ready for something new.

Unfortunately, due to their total suppression during the Seichō years, the veteran *honkaku* writers had virtually disappeared, so that when the first young *shin honkaku* novelists made their debut, the only experienced detective novelists were those from the social school, which is why the writers who made the *shin honkaku* movement possible were all so young. This was an unprecedented happening, even when seen in an international context. It didn't take long for the traditional Japanese mechanisms to start, with the older generation reprimanding this younger generation of novelists and verbally abusing them under the pretext of "helping them grow up." The young *shin honkaku* generation was thus treated coldly at first.

With hindsight, these young novelists, who had mostly belonged to university mystery clubs, had a very narrow definition of what *honkaku* mystery fiction actually entailed. Their ideal was the country house murder mystery, as advocated by the American S.S. Van Dine. They looked at what Van Dine had written and said during his lifetime and found their ideal format for a *shin honkaku* detective story, which would have all or most of the following elements: the suspicious country house or mansion with its equally suspicious inhabitants; the necessary information about the characters all presented to the reader at an early stage. A locked room murder occurs with no apparent motive. A great detective is invited to the mansion from the outside world, who uses only information the reader also has to make their deductions. A second murder occurs. And in the end, the detective outsmarts the reader by pointing out the surprising murderer and logically explains how they arrived at their conclusion.

Based on their knowledge of the history of modern detective fiction, the young *shin honkaku* generation had decided that the genre's apex was this approach of S.S. Van Dine. They followed the format and expected others to adhere to its rules. As explained above, there were no veterans who could correct their narrow views, and so this limited vision of what *shin honkaku* detective fiction should be would bind the industry in precisely the same way that the Spell of Seichō had done before.

The fact that Ayatsuji's novel, the first work in the *shin honkaku* movement, followed the Van Dine format led to much praise from university mystery club fans. But, in reality, *The Decagon House Murders* was written with very different intentions. Whilst conforming to the country house murder mystery format, the novel was written using narrative techniques concepts that Van Dine never employed. The *shin honkaku* movement was able to bring forth revolutionary change in the world of mystery fiction, precisely because *The Decagon House Murders* was not blindly following an existing format.

But, in a way reminiscent of the Rampo era, those who followed in Ayatsuji's footsteps missed that point or intentionally ignored it. Adherence to S.S. Van Dine's ideal format became a requirement for commercial success. So it was that Takemaru Abiko, a gifted and versatile author in his own right, wrote *The 8 Mansion Murders* to follow the simple format of the country house murder mystery without adding much by way of plot (but much by way of humour). As with Rampo and Seichō, the mass production of stories in a predetermined style did not lead to the kind of originality that lasts for generations, but it was nevertheless the style which would come to rule the literary world of Japanese detective fiction for another twenty years.

But rigid adherence to one particular style eventually has a stifling effect on originality, and *shin honkaku* began to suffer the same fate

11

as the Rampo style and the Spell of Seichō had done before. Its myriad supporters, still loyal to the closed circle setting and the country manor, were nevertheless getting frustrated by the lack of new ideas and yearned for the kind of impetus that *The Decagon House Murders* had created. After a long wait, a new mansion appeared like manna from heaven. It was the Villa Violet of *Death Among the Undead*.

It would not be an exaggeration to say that fans of *shin honkaku* fiction metaphorically danced for joy as they welcomed this novel. That is basically what really happened. Japanese fans of *shin honkaku* fiction loved the closed circle situation and had thus long awaited a work like this. This is one of the reasons why, when *Death Among the Undead* won the Ayukawa Tetsuya Award, every praise imaginable was heaped upon the book.

Masahiro Imamura, author of *Death Among the Undead*, correctly noted that *The Decagon House Murders*, the starting point of *shin honkaku*, was at its core a closed circle murder mystery, but with unique narrative techniques used to present the tale. He knew that, just like Ayatsuji before him, he needed to add an extra original factor to the core format. Imamura's choice: zombies.

At first sight, the concept of zombies might sound outrageous, but in *Death Among the Undead* their supernatural powers double, nay, triple the amount of entertainment the book provides. The almost manga-like presence of these beings brings thrills and suspense to the story, and provides unexpected new developments of the country house murder mystery we thought we knew inside-out. This is because Imamura simultaneously maintains the necessary rigour of the locked room mystery by making the zombies bound by strict rules governing their behaviour and even their existence.

Despite the rigour, the plot of *Death Among the Undead* does signal a revolutionary change for the mystery genre. The core elements of any classic murder mystery are the killer, the victim and the murder weapon, and the lines between these three elements are never crossed. Zombies, however, can change from one element to another. A zombie can be the killer, the victim and even a powerful murder weapon. Such a concept changes the very foundations of the mystery story, which is why *Death Among the Undead* is a masterpiece of the genre.

It had always been an iron law in mystery fiction to only build on reality. It was feared that ignoring this rule by incorporating sci-fi or horror elements would lead too easily to perfect crimes. Many traditional fans of the detective genre are against violating the rule of realism for that reason.

But this law is perhaps already outdated. In a time where technology has enveloped society in a web of computer networks, authors are likely to try their hands at fantastical elements in near-futuristic settings, like zombies. The detective stories of Poe and Doyle were a result of the absolute belief in the science of that time, so one can't dismiss the new changes appropriate to our own times.

We are entering a time in Asian regions where we are looking for stories that add something new and original when it comes to creative *honkaku* fiction. For the Soji Shimada Mystery Award held in Taiwan, I myself have been advocating the notion of "twenty-first century *honkaku*" and, lately, I have seen country house murder mysteries which utilise artificial intelligence as a new and original element.

Whether these movements will open up new grounds like *shin honkaku* did in the past is something we need to keep an eye on. However things ultimately turn out, *Death Among the Undead* is undeniably the work that has forced our first steps towards this new world, and in that regard I feel that it is a work of great importance.

Sōji Shimada

Tokyo, August 7, 2021

LIST OF CHARACTERS

Yuzuru Hamura: Economics student at Shinkō University (1st yr). Mystery Society member.

Kyōsuke Akechi: Science (3rd yr). President of the Mystery Society. The Holmes of Shinkō.

Hiruko Kenzaki: Literature (2nd yr). Detective who has helped solve numerous cases.

Ayumu Shindō: Arts (3rd yr). President of the Film Club.

Reika Hoshikawa: Arts (3rd yr). Drama Club member. Shindō's girlfriend.

Sumie Nabari: Arts (2nd yr). Drama Club member. Nervous personality.

Rin Takagi: Economics (3rd yr). Film Club member. Looks after others.

Mifuyu Shizuhara: Medicine (1st yr). Film Club member. Mild-mannered.

Takako Kudamatsu: Sociology (3rd yr). Film Club member. Cheerful and determined.

Mitsuru Shigemoto: Science (2nd yr). Film Club member. Fan of a certain film genre.

Kanemitsu Nanamiya: Film Club alumnus. Son of the owner of the Villa Violet.

Tobio Deme: Shinkō University alumnus. Nanamiya's friend.

Haruya Tatsunami: Shinkō University alumnus. Nanamiya's friend.

Yuito Kanno: Manager of the Villa Violet.

Tomonori Hamasaka: Associate-professor in biology at Gisen University.

Eitatsu Madarame: Person of wealth from Okayama Prefecture. Founder of the Madarame Organisation.

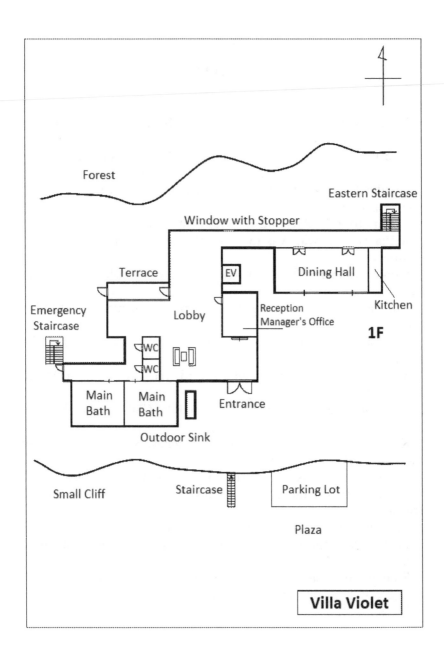

Forest

Eastern Staircase

Window with Stopper

Terrace

EV

Dining Hall

Kitchen

Emergency
Staircase

Lobby

Reception
Manager's Office

1F

WC

WC

Main
Bath

Main
Bath

Entrance

Outdoor Sink

Small Cliff

Staircase

Parking Lot

Plaza

Villa Violet

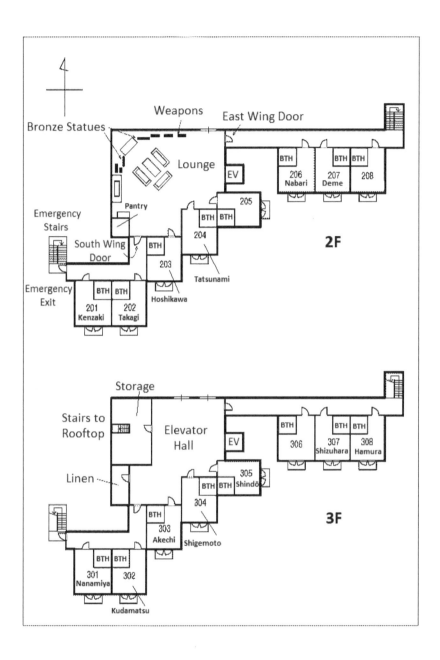

PROLOGUE

Dear Hiruko Kenzaki,

I trust you are well. Small talk is not my forte, so allow me to get right to the point. Attached you will find the requested report, with my findings concerning the group known as The Madarame Organisation.

I myself have found the information detailed within to be extremely singular and highly disturbing. During my work on the report, I also happened to stumble unexpectedly upon top secret files of the Public Security Intelligence Agency.

Please understand that it is for that reason the assignment was handled completely by myself, personally, independent of the agency. None of my co-workers has any knowledge of the findings. Bear in mind not to copy the report or mention its contents to others.I strongly advise you to destroy all documents once you have read them.

The Madarame Organisation.

A research institute set up by Eitatsu Madarame, a person of means from the Okayama prefecture. The organisation was established after World War II, although the exact date is unknown.

Its facilities were located in the mountains of xxx City, Okayama prefecture, far away from any other buildings. The official account is that medicinal research was performed there. The facility was of a considerable size, with several subterranean levels. Multiple testimonies claim that academics and researchers considered "crazy" from all across the country had been assembled there to perform interdisciplinary research, day and night. However, the outside world was largely unaware of the institute's activities.

According to an elderly local who once wandered onto the grounds of the facility, uncanny living creatures, the likes of which he had never seen before, were kept there. Some rumours suggest research from Nazi experiments had been brought there after World War II. Such occult stories are numerous, and further details are included in the attachments.

The Madarame Organisation continued its activities for forty years after its foundation, but in 1985 the organisation was designated by

Public Security as what we now call a "group of significance" and, shortly after a search of the premises, the institute was dismantled. According to the accounts, the Nakasōne Cabinet had strongly argued for such an intervention, which suggests that the institute had become so influential that the government had felt compelled to step in.

However, there are no records whatsoever concerning the confiscated research data, and it remains unclear what exactly the people at The Madarame Organisation were researching.

The situation changed considerably because of Tomonori Hamasaka, associate-professor in biology at Gisen University. He had close ties with ultra-left groups and three years ago, Public Security started keeping an eye on him. This summer, his house and office were searched and, in his home, old research files believed to be of The Madarame Organisation were discovered. Hamasaka himself, however, disappeared, together with the experiment results he had been keeping at his university office.

Hamasaka is the mastermind behind the major bioterrorism attack at Lake Sabea in August, in which you were involved.

CHAPTER ONE
A CURIOUS DEAL

1

'Udon noodles in curry soup do not make for proper mystery fiction,' I declared.

I was, of course, aware of the fact that using udon noodles in curry soup was not a traditional way to serve udon in the first place. Curry udon was therefore neither proper mystery fiction, nor even proper Chinese-style cuisine. What I meant was that curry udon as an answer was illogical.

'I'll have to consider that a declaration of war,' he said as he glared back at me. He was sitting straight up in his chair. His small eyes flickered from behind his rimless spectacles, as if to challenge me. His intimidating posture was reinforced by his tall stature.

'Feel free to do so. But I already know the outcome of this battle. In fact, I can't even imagine why you'd even pick curry udon.'

I crossed my arms and pointed with my chin as I turned back to look at the female college student we were watching. The blue tray she was holding was empty. She was standing in front of the "NOODLES" menu, staring at the sign and lost in thought. It was obvious she was thinking about what she would order. We were sitting at a table about ten metres away from her.

'If you have trouble following my train of thought, I suppose I'll have to explain it step by step to you.'

He smirked.

'Take a look at her appearance. Despite the burning midsummer heat outside, she's wearing a long-sleeved hooded sweatshirt.'

As he pointed out, the student in question stood out amongst all the other students around us, who were wearing short sleeved shirts, and trousers and skirts that only reached to the knees.

'That means the air conditioning in the lecture halls and cafeteria is too chilly for her. Especially in the cafeteria here, where the temperature is set rather low, due to the glass windows which allow for the sun to shine directly inside. From there, it's the simplest thing to deduce that someone who's sensitive to cold will opt for warm food.'

'That I can accept. However, udon isn't the only warm noodle dish they serve here. They also have ramen noodles. So how can you eliminate ramen noodles as an option?'

'Time, my dear Hamura.'

His lips formed a grin. He looked as if he were an evil genius scheming to take over the country, but we were merely chatting about why a student wouldn't pick ramen noodles. It was rather sad, actually. But I didn't say anything, as it would have ruined the mood.

'Time?' I repeated.

'Yes. She entered the cafeteria with two friends. Her companions have already received their orders and are now at the cashier. She needs to hurry up if she doesn't want to keep her friends waiting. And now I ask you, which one will be served faster, ramen or udon?'

Normally, the boiling time for the thinner ramen noodles would be shorter. But....

'Without any doubt, udon,' I replied, and he nodded slowly in response.

Indeed, we ourselves had experienced this fact ourselves. The cooks here really love their udon noodles, for some reason, and freshly kneaded batches made at a nearby factory are delivered here twice a day. The udon dishes are therefore extremely popular among the students and,since there is always a rush of udon orders around the lunch hour, the cooks always make sure to boil batches in advance. Which is why udon orders are served relatively swiftly here. Ramen noodles receive less attention from the cooks, and the tasteless noodles are not popular at all. Because the cooks will only start boiling noodles upon an incoming order, empty stomachs always have to endure an insufferable wait before they are filled.

'Exactly, nobody in a hurry would ever order ramen noodles.'

His line of reasoning did sound logical.

'I can agree with you up to a point. But they serve two warm udon dishes here. Curry udon, and plain udon noodles in a warm broth. Why would she choose the curry udon?'

'She hasn't moved one step from that spot since she arrived there. She has no intention of ordering any side dishes. Plain udon is hardly enough for lunch. But curry udon is a different story. Because it's curry, rich and flavourful!'

The quality of his deductions seemed to take a turn for the worse. Arriving at an answer based on your own expectations or whatever works best for you personally does not make for proper mystery fiction.

'But that doesn't eliminate plain udon. She might be trying to save on expenses, or perhaps she's on a diet. And you missed one important fact.'

'Hah. And what would that be?'

So he really hadn't noticed it. I savoured the sensation of superiority for a moment, before I answered his question.

'Look at the hooded sweatshirt she's wearing. It's white. Would you order curry udon wearing that?'

Curry stains are the arch-enemy of white clothing. A woman her age would never be oblivious to such risks. He refused to back down, however.

'Stupid, she can just take it off!'

'You can't mean that!'

I couldn't believe it. If she could just take it off, his whole premise of her being sensitive to cold would collapse!

'First of all, if she was trying to save on money or on a diet, her options would have been very limited from the start. Why would she take such a long time to make up her mind?'

'It's precisely because she's on a diet and can eat so little that she's trying to considerher choice carefully.'

While we were having our discussion, the student had already passed the cashier and walked right past us. We stopped our argument and surreptitiously turned our heads towards her to take a look at her tray. Cards on the table!

Her lunch was... the daily special: soy sauce-flavoured cooledudon with grated *daikon* and tuna.

We both wanted to cry out loud.It was an absolutely ordinary lunch, of course. But wasn't she supposed to be sensitive to the cold!?

'Guess it's another draw.'

I added the third cross today in the corner of my notepad. He looked disappointed ashe reached for his glass, which was covered in drops of condensation, and drank the remainder of the water.

Of the various cafeterias located on the campus of Shinkō University, a well-known private college in the western Kansai region of Japan, the Central Union cafeteria was the one frequented most by the students. The interior is fancy, as you would expect from a place with cafeteria, bistro or some similar word of foreign origin in its name. The natural light shining in through the glass walls and lighting windows brightens the moods of its customers. The cafeteria could probably house at least four tennis courts, and the eye-catching feature of the interior was the wall decorated with a gigantic mosaic picture of the ocean. About seventy percent of the many long tables inside were being used by students at the moment. Appetising smells escaped from the kitchen in the back. The most fragrant smell came from the demi-glace sauce used in the daily special.

The students having lunch looked cheerful. With the two-week test period finally ending that morning, they were all talking excitedly about their plans for the summer holiday.

I envied them. All that awaited me was not excitement, but anxiety.The greatest reason for my worries was sitting opposite me: Kyōsuke Akechi, third year student in the Faculty of Science. He was clutching my notepad with all the crosses and glaring at it, so I doubted he was even aware of his role in my concerns.

'Blast! Why can't people act according to what logic dictates?' Akechi groaned.

It was up for debate whether his "deductions" could be considered logical, but I did agree that humans do not act as predictably as they do in books. People eat ice cream in the winter whilst huddling against a stove, and it was no good complaining about the girl with the hooded sweatshirt, who nevertheless decided to have cold udon noodles.

Whenever we had the time, Akechi and I would hold these battles of deduction, but winning them in a clear-cut manner was a rare occasion for either of us. Over the course of nearly a hundred such matches, there was one sad fact we had learned: rather than following your own convoluted reasoning, you had better odds by simply picking the daily or chef's special. But that would, of course, only invite accusations from the opponent of running away from the intellectual fight, so we kept on repeating the same process of not so much inferring, but fantasising, and ultimately have it all blow up in our faces. We weren't the types to learn from earlier mistakes.

As for the reason why I was sitting here with Kyōsuke Akechi, someone two years my senior,who wears rimless glasses on his long face and bears a name reminiscent of two fictional detectives? To answer that question, we have to go back to April, soon after I entered Shinkō University.

The same sight awaits new students setting foot on campus at nearly all universities at the start of the new academic year: a bewildering choice of clubs and circles trying to lure in new members. With both officially sanctioned and unofficial clubs, there are many more than in high school, and the attempts to secure new members are therefore more desperate.

At first I had been planning to join the Mystery Club. My teenage years had been quite uneventful and uninteresting. Being alone never made me feel lonely, I barely had any experience with sports, and I had nobody I could call a close friend, not even a cute childhood friend. But I reasoned that I should at least attempt to maintain some human contact at university. Considering the social system there was completely different from high school, I felt sure it was important to get advice from seniors, or exchange information with friends, in order to survive.

I had always liked mystery fiction, so when I noticed the Mystery Club in a tiny corner of the club guide, I attended a couple of open sessions. To be honest, it had been an utter disappointment. The Mystery Club had about fifteen members who occupied a room in the club building, but their only official activity was a critical booklet they published once a year, and for the rest of the year the members just hung around in the room to chat. Although the club had a free atmosphere, I couldn't sense any love for the mystery genre from the senior club members with whom I talked. Whenever I asked them about their favourite works or themes, the answer would be "I don't know," or "I haven't read that one," and I even had to explain to them who Van Dine and Michio Tsuzuki were! It was the same story each time I tried, so after a while, both sides had had enough of each other. The second session I attended ended up exactly the same way, so I left the club room, having lost any desire to join the club.

It was just then that a tall man blocked my way and asked me: "The *Nationality* series was written by Queen. The *House* series by YukitoAyatsuji. So, who wrote the *Flower Burial* series?"

I was about to ask who he was and what this was all about, but I replied instinctively.

'Err, MikihikoRenjō.'

The next moment, he was holding my hand, which I hadn't even offered him. He had big hands.

'You're promising. How about becoming my assistant?'

Whereupon, he took me to a nearby café. I was completely befuddled, but he said it was his treat, so I ordered a cream soda. He didn't wait for our drinks and introduced himself.

'The name's Kyōsuke Akechi, third year in Science. I'm also the president of the Mystery Society.'

The Mystery Society? Was that any different from the Mystery Club?

'So a rip-off of the Mystery Club?'

'No, absolutely not!'

The question I blurted out was struck down as fast as lightning. According to Akechi, the Mystery Society was the true home for fans of mystery fiction.

'Don't ever compare the Mystery Society to those guys who don't even know their Van Dine or Michio Tsuzuki!'

It was as if I had found my long-lost twin.I listened to what he had to tell me whilst sipping my drink. He, too, had been a member of the Mystery Club when he first entered university. And, just like me, he soon grew fed up with how their discussions never went the way he wanted, so he soon left the club and started his own Mystery Society. He had been chasing after mysteries that occurred around him, polishing his deductive skills like a true fan of the mystery genre ever since. At least, that's how he explained it.

A few days ago, he had got wind of a promising new student called Yuzuru Hamura (that's me) who had appeared at the Mystery Club and, after the little quiz as a test, he intended to headhunt me as a member.

'Surely you're not going to spend four years with those people there?'

He was right, of course. The people at the Mystery Club liked what I would call the light mystery fiction that's popular nowadays, focusing on unique characters and relying heavily on tropes from romance and YA fiction. Don't get me wrong, that's also mystery fiction of sorts. Saying otherwise would only earn me more enemies. But, as someone who likes classic, orthodox mystery fiction, I have to be honest and say that people who have no interest in the classics don't have any right to call themselves the Mystery Club.

'Yes, I will join the Mystery Society.'

It wasn't as if he had struck a chord with me, nor had it been his conversational skill which had managed to sell the Society to me, but I decided to accept his offer anyway. Why then? Up until that moment, I had always gone straight home after school and had never been a member of any club. Akechi was the first upper-classman who had ever bought me a drink: that was my sole reason.

That is how I became his assistant, joined an unofficial university club,and started spending all those unproductive days. To my knowledge, no other students are planning to join.

'By the way, what are your plans for late August?' Akechi asked me, as his eyes followed the backs of the students leaving the cafeteria.

'Nothing, of course. Another cat we have to find?'

'Fool, there are more enjoyable things to do than to chase a cat's behind in this heat!'

He started chewing loudly on the ice cubes from his glass of water.

Looking for lost cats was a part-time job we were sometimes offered by the Tanuma Detective Agency, located near the campus.

Akechi, a great lover of mysteries both real and fictional, was always hoping for some incident to occur around him. Which wouldn't be much of a problem if he would be content with just waiting for something to turn up, but he had the nasty habit of wanting to jump in on his own. He had his own business cards made (with the title "President of the Mystery Society" on it), which he circulated amongst various clubs with the message that they could call on him whenever they needed his services. He had been doing so for over two years, so it was hardly surprising that he was quite well-known across the campus. When he told me I should have some cards made as well, I firmly declined.

That his enthusiasm isn't just for show, however, is proved by the fact that he has indeed solved several cases in which people around campus asked for his help. Even limiting myself to the short period since I entered university, I can tell you he was involved in The Case of the Leaked Theology Tests (Tentative Title) and The Case of the Central Ground Diggings (Tentative Title). When he's working on an actual case, Akechi shows off what his sharp mind is truly capable of. Sometimes, at least. Sometimes, he doesn't show it.

Akechi wasn't content with just the campus as his territory, so he also handed out business cards to nearby detective agencies and the local police station, which is how he became acquainted with the people at the Tanuma Detective Agency. They were the friendly ones who sometimes got us part-time work. Meanwhile, the police were probably viewing Akechi as a highly suspicious character, considering that he always tried to enter a crime scene whenever something had happened. I was not only Akechi's assistant, but also functioned as his brakes. As his junior, it was my responsibility to make sure that his enthusiasm wouldn't cause problems for others. Asking me what my plans were for the summer holiday was therefore a reason for great concern.

Akechi got a new glass of water from the self-service corner and then started to explain himself.

'You see, I heard through the grapevine that the folks at the Film Club are going to have a fun outing this summer.'

I didn't even know there was such a club.

'They are going to rent a boarding house somewhere and try to catch paranormal activity on camera.'

'Like going to a place with rumours of ghosts, and see which of them is courageous enough to actually stay there for the night?'

'No, not like that. They're going to make a short film using a camcorder. I think they call that POV style? Where it's filmed from the perspective of the protagonist, as in *The Blair Witch Project* and *Paranormal Activity*. Their project will be short though, only a few minutes long. You know, like those special television programmes which air in the summer.'

He was talking about the specials with footage of spirits and UFOs. To be honest, I don't dislike them.

'That sounds like fun.'

'Yes, they're interesting, but I've had quite enough of the young, attractive singer who breaks down in some haunted place. It's getting old.'

'I agree with you completely.'

Personally, I also thought those longwinded exorcism scenes you see in foreign films had overstayed their welcome.

'What are they filming it for? Are they going to upload it to a video sharing site, or show it at the university festival?'

'It's probably also part of their club activities, but I believe they have plans to publish it online somewhere. If the end result is good enough, the film might be bought by a film company, even if it's produced by amateurs. Which means some income. The whole project would be deemed a great success if they managed to get the film shown on one of those programmes.'

Aha, so it would be a club activity, a source of income and a special summer memory as well. What's not to like about that?

'So I was thinking it might be nice if we could be a part of that as well.'

'Eh!' I cried out upon hearing this unexpected turn of events.

'But when I asked the club president if we could come along, my offer to join them was rejected.'

28

'I could have seen that coming.'

'Three times I have asked since last month, but the answer remains the same.'

'How wonderful it must be, to have a mind strong-willed enough to be able to ask the same question again, even after getting rejected twice.'

Akechi's energy was commendable, but his one flaw was that he couldn't take a hint. But it was a gigantic flaw. Anyone could understand that the people of the Film Clubwouldn't want any outsiders hanging around during their club's summer event.

Akechi, however, didn't seem to have given up yet. He crossed his arms and started swaying his upper body.

'But Hamura, picture it! A boarding house. A boarding house in the summer. And a group of young people gathering there. Don't you think it's the perfect place for some incident to occur?'

It wasn't as if they were going to the Villa Lilac from the Tetsuya Ayukawa novel!As a modest fan of mystery fiction myself, my brain has also been poisoned, to the point that I get excited just by hearing phrases like country houses, remote islands or boarding houses. Sometimes, I even accidentally react to mentions of the Ijinkan foreign settlement in Kōbe, or the Glover Residence in Nagasaki. But still, I didn't like causing trouble for others.

'Please refrain from doing things that annoy others. People on the campus know your face.'

'Man, if there was some way we could go with them!'

Akechi clearly still hadn't given up, but I guess that's who he was. That's exactly who he was.

3

It was now August. Akechi and I had spent almost every day hanging around in a café near the university, because we simply had too much free time on our hands. It was the place Akechi had taken me to the first time we had met. It was not a place which served fancy lunches, but a café with a retro atmosphere and a limited menu, where the owner and the one waitress made their customers feel welcome. Stained glass was set in the small windows of the dimly lit establishment, and moody music played from vinyl records. Normally almost all of the seats were taken by students, but as summer holiday had already begun, it was quite empty. The smell of coffee beans was stronger than usual.

'And another no,' Akechi blurted out, as he sat in the worn-out coffee-coloured chair, his long legs stretched out beneath the low table. There was a cup of coffee in front of him and emerald green cream soda for me.He still hadn't given up on the Film Club's summer trip.

'You really should stop doing that.'

'Doing what?'

He really didn't understand.

'Keep pressing on, incessantly and persistently. The answer was no, so it's no. It's not like a fortune cookie, where you can keep on opening new ones to see what'll come out next. A detective only looks cool if he becomes involved with a case nonchalantly.'

'All I do is plead with them. I'm not causing them any trouble.'

'That's exactly what all wacky types think of themselves.'

'But we can't spend this whole summer without getting our hands on even a single case. We have to do something.'

It was hopeless. The magic words "boarding house" and the summer heat must have gone to his head. As I scratched my head to come up with a way to distract Akechi from the summer trip, I heard the bell that sounded whenever the café's doors opened. I looked over my shoulder and saw a young woman. She looked slowly around, and then came straight towards us. She stopped diagonally behind my back.

'Excuse me. Kyōsuke Akechi and Yuzuru Hamura of the Mystery Society, I presume?'

I was surprised at suddenly hearing our names, and I was surprised again when I looked her straight in the face.

She was a very pretty girl. (Girl was probably not the right word.) She wore a black blouse and skirt, and her hair, reaching just below her shoulders, was also black. She was about 150 centimetres tall and looked slender, as she wore her skirt high. Cute wouldn't begin to describe her. She was quite simply beautiful. She was both a girl and a woman at the same time. At any rate, she was in a completely different class from the average female student walking around campus.

'And to whom are we speaking?'

Akechi had shed his previously listless attitude as he addressed the woman. Given that she knew about the Mystery Society, she was probably a student like us, but even Akechi, with his wide network of connections, did not seem to recognise her.

30

'I'm Hiruko Kenzaki, second year student in the Faculty of Literature. Pleased to make your acquaintance.'

She didn't seem to have any direct connection with Akechi from Science, nor me from Economics. Whilst Akechi's name might be well-known on campus, how had she learnt my name? Who could she be?

'...Kenzaki... Kenzaki.' Akechi repeated her name as if it rang a bell. 'And what business brought you here?'

'Let's make a deal,' she said bluntly. 'Mr. Akechi, I believe you wish to join the summer outing of the Film Club.'

'How did you learn about that?'

'I happened to hear about you from a friend in the club. I was told you were rather persistent.'

He shrugged.

'The answers I got were pretty rude.'

Rude? With the way he kept pushing, he should be grateful they hadn't got physical. But upon hearing Akechi's answer, a smile appeared on the beautiful girl's face.

'From your reaction, I gather you don't know the reason why you were rejected.'

'The reason?'

'Will you listen to what I have to tell you?'

She smiled. She had taken the initiative in the conversation. I moved over one seat, and made room for her.

'Thank you.'

We waited for her coffee to arrive, after which Akechi asked her: 'The reason why they said no to me? I thought they just didn't want an outsider to come along.'

'That is not the only reason. At least, not according to my friend,' said Kenzaki, setting the mood.'The main goal of the summer outing is not to shoot a film, but to act as a social event for the men and women of the club, what some might call a group dating party. A perfect event for the summer. The boarding house in question is owned by the parents of an alumnus of Shinkō University, who used to belong to the Film Club. They will have the whole place to themselves, at no cost. However, due to the limited number of rooms, only select members are able to participate in the event. They call it the club's summer outing, but basically, it's an event you have to be invited to. So that's why there is no room for outsiders.'

What student in the prime of their lives wouldn't dream of spending a holiday in their own private boarding house? It was already hard to get invited, so no wonder they didn't want some outsider trying to get in as well. Hopefully, Akechi would give up on the idea now.

'However, circumstances have recently changed.'

That didn't sound good.

'With only two weeks left before the trip, many of the club members have cancelled. My friend is one of those people.'

'And what would their reason be?'

Akechi had not touched his coffee at all during the conversation. His mind was completely focused on Kenzaki's story.

'There was a threatening note.'

She sipped her cup of coffee, as if to make the scene look more dramatic.

'It was my friend who found the note. One day she happened to be the first into the club room, and a piece of paper had been left on the table.'

'What did the note say?'

'"Who will be the sacrifice this year?" It was written with a red marker, in such a manner as to hide the author's handwriting.'

I cocked my head.

'What an odd message. It doesn't say kill or curse, nothing to indicate the author's intention to do harm to others. So technically, it's not even a threat.'

'Exactly. However, it appears the members had an inkling of what it alluded to.'

She suddenly lowered her voice as if she feared someone was listening in.

'I heard that a female club member who went on the trip last year committed suicide after the summer holiday ended. Mr. Akechi, did you hear about that?'

'Ah, now you mention it, I think I did look into it. But in the end, there didn't seem to be much behind it—at least, it didn't become a big topic in the news.'

'The direct connection between her suicide and the summer outing was not clear, but according to multiple club members, there was a ghostly face in the haunted video they shot, and it was not a fake apparition they had engineered themselves.'

'So now they think there's some kind of curse?' I frowned.

'It's just a rumour. But there's a silent understanding amongst the club members that the summer outing is what caused her suicide. It wasn't just the suicide, other people also left the club, or even the university. Even so, plans for this year's outing had been continuing as usual.'

'But then that note started to spoil the party,' concluded Akechi.

'Exactly.'

'So did all the people who withdrew take that note seriously?' I asked. That part didn't make much sense to me. The note might be a bit creepy, but would so many young persons, in this time and age, decide to not go, just because of such a note? Kenzaki nodded.

'There's more to the story. Immediately after my friend discovered the note, the club president came into the room.'

'Oh, that would be Shindō, would it not?' asked Akechi. It was probably the guy he had been stalking for an invitation.

'Yes. But, the moment he laid eyes on the note, he insisted harshly that my friend keep silent about it. Shindō was actually one of the few members who also went on the summer outing last year. Sensing there was something suspicious about his behaviour, my friend decided the contents of the note should not be kept secret. She told the truth to the other members and said she wouldn't go on the trip. That was the start of a whole series of cancellations.'

It was only natural that the women, in particular, would become worried if the president, who presumably would know what had happened the previous year, was acting suspiciously about everything.

'The situation is clear to me now.' Akechi nodded before carefully choosing his words. 'You mentioned a deal. Would you care to explain yourself?'

'It appears that Shindō fears he might have to cancel the event due to a lack of participants, even though the alumnus went through all the trouble of arranging accommodation for them.'

'And yet he didn't invite us.'

'That's because you are both men,' retorted Kenzaki. 'The alumnus issued the invitation because he wanted a dating party, so naturally, women needed to be present. That's what's worrying Shindō. And that's where we come in. Would you two join me and participate in the outing?'

Upon hearing the offer, Akechi's eyes opened wide behind his glasses.

'I believe you have a reputation as the Holmes of Shinkō. We have a suspicious trip and an anonymous threatening note. Surely it's exactly the kind of case that should interest you?'

'…Hmmm.'

What was he holding out for? It was obvious that Akechi had been completely taken in by Kenzaki's story. He could barely contain his excitement. The rumbling noise of the tableware was probably caused by him shaking his legs beneath the table. But he wasn't aware that his feelings were as easy to read as an open book. He coughed in a dramatic manner.

'Ahem. Well, I suppose you could say the case has some particulars that interest me.'

'I've already made arrangements with president Shindō. It seems he has had trouble finding enough female participants, and has even invited girls from the Drama Club. He agreed that if I would go, I could bring two men along with me.'

She certainly knew how to get things done. For us, or at least for Akechi, things couldn't have turned out any better. Which was exactly why I thought something was amiss, so I had to throw in a question of my own.

'Wait. You just said this was a deal. But as things are now, only we benefit from this. Why did you approach us in the first place?'

Perhaps it was my imagination, but for a moment I thought I saw a fang peeking through her lips. But that split-second smile was immediately hidden as she bowed her head.

'Please don't ask me about my reasons. That is your part of the deal.'

What a curious deal. Hiruko Kenzaki, the woman who suddenly appeared before us, had invited us to join her on a suspicious-sounding outing. None of it made any sense, but that was exactly the reason why Akechi wouldn't back out.

'It's a deal.'

A broad grin spread slowly across his face.

CHAPTER TWO
THE VILLA VIOLET

1

The strong morning sun shone inside the mouldy concrete building. There were no curtains or glass in the window frames to block out the light.

It was an abandoned hotel in the mountains. Nearly twenty years had passed since it was last occupied and, as there were no other buildings in the vicinity, even the locals rarely approached it. The sky was almost comically clear. Hamasaka squinted as he looked up, thinking that this would be a good day to die.

Someone called out to him from behind.

'Hamasaka. Just got a call from Gondō. Seems as though the police or Public Security went through your lab yesterday.'

'Aha.'

Hamasaka had spent about twenty years of his life on research. And now his laboratory at the university, the place to which he had dedicated his entire working life, had fallen into the hands of the enemy. But Hamasaka felt neither anger nor resentment. His mind was calm, almost drained of emotion. He had taken all the results of his experiments with him. All the data on his computer had been erased. There was nothing of importance in the files he had left behind. The lab was like an empty, cast-off husk. The authorities could play there as much as they wanted.

Only one mission remained. He would let the world know what he had accomplished.There were five other men in the ruined building. Some of them he had known for a long time, some he had only met for the first time a few days ago. But that was of no consequence. Everything would end today.

'It's about time to make a move. The roads might be crowded later. It will have been all for nothing if we can't get in before the designated time,' said Hamasaka.

'Of course.' The man who had called out to him lifted a package above his head. He cried to the others: 'Our holy war is about to start. Let's go!'

35

The men responded by shouting feverishly and raising their fists in the air. One of them bellowed: 'Here we come! We'll open Pandora's Box!'

They imagined themselves to be warriors of salvation. Hamasaka coolly observed the one who had shouted. He had graduated from one of the top universities, but soon after he started working for a company, he realised the environment was not for him, and he left. In the eyes of society, he was nothing but a loser. He was cursing at the world when Hamasaka recruited him. Now he had found a purpose through Hamasaka's plan, and was willing to give his life for it.

Although they formed a group, they were not comrades. They were just working ants Hamasaka had gathered to execute his plan. Nevertheless, he understood very well that nothing would have been accomplished without their help.

But they did not fully comprehend the situation.This wasn't Pandora's Box. This was a whole Cabinet. A cabinet left by the group called The Madarame Organisation. What they were opening today, was only one drawer of many.

2

On the early morning of the day of the outing, Akechi, Kenzaki, and I met at the train station closest to the university and boarded the train. The boarding house in question was located near Lake Sabea in S Prefecture and every participant was supposed to meet at the nearest station there. The region surrounding the lake was known for its summer resorts, and there were many private holiday homes and camp grounds there. To be able to spend three days there as part of club activities was like a dream come true.

'What's the matter, Hamura? You look so gloomy this morning!'

Akechi, who was wearing an Aloha shirt that didn't suit him, was naturally ecstatic, with the boarding house and the mystery of the threatening note to look forward to.

I, on the other hand, was wearing a long face. I couldn't even get along with the people at the Mystery Club, so what was I going to do, staying several days together with a group of men and women I had never met?

'I was born with this face. And we don't know anything about this trip except that we'll be there for three days. We don't even know who's going to show up. Doesn't that bother you?'

'I'm quite sure they'll understand Japanese. It's not as if we're being deployed to a Middle-East warzone, so why the worries? Something unexpected will inevitably happen, so relax and enjoy yourself until then.'

However, it wasn't not being able to communicate, or whether some incident would occur, that I was worried about. Neither was it the creepy threatening note; it was having the overly-excited Akechi mingle with a gathering of young people. I could easily imagine him standing in front of them, asking them whether the rumours were true that one of the participants in the previous year's outing had committed suicide, and whether anyone had noticed anything odd about her before her death.

Kenzaki turned to me and apologised. I was sitting between the two of them.

'Sorry about that, I should have asked for more details about the trip.'

'Ah, no, it's nothing important, it's all right.'

I turned my face away from her clear eyes. I wasn't any good with beautiful women. Today, she was wearing something completely different from the black outfit she had worn in the café: a sleeveless one-piece dress with lace decorations. She was the stereotype of A Young Lady in Summer Dress. The chest of her white dress was adorned with a large ribbon bow, a simple but colourful decoration. The straw hat on her head made her look like a teenager, and having her apologise to me pained my heart.

'There.'

Kenzaki sat on her knees and pushed the window up. The cold of the air conditioner was replaced by a pleasant cool wind, which lifted her hat.

'Ooooh!'

She had to use both hands to keep it on her head. Fair underarms. I forced myself to look outside. The fresh rice in the paddy-fields swayed in the wind, creating a wave, and making it appear as if the four-carriage train was moving slowly.

'That alumnus of the Film Club must be very generous, arranging the whole place for the club,' I said.

'I think his parents run a film production company.'

Kenzaki spoke in a friendlier, less formal manner to me compared to Akechi. After she had enjoyed the breeze for a while, she seemed to be satisfied and moved to close the window. Her long hair suddenly flew up, covering her face.

'Aaah!'

Whilst she was holding down her hair, I closed the window for her.

'Thank youummmhh.'

I snorted as I watched Kenzaki pull the last strand of hair out of her mouth.

'You were laughing at me!'

'I wasn't.'

'So you do have more than that long face of yours,' she said as she pouted. When we had first met in the café, I thought she was a cold, distant person, but for the first time she actually seemed friendly. I suddenly realised she was staring at me, and I instantly knew why. She was looking at the old scar across my left temple. It was a cut of about four or five centimetres, so it stood out. Usually I let my hair grow to cover it up, but the wind blowing though my hair must have made it visible.

'What happened?'

'There was an earthquake a long time ago, and a piece of rubble hit my head.'

I tried to downplay the injury, but she clearly seemed to find it alarming.

'How horrible. Any trauma?'

'Fortunately not. I just look gloomy at times, scaring people away.'

'Poor thing.'

Before I knew it, Kenzaki's slender fingers were feeling my scar. I shivered at her cool, soft touch on my temple. Taken by surprise, I wasn't able to say anything before she removed her fingers as if nothing had occurred, and started to tidy her hair.

She fascinated me immensely. The previous day, she had come to us with an intricately planned deal we weren't able to refuse, and now she was being so innocently straightforward. What a fearsome person she must be if all of this was calculated, but for some reason I felt as though the latter persona was her true self.

Hiruko Kenzaki. Akechi had shared information about her with me before we had come.

3

'Hiruko Kenzaki. I thought the name sounded familiar, and now I remember. When I went to the police to hand out my business card, there was a detective who noticed I was from Shinkō University and mentioned her name. She's a female detective who has taken on many

38

difficult and downright inexplicable cases that even the police couldn't handle, and managed to solve them with her matchless powers of reasoning.'

Akechi had told me that, just before Kenzaki's arrival at our meeting spot.

I knew she was no ordinary person, but who could have imagined her to be a detective?

'Sounds like something out of a detective novel. But if that's true, wouldn't the media be all over this news?'

Considering her looks, I could easily imagine the impact it would have if the media focused on Kenzaki, who was far more attractive than your second-rate model or singing idol.

'That aroused my interest, so I asked Mr. Tanuma what he could find out about her. Apparently, she comes from an illustrious Yokohama family with a long history, and each time she's involved in a case, strict restraints are put on the media. Something about the honour of the family.'

'So she's the daughter of a distinguished family, beautiful and a detective? How awesome can you get!? And getting involved with difficult cases reminds me of you. So why haven't you tried to contact her before?'

Considering Akechi's personality, I was sure the moment he'd learnt about such a unique girl at our university, he'd have done everything possible to meet her. He replied reluctantly to my question.

'I have my pride, too.'

'Huh?'

'Her accomplishments are the real thing. They may not have been made public, but she has been awarded a commendation for her assistance to the police. What have I ever done? It was too soon for me to meet her.'

Apparently Akechi considered Kenzaki as his rival detective. Meeting her would probably be an admission she was superior to him in his eyes. But this made things even more curious. If she was such an accomplished detective, why would she be interested in a threatening note addressed to some university club? I also still didn't understand why she had asked us to join her. She couldn't possibly be counting on our skills, could she?

'My dear Hamura, I know exactly what this is,' said Akechi seriously.

'What?'

'This is a challenge from one of Japan's greatest detectives to us, the dynamic duo of Shinkō University.'

'We're the dynamic duo?'

'Of course. You are my assistant.'

That did have a nice ring to it.

'Anyway, we still don't know what's on her mind. The true purpose of her deal is still unclear, so we'd better be careful.'

4

We had an early lunch at one of the stations en route. After changing from the JR line, it would still be another thirty minutes on a private railway line until we arrived at our destination station. The station building had once been a vibrant pastel green, but the colours of the steel frame building had faded. There was no staff nearby, so perhaps this was an unmanned station.

We were about to go down the platform steps when someone called out to us.

'Akechi, Kenzaki.'

We turned around to find a man and a woman standing there. They had apparently been in a different carriage of the same train.

Akechi recognised the man who had addressed us.

'Ah, Shindō! Thank you for allowing us to come along.'

An awkward smile appeared on Shindō's face. So this was the president of the Film Club. A lean figure, wearing glasses and looking nondescript, ahem, I mean, earnest.

'Usually I wouldn't have given the okay, but with Kenzaki's offer, and what's going on, it is what it is. Let's try and have a nice trip.'

The way he chose his words made it clear it was never his intention to invite Akechi, whose persistence must have been a real nuisance. The couple then turned to me and introduced themselves.

'I'm Ayumu Shindō, third year in Arts and president of the Film Club. And this is…'

'Reika Hoshikawa, also third year in Arts. I'm in the Drama Club, and I have a role in the film. Nice to meet you.'

She had a charming face that could pass for an actress and auburn, wavy hair. She was also beautiful, but in a different way from Kenzaki. Shindō and she were wearing matching rings. They were probably dating.

We introduced ourselves in turn. When Kenzaki was done, Shindō said, bowing to her: 'Thank you very much for coming. We had

40

trouble finding enough people.' He treated her very differently from Akechi. Even though he was one year her senior, he still spoke very politely to her. Hiruko, however, did not return the favour.

'I was interested in the trip myself, as well.'

Interested? I tried to read her face, but it was of no use.

'Who else is coming?'

Akechi looked around the empty platform. We didn't know how many others were due to come. It was another fifteen minutes until the designated time.

'Two club members drove directly to the boarding house with our equipment and props, so we should be meeting three more people here,' replied Shindō.

As soon as we passed through the ticket gates, we were greeted by the intense sun and the noise of cicadas. The world in front of me turned white for a moment, reminding me of the summer holidays I had spent in the rural village where my deceased grandfather once lived.

'Oh, look.'

There was a large van parked in the small station square.

'I want to go the bathroom first. You go on ahead,' said Hoshikawa as we approached the van. A man stepped down from the driver's seat. He had a sincere-looking face and wore glasses. He was older than Akechi, probably in his thirties.

'Hello, you're the guests from Shinkō University, I assume? I'm Yuito Kanno, the manager of the boarding house.'

'Did last year's manager quit?' asked Shindō in a slightly puzzled manner.

'Yes, I've had the pleasure of working there since last November. The other members of your party are already waiting in the van.'

Smiling broadly, Kanno opened the sliding door. The three early arrivals were sitting inside. But the moment I saw how they were seated, I knew there was something odd. There were four rows of seats in the van, from front to back: a row of two seats, then two seats, three seats, and three seats. There were nine of us, including the driver Kanno, so you would expect the first three people inside would take either the third or the fourth rows. However, only two of the early arrivals had taken the last row, whilst the other person had taken the passenger's seat, the furthest possible position from the others, as if they were the opposing poles of a magnet.

Shindō seemed to have noticed this as well, and frowned for a second, but said nothing and sat down in the second row. Akechi took the seat next to him. Kenzaki and I took the third row, and Hoshikawa would probably take the seat next to us. But why was that woman sitting in the passenger's seat? Even if she didn't get along with the two in the back, why would she take the passenger's seat?

She seemed to have noticed our looks, and turned to us to explain that she suffered from motion sickness.She seemed intelligent and charming. Akechi, who was sitting nearest to her, said: 'Don't worry. My name is Akechi, and these two are Hamura and Kenzaki.'

'I'm Sumie Nabari. Second year in Arts,' said the woman, turning back towards the windshield. She looked a bit nervous. A voice called out to us awkwardly from behind.

'I'm Takagi and this is Shizuhara.'

The two girls sitting in the back row looked like an odd couple. The tall girl on the right (about a head taller than the other) looked quite strong-willed. Her name was Takagi, and the small, quiet girl on the left was Shizuhara. Both looked quite charming. Takagi was a striking figure, with her boyish short hair and clear-cut features. Shizuhara was a more feminine type, with black hair. They sounded rather curt, as they hadn't even said what their majors were. In fact, the three women in the car hardly seemed to be having a good time. Shindō's selection of people had been rather poor.

'Sorry to have kept you waiting.'

Hoshikawa came at just the right time to break the icy mood, and the van soon drove off. Ten minutes after our departure,we were already quite deep into nature, with not a single house in sight. Surprisingly enough, one side of the road was jammed with cars, and we were hardly able to move forward.

'Is it always so crowded here?'

Kanno looked back via the rear-view mirror at Shindō, who had asked the question.

'No, it's usually empty around here. But there's a big outdoor event today and tomorrow, in a park nearby.'

'What kind of event?'

'The Sabea Rock Festival,' said Takagi, from the back row. 'I had heard about it before, but this time it seems as though some famous bands are going to perform. Is that right, Mifuyu?'

Shizuhara nodded by way of reply. Takagi seemed quite relaxed. She was probably a third-year student like Shindō.

'I think the timing of last year's trip was off by a week,' remarked Takagi, which I found curious.

'So, did you come here last year as well?' I asked. She merely mumbled in the positive. It seemed as though she wasn't all that thrilled by our presence.

'She and I are the only ones who were also here last year,' explained Shindō, following Takagi's grunted reply. So if there were any people who had knowledge about what happened last year, it would be these two.I'd better keep that in mind.

'I'll hand out the schedule for the coming days.'

Hoshikawa handed each of us a small booklet of six pages stapled together. The cover was an illustration of animals playing near a lake. One of the Art students had probably drawn it.

'This looks quite impressive,' I said.

'Thank you, I drew that,' replied Hoshikawa.

Inside the booklet was the schedule for the coming three days, with a plan showing the allocation of rooms. The name of the boarding house was the Villa Violet. There were ten students on the trip, from the Film and Drama clubs, and we outsiders. However, it was what hadn't been written in the booklet that stood out. There were a total of sixteen guest rooms in the boarding house, spread across the second and third floor of the building, but six of the rooms had no name assigned to them.

Akechi said: 'It's smaller than I imagined. How many of your club usually come along?'

'Not even half of the members. It's technically a club outing, but participation is not mandatory. It's just an opportunity to make some income, if we manage to make a good film and sell it to the film production company of one of our alumni's parents. Oh, he's also bringing along two old classmates.'

Shindō's lengthy explanation didn't seem to answer why so few members of the club had come along on the trip, however.

Whilst we were talking, the other women besides Hoshikawa hardly made a noise, and only the voices of the men could be heard in the van. Eventually the conversation turned to the Mystery Society. Uncomfortably, I talked about the books I liked, and fortunately the cinephiles among them also mentioned a few mystery films. Then Hoshikawa raised a taboo topic.

'I've only just realised it, but you're not the Mystery Club. I mixed you up.'

'Hahaha, I'll admit that at the very least, they are better known than we are,' replied Akechi.

'Sorry, but why are there two similar clubs at our university anyway?'

Don't bring that up, Akechi's going to explode, I was screaming to myself.

I was sitting behind Akechi, but I could vividly imagine the grimace on his face, being placed in the same category as those ignorant people of the Mystery Club. But Hoshikawa didn't relent and charged right on.

'So what do you usually do at the Mystery Society?'

Her bright eyes were aimed at me this time. Don't ask. Sticking our heads in businesses that don't concern us is what we usually do. But rescue came from an unexpected angle.

'These two are not just fans of detective stories. They have solved several incidents that have occurred on campus,' said Kenzaki from her seat next to me.

Upon hearing that, several people in the car, Hoshikawa and Shindō, and perhaps even Kanno in the driver's seat, seemed to react in an interested, or perhaps uneasy manner. In my mind, I thanked Kenzaki for her help. Nice job!

I assumed Akechi would be pleased too, but he remained silent, facing forward. Given that she had solved cases all over the country, Akechi probably considered her "help" nothing more than a straight challenge to us.

But what Kenzaki said next was totally unexpected.

'You all have such nice hobbies, films and books. I don't really know much about such things.'

'You don't read detective stories?' I asked.

'When I was a child, I read a little of Holmes and Lupin in the school library, but I don't remember much about the stories.'

Akechi, too,must have thought this was interesting, as almost half of his face was now turned our way. In his mind, a real-life detective and detective fiction probably formed one inseparable combination.

'I think you will enjoy your stay in our boarding house then,' said Kanno in a cheery voice.

'Why, is there some dark past there?' Akechi raised his voice, his interest piqued.

'No, no, I have no knowledge of that. However, you'll find the place decorated with countless foreign weapons. It's a hobby of the owner. Swords, spears, it's quite an impressive sight.'

'Ah, that's right. Mr. Nanamiya tried to scare us last year, saying some of those weapons had really been used on the battlefield to kill people,' added Shindō. Nanamiya was probably one of the alumni.

'Hmm, weapons.'

Akechi's reaction was a bit weak. Probably because weapons didn't have a direct connection to the mystery genre.

Kanno continued: 'When I think of summer, leisure and a group of young people, I'm more inclined to think of panic horror films than detective stories.'

'You mean with zombies, and Jason, and all that?'

'Yes. Those stories usually occur in the summer, don't they? And the people who let loose too much are the first to fall victim.'

'So we're going to become victims?'

Shindō's out-of-character joke was answered by a loud snort from Takagi in the back row.

5

An enormous lake came into view as we advanced along the road. You could almost mistake it for the sea because of its size. It was Lake Sabea, only one fifth the size of Lake Biwa, the largest lake in Japan, but big enough to amaze us. It was crescent-shaped, like a cartoon smile, and we were now driving along the upper line of the arc, from the centre heading towards the upper left corner. Unlike the sea, the azure surface of the lake was serene. The two-lane road followed the gentle lakeside curve, and as we approached the mountainside on the north, we could catch glimpses of the roofs of the holiday villas there. The long line of cars eventually took a turn in the direction of the mountains, which finally freed us.According to the signs, the park where the rock festival was going to be held was on the other side of the mountains.

Our van drove along the lake for a while longer, skirting the mountains. Eventually, Kanno said: 'There it is.'

A red-brown roof and a balcony became briefly visible through the thickly-grown trees, then Kanno turned onto a narrow path to the right and started climbing a slope.

It soon flattened out,and we arrived at an open place in the woods, where the boarding house whose roof we had spotted moments earlier was standing. The Western-style half-timbered building had been erected on the terraced mountainside, and its white walls formed a brilliant contrast with the wooden frames. I was extremely impressed.

'Wow, it looks so stunning. I was expecting it to be much smaller.'

The house was about the size of a rural elementary school and stood on the upper level of the terraced mountainside. An open space area on the lower level served as a plaza, with a roofed parking lot. According to the guide, we were going to have a barbecue party there that night.

There were two other cars already parked there. One probably belonged to the people who had come earlier with the props and equipment, and I assumed the other belonged to the alumni who were joining us.

'A red GT-R. That's the last car you'd expect to find in the woods.'

'That's Mr. Nanamiya's car. He's the son of the house's owners,' explained Kanno, with a wry smile on his face. 'It is indeed a rather luxurious car.'

As we sat admiring the vehicle, which had probably cost close to ten million yen, we heard someone make fun of it from behind us.

'Pfft. That guy never learns. Last year he nearly lost it because he scratched the underside on the slope.'

I turned around to see Takagi, who had spoken earlier. She had also come here last year, but didn't seem to think much of the other alumni.

'I'll show you inside.'

Led by Kanno, we ascended the steel staircase leading to the upper level and the entrance hall of the Villa Violet. The building had three stories, but had a rather peculiar shape. Looking at the room assignment in the schedule, it appeared to be in the shape of a pistol pointing sideways, with the guest rooms all located on the south side.

The floor of the main hall was covered by a crimson carpet. Opposite the main doors was the reception desk with a glass divider. Further back was a terrace that faced a small garden. The lobby area to the left of the reception desk was about as wide as a volleyball field. The sun shone generously through the large windows, making any additional lighting unnecessary. Three men were seated there, on sofas surrounding a table.

One of them turned to look at us. His wide-set bulging eyes and his buzzcut hairstyle made him look like a fish. He exclaimed, in a nagging voice: 'You're late! I've been looking forward to some female charm since this morning, but all I got was some fat bloke! I was about to throw up.'

We were perplexed by the sudden rude outburst, but Shindō stepped forward and bowed.

46

'Sorry, the roads were very busy. But didn't a woman arrive with him?'

'I don't know, nobody's come down to see us,' continued the fish, stretched out on the sofa. What a stuck-up guy. I assumed he was the son of the owner.

'Shut it, Deme. You're making even us feel bad,' said a man with a tan. He had his straight hair tied back and was wearing a white shirt, with a silver necklace. A handsome guy, with something reckless about him. He was probably somewhere in his mid or late twenties.

'Welcome, students of Shinkō University. We're not from the Film Club, but we also studied at Shinkō and are friends of Nanamiya. We're invited here every summer. I'm Haruya Tatsunami. The loud one is Tobio Deme.'

To my surprise, the fish called Deme was one of the invited guests, just like us. Shindō and Deme must have met last year, but even so, how could he act so arrogantly in someone else'shouse?

Deme fell silent with a sour look, and the small man who had been addressed as Nanamiya stood up. His face had regular features, but his skin was pale, and his eyes and mouth were rather small. Because he, too, had his hair straight back, his face almost looked like a mask. He smacked his temple with his fist.

'Shindō, are there even fewer girls here than you told me earlier? Can't you do anything right?'

The awful remarks continued.

'Oh, err, unfortunately, a couple of people couldn't make it after all, due to circumstances....'

Nanamiya didn't bother to listen to Shindō's excuses, but nodded to Kanno.

'Show them their rooms. Shindō, you were planning to film now, weren't you?'

'Yes.'

'Barbecue is at six. Don't be late.'

After reminding us of the schedule, the three older men left the building and went down to the parking lot. The manner in which Nanamiya and Deme leered at the women as they went past was disgusting.

'What's up with them? What a beastly bunch.'

It was Hoshikawa who voiced what we were all thinking.We all knew that this trip was to serve as a kind of hook-up party, but none of us had expected that there would be people so crude about their reasons to be here. They were treating the women as mere entertainment. Akechi asked more about the three who had just left.

'I presume that was the son of the owners?'

'Yes, he used to be in the Film Club, graduated three or four years ago. He still arranges things so current members can stay for free here, which is pretty generous. And Mr. Deme isn't really as bad a person as he first appears. So don't be worried about them,' explained Shindō rapidly, sweating nervously. But the women were obviously still concerned.

Only Kenzaki seemed undisturbed. She was perusing the booklet as she addressed Shindō.

'So those three are staying in the rooms that are shown as empty on the room assignment, correct?'

Besides the ten rooms assigned to us, there were six that had been left empty, which meant that three of the rooms had been assigned to those three.

'That's right.' Shindō nodded awkwardly.

'Seriously?'

The women checked the room assignments together. There were four empty rooms on the second floor, and two on the third. If those three men were going to stay in those rooms, the people who might be occupying a room next to them would be Hoshikawa in 203, Nabari in 206, Kudamatsu in 302 and Shizuhara in 307. I was relieved to see that the tall beauty Takagi was in the room next to Kenzaki's 201. Fortunately, my own room was at the far end of the third floor, and my neighbour was the other half of the odd couple: the small, quiet Shizuhara. So, at least I wouldn't end up next to any of the alumni. Suddenly I felt a gaze upon me, and I turned to see Takagi staring coolly at me. Was she acting as Shizuhara's bodyguard? Her eyes told me very clearly that if I dared pull some funny business with her friend, I would regret it. It would probably be better to forego any awkward attempts at befriending Shizuhara.

Kanno unlocked the reception desk and brought out a bundle of cards.

'I will hand you the keycards to your doors now. Inside your rooms, you'll find a second holder installed in the wall right next to the door. Please insert your keycard there to turn the power on in your room. The doors lock automatically, so please be careful not to leave your card inside when you leave. You do not need to leave your keycards here at reception when you go out.'

Kanno then looked to his right.

'The elevator here is rather small and can only carry about four people at a time. You can't all use the elevator together, so if some of you could use the stairs....'

The east corridor to the left of the elevator led to the stairs. It was a detour, but as my room was closer to the stairs anyway, I decided to go up that way.Akechi called out to me as he checked his wristwatch.

'The others are going to work on their film after they've put their luggage in their rooms. What shall we do?'

After a short deliberation, we decided to join them. To be honest, I would have preferred to take a relaxed walk around Lake Sabea, but it would be bad manners to come along on another club's trip and then go our own way. And I was genuinely curious as to how they were going to make a film with ghosts.

'What are you going to do, err, Kenzaki?' I asked.

'Eh? I'll come with you of course.'

She seemed surprised that I had asked her in the first place. Her plan had obviously been to stick with us.She raised her index finger as she looked at me, and added:

'And please don't call me "Kenzaki" again. You know that the "ken" in my surname means "sword," which sounds so violent. You can call me Hiruko.'

'...Okay, Hiruko.'

'Good, good.'

As "hiru" also meant "leech" in Japanese, I thought that sounded a bit rude, but she had given me permission to call her by her given name. Perhaps she liked me better than I imagined.

We left the others at the elevator, and took the eastern staircase. Hiruko was in 201, so we agreed we'd meet up later and left her on the second floor, whilst Akechi and I went on up to the third floor. Akechi occupied 303, right next to the elevator hall.

'When I first heard about this boarding house, I did expect the kind of events you see in a gothic adventure,' mumbled Akechi, as we stood in front of my room 308. 'But this trip has turned out trickier than I imagined.'

Akechi was absolutely right. The attitude of the participants was curious, and I also found it odd that all the women who had come along were good-looking. It felt as if all the women I had met today were attractive in one way or another. From the way Deme spoke, it seemed as though Shindō had selected the women especially for the trio of alumni.

'Anyway, a true detective remains calm, regardless of whatever circumstances they become involved in. Let's have a short rest and meet in the lobby at two o'clock, as per schedule.'

I glanced at my wristwatch. The hands on the dial were pointing to precisely half past one.

6

The room number was printed on the front of the keycard, which had a magnetic strip on the back. Inserting the keycard in the reader built into the door resulted in a beep, and the door opened.

'Wow!'

I was surprised that the door opened outwards into the corridor. As far as I could remember, at all the business hotels I had ever stayed in, the doors opened into the room. I had heard that doors opening outwards could block the corridor during emergencies, but there was another view which held that doors opening outwards were preferable, because if someone collapsed inside the room next to the door, they could block the door and prevent help from entering. So perhaps outward-opening doors weren't as rare as I had thought.

I removed the card, stepped inside, and closed the door behind me. I could hear it locking automatically. There was also a swing bar door guard attached to the door. With the door guard on, the door could only be opened for about ten centimetres. You could also use it as a kind of doorstop to keep the door ajar.

The power in the room was activated,just as in business hotels, by inserting the same keycard into the holder in the wall.

The first thing that struck me as I stepped inside the room was the fantastic view through the large windows. Beneath the clear sky and beyond the forest was the majestic shape of Lake Sabea, as wide as the sea.

The room itself was larger than I had expected, with the floor covered with the same crimson carpet as in the corridor. The furniture included a wide single bed, a nightstand with a telephone, and a desk with a mirror. Hanging from the wall was a digital clock, a rare sight. It indicated the same time as my own watch. It was a radio-controlled clock with a simple design which only indicated the current time on its digital display. The timepiece could be synchronised via a radio transmitter.

French windows opening outwards led to the narrow balcony which provided just enough space for the doors. You couldn't place a sofa there, but it was quite wide enough to enjoy the breeze outside. Standing on the balcony and looking to my right, I could see the other guest rooms in a cascading line.

There was still enough time until our meeting, so I decided to have a look around. I went out into the corridor and turned left, towards the elevator hall. Passing Shizuhara's room next door, the first thing that caught my eye was the door at the end of the corridor, leading to the elevator hall. It was open now, but I wondered why there was a door there in the first place. It was made of wood, so it was not a fire door. A closer look told me that it had a keyhole on both sides, meaning it could be locked from either side.

According to the floor plan in the schedule booklet, the second and third floors were divided into east, central and south wings through such doors. The area on this side of the door, where Shizuhara and my rooms were, was the east wing. The elevator hall was in the central wing and, passing through that area and beyond another similar door, was the south wing. Each wing had two or three rooms.

The three rooms in the central wing of the third floor were occupied by Shindō, Shigemoto and Akechi, respectively, starting from the east wing side. I hadn't met this Shigemoto yet, so he was probably one of the people who had arrived earlier with the equipment. Shindō's 305 was the only room where the door was oriented differently and set in a rather narrow place. The reason why some of the doors opened to the left and some to the right, was probably due to the way the gas and water pipes were laid out, resulting in rooms that were mirrored in terms of layout. Apart from the guest rooms, the elevator hall also provided access to two more doors. The plates on those doors said Storage and Linen.

At that moment, a woman appeared from the south corridor. I hadn't met her before. As soon as she saw me, she cocked her head in surprise.

'Who are you? Oh, are you from the Mystery Club?'

Another one who got it wrong. I needed to correct her before Akechi could hear her.

'Not the Mystery Club. It's the Mystery Society. I'm Hamura, first year student.'

'Ah, so still a detective-in-training. I'm Takako Kudamatsu, third year in Sociology. Nice to meet you.'

She saluted me as if she was in the Self-Defence Force. It seemed like ages since I'd last met someone cheerful. Kudamatsu was also an attractive woman, but she felt very different from the others in our

51

group. With her permed hair dyed blonde in a ponytail and perfectly applied make-up, she came across as someone into the *gyaru* subculture. She was very much like a modern city girl. I could feel my heart jump as I almost peeked inside the wide neckline of her t-shirt.

'Heard you went through a lot of trouble to get invited here? Some girl you're after? Gotta warn you, the girls this year are on their guard.'

Unlike Takagi and Shizuhara, Kudamatsu was overly perky. Didn't she know about the threatening note and the rumours surrounding last year's trip, or was she the type who didn't care?

'Nooooono!' I shook my head at the suggestion that girl-hunting was my reason to be there.

'Huh, you're not? Oh wait, don't tell me you're another rival?'

Her remark piqued my interest.

'Rival? In what?'

'Oh, I guess you don't know, then. I really shouldn't talk about this though,' Kudamatsu continued, although it didn't really seem as though she was planning to keep it a secret from me. She did look around the hall first before she spoke, however.

'You know Mr. Nanamiya, the guywho arranged this place for us?'

'Yeah, we just met him downstairs.'

'His parents run a well-known film company. So they say that if he likes you, he can help you get a job there.'

Getting people a job through his connections. Sounds simple enough, though I wondered whether Nanamiya really could pull such strings.

'So you're here because you believe those stories?'

'Of course.I'm never going to get into a good place with my grades, and the very thought of having to take recruiting exams at dozens of companies makes me tired. Why else would I come here? Just to entertain some spoiled rich kid? Oops.'

She covered her mouth dramatically as she looked around the hall again to see if anyone was listening.

'Anyway, it's not just baseless rumours. There's someone who did get a job there last year. I guess his parents must be big softies, as they also let him use a boarding house like this.'

So this woman had her own reasons for coming on this trip. And to accomplish her goals, she was willing to go a long way to humour Nanamiya's whims. Kudamatsu seemed as though she was willing to play an open hand, so I decided to ask her about something that had been intriguing me for a while now.

'You just asked whether I was *another* rival. So are there other people here who are here hoping to land a job?'

A smirk appeared on Kudamatsu's face as she indicated a corner of the hall.

'Him over there. Our prez.'

She pouted her lips as she pointed at a door. Shindō's room.

'Shindō?'

'Yep. Some people are fooled by how he looks and behaves, but he's really not that smart. Who would ever think of bringing his own girlfriend along on an outing like this if not for the employment bait? That's why he's so desperate to get on Nanamiya's good side. But still, he's a man, so I have the advantage.'

Her well-endowed chest heaved up and down while she laughed loudly. She was probably correct that a woman was more likely to get the attention of those three.

I had been taken aback by this revelation, however. I had imagined Shindō to be a more thoughtful individual, but I suppose he had his own machinations. That would explain why he tried to hide the affair of the threatening note, and what had occurred here last year. Things were much murkier than they appeared on the surface.

'Ah, I still have to get things ready for the filming. You coming along too?'

'Yes, all three of us will be there if you need a hand with something.'

'Okay, see you later then.'

Kudamatsu waved airily to me and went down in the elevator.

I proceeded on my way and went through the next door to enter the south wing, which contained two rooms. Room 302 was occupied by Kudamatsu and the room at the back had been left empty, according to the booklet. One of the three alumni might be staying there. The corridor ended at the emergency exit, leading to the emergency staircase outside.

I returned to the central wing and went down to the second floor. As Kanno had told us, the elevator was rather cramped. He said it could hold four people, but I heard that was based on an average weight of 65 kilograms per person. So, 260 kilograms in total. It could probably barely carry three adult men with luggage.

I was surprised at the sight which awaited me on the second floor. Unlike the floor above, it had a spacious lounge area. It was almost as if they had moved the living room of some fancy apartment here. There was a 60-inch television in the corner of the lounge, with an expensive-looking set of sofas in front of it. Near the wall was the same kind of telephone we had in our own rooms. There were even a water dispenser and coffee machine, but what attracted my attention the most was something else.

'Wow!'

One wall of the lounge was decorated with impressive replicas of weapons. It was the collection Kanno had mentioned earlier. Besides Japanese katanas,I could also spot Western-style swords, spears and war hammers shining coldly on the wall. It was the kind of equipment you'd often see in fantasy videogames or anime, but this was the first time I had seen the real thing for myself. I had to think back to the time I borrowed the *Weapons Almanac* from my little sister, a gamer at heart. I tried to recall the names of the weapons present. What first caught my eye were the various kinds of swords. A buster sword which could be used both single and double-handed, a magnificently curved shamshir, the long but thin rapier... no, the straight and simple sword guard meant it was probably a tuck. Most of the spears were short, but even so they were nearly two metres long. In the knife category were daggers and kukris, and didn't I spot a crossbow and even a mace somewhere? In front of the wall stood an acrylic display case with medieval battlefield miniatures.

'It's quite a sight, isn't it?'

I turned around to find Kanno wearing a green apron. He had just arrived from the eastern staircase. He was holding bags of coffee creamer and paper cups in his hands. He was probably busy refilling supplies.

'I was surprised as well, when I first saw this wall. I don't know anything about the value of this collection, but the owner is quite a fan of Middle-Age battlefields.'

'Are they replicas?'

'I believe so. Although the blades have been blunted, the material itself is all real. I have been instructed to dust and clean them once a month.'

'What are those?'

Standing guard by the side of the television stood nine statues which came up to my waist, so about one metre high. There were four to the left of the television, and five to the right. From the bluish, dull colour, I imagined them to be made of bronze.

'They are bronze statues of the Nine, err, what was it again, the Nine Worthies. Famous in the Western world. The owner got quite mad at me for not knowing them. There's King Arthur, King David and Caesar, and… Oh, I forgot again.'

The Nine Worthies? I had heard about them. I think they were considered heroes embodying chivalry in the Middle Ages in Europe. The ones I could remember were Alexander the Great and Hector. The owner of the house had quite a unique collection of weapons and bronze statues. I had a look around and observed: 'But it's a relief you don't have rifles hanging around here.'

In detective stories, country houses or manors with rifles hanging around always result in death.

'I believe they had them here several years ago.'

'Huh?'

'But the owner had them removed because his son had taken them down and fired them in secret.'

The guy was really a hopeless cause.

'Is the Villa Violet not generally open to the public? There are some strangely located doors, and you're the only one working here.'

Kanno smiled and nodded.

'The building used to be the owner's holiday villa, but he had it renovated so it could function as a training and recreational facility for his company. The doors at the end of each corridor are still a reminder of the old days. The Villa Violet is a boarding house, but it's only open for employees and their families, so I don't have much to do, although I do sometimes have a part-timer to assist me.'

At that moment, muffled voices interrupted our talk.

'Ayumu, you said it would be all right! You really think that was all right!?'

'But I already… and there's… so please….'

People were speaking on the other side of the door behind us. Surprised by the outburst, Kanno and I stopped talking.

'That's not what I meant! Why didn't you say anything to them!'

'But… just me… So….'

One of them was probably Hoshikawa. The other was a male, who was speaking so softly that I was unable to recognise him. It was apparent, however, that the voices were coming from the room in the corner of the central wing, which was Hoshikawa's own 203. I assumed she was talkingto Shindō. I seem to remember his given name was Ayumu.

'Three days with creeps like them? If anything happens, it's all your fault!'

Although she had seemed perfectly fine in the van, Hoshikawa now appeared to be furious. If the creeps she was talking about referred to the trio, then their attitude earlier in the lobby must have left the worst possible impression on the girls present. I couldn't make out Shindō's reply. It was a very awkward conversation to overhear.

'That sounds serious. Fights and confessions of love are subjects to avoid on the first day of a trip,' whisperedKanno.

Please don't fight, I pleaded in my mind. If those two were going to argue, our whole group would fall apart. Their argument still continued, but as it was almost time to meet, I went downstairs alone.

I found Hiruko already waiting in the lobby. We spoke about the weapons in the lounge upstairs, when Akechi appeared, two minutes early. His smartphone had trouble getting a signal, so he walked up and down the lobby. Eventually he spoke up.

'It's going to rain tomorrow.'

He didn't sound disappointed.

'A closed circle situation?' I asked.

'Closed circle?' Hiruko repeated. 'You mean, like closed off?'

'The closed circle is a common trope in mystery fiction, where nobody is able to leave the crime scene because it's closed off from the outside world,either because of bad weather, or because the roads are blocked,' I explained.'That prevents the police from coming, meaning it's more difficult to gather clues to aid in the investigation. So there are more moments where the characters have to rely solely on their powers of reasoning to work out what's happening.'

'But it's not as if there's a storm coming, and there's more than one road leading here. So, unfortunately, it's unlikely for this place to become a closed circle,' sighedAkechi.

Whilst we were discussing this, the members of the Film Club started to arrive in the lobby. Most faces I already knew, but there was one man I hadn't met before. He was rather chubby, and wore thick-rimmed glasses and a checkered shirt over his t-shirt. This was probably Shigemoto.

Akechi asked Shindō about what we were going to do.

'Are we going to film in the neighbourhood?'

'No, there's an abandoned hotel a short drive away. We'll be filming there.'

As he said that, Shindō glanced at Hiruko's feet.

'The hotel is basically a ruin now, so bare feet in sandals might be dangerous.'

'Oh, I didn't know we were going to go to a ruin, how careless of me.'

'Well, I guess you'll be fine as long as you're careful.'

Shindō's attitude towards Hiruko was still much better than towards us.

'You could also wear my shoes when we're there.'

It was Hoshikawa who made the kind offer. Nothing about her attitude even hinted at the big row she'd had with Shindō just moments ago in her room, but I suppose that's what makes her a member of the Drama Club. A puzzled look appeared on Shindō's face as he looked at the white court shoes Hoshikawa was wearing.

'But I thought you didn't bring any spare shoes with you?'

'No, but I have to take my shoes off anyway, when I'm playing the ghost.'

'Ah, of course, the ghost has to be barefoot. We'll have to sweep the set first anyway, to make sure nobody gets hurt.'

Then the cheery Kudamatsu I had met earlier cried out: 'But prez, we won't fit in one car with the detectives coming along too! There's also the stuff we have to bring along.'

She called the club president Shindō "prez" and, going by our earlier conversation, there was probably a mocking undertone to her use of it.

'No problem, we'll borrow Mr. Kanno's van and go in two cars.'

'I don't know the place, so you'll have to lead the way.' Shigemoto pouted.

'Of course. But to be honest, I'm not sure whether I can drive a van that size.'

Shindō wasn't a good driver, apparently. But we couldn't ask Kanno to drive us, as he had his own work and the barbecue to attend to. It was then that Akechi raised his hand.

'Allow me to drive, then. Don't worry, I have a license for heavy vehicles.'

CHAPTER THREE
AN EVENT UNTOLD

1

Attendees were crawling everywhere, and there was an excited commotion as coloured smoke split the sky. Activities had begun around the steel live stages set up on the far-stretching festival grounds.

A sweating Hamasaka had made his way through the masses to return to the car. More than half of his comrades had already returned to the parking lot. It appeared that none of them had messed up.

'Done?'

'Yes. News from the others?'

'No problems there. Now it's just a question of waiting for the final stage.'

A pregnant pause followed those words.

There were three areas with live stages set up in the park. The comrades had split up and mingled with the crowd in each of the areas, injecting dozens of people there with the substance, using hypodermic needles. Some of them might have sensed a bit of pain, but most of them noticed nothing, due to their excited state. By the time the symptoms appeared, the crowd would already be going crazy around the live stages, making it impossible for anyone to escape.

'And now for our last mission.'

When everyone had returned, they all got into the van, which was now a sauna, due to the hot sun. A duralumin suitcase was taken out of a cooler box. A syringe with the substance was handed to each of the men in the car.There was no turning back now. This was the start of their revolution, the end of their human existence. None of them would ever witness the results of their revolution, and even if they could see it, by that time they would not comprehend the meaning of their actions anymore. The men looked at each other, waiting for the sign.

Hamasaka sighed gently. He injected the needle in his own arm.

'Let's go. We're the vanguard of the revolution!'

'Yeah!'

'Madarame, banzai!'

Everyone reacted feverishly to Hamasaka's dramatic cry and they each plunged a needle into their own skin. The scientist watched how the substance he had dedicated his life and research to disappeared into each of their bodies. He excitedly imagined the upcoming horror which would shake the world, and lamented the fate of these men, who imagined themselves to be heroes, even though they were nothing more than his worker ants.But that was of no consequence any more. It was all over now.

Hamasaka thought about the notebook he had left in the abandoned hotel, unknown to his comrades. He didn't like the idea of his research falling into the hands of some talentless hack, but it would please him if his notes were to be found by a curious-minded person who could understand its contents. It was almost farcical. For twenty years, he had been preparing for this moment in total secrecy, but now the time had come, he couldn't contain this urge to let someone acknowledge the time and energy he had spent on his research.

Everyone had finished injecting themselves.

'Let's enjoy the time we have left, then.'

He opened the door, and the men, who had now become carriers, all stepped out.

2

After about ten minutes driving in the mountains, with the four men and six women divided into two cars, they arrived at the abandoned hotel. It was located at a higher level than the Villa Violet, and must have boasted a fantastic view back in the time when it was still in business, but now the view was blocked by trees and plants. The building had been completely absorbed by the surrounding forest.

We carried the essential equipment out of the van and waited for the Drama Club members, Hoshikawa and Nabari,to get dressed, after which we all entered the hotel. There was no power anymore, so even though it was still afternoon, it was quite dark inside the concrete building.

'Mind your step.'

Shindō let the way down a gloomy corridor strewn with rubble. When we arrived at a room which had presumably been the lobby, we set down our luggage and started preparing for filming. Takagi and Shizuhara went over the outfits and make up of the two ghosts, whilst Shindō and Kudamatsu went over the script again. Shigemoto made sure the equipment was running. We cleaned the area so the actors would not hurt their feet, and then waited silently in a corner, so as not to not disturb the others in their work.

It was then that I noticed that one corner of the lobby had been vandalised with graffiti, and there were cigarette stubs and plastic bags from a convenience store lying around. The rubble and debris that had been strewn everywhere in the other rooms and corridors had been clearly moved over to one side to clear a space there. It was as if someone had been staying in the abandoned hotel.

As far I as I could piece together from the Film Club members' conversation, they would basically film as follows: Shindō and Kudamatsu would play two people entering the abandoned building as the result of a Trial of Courage dare. Shindō would be recording their movements with a camcorder as they explored the premises. They would look inside each room as they advance deeper and deeper, and eventually Shindō would aim his camcorder at a mirror, which would show the reflection of a ghostly woman. The two explorers would then flee in a panic towards the emergency stairs. When they turned to look back, they would be relieved to see the ghost had not followed them, but then, as Shindō turned back to look at Kudamatsu, the ghost would be standing behind her.

Basically, the trick was that Hoshikawa and Nabari, who were of similar height, would play the same ghost. The hard thing about the film, however, was that everything had to be filmed in one continuous sequence. If they messed up the timing of the ghost's appearance, they would have to start all over again, so they were rehearsing first. Shigemoto was one of the few men in the party, and it was his job to save the rehearsal footage on his laptop. He did his job silently, like a veteran. Shizuhara carefully checked the hair and make up of the ghosts to make sure nobody would notice that they were actually two different actresses.

Takagi was just standing there with her arms crossed, looking at the people who walked up and down from the corridor to the rooms, to the stairs. She probably would have had more to do if it had been a bigger project, but this time it was to be filmed as a home video, so as a stagehand, there was little for her to do. Akechi nonchalantly made his way towards her.

'Is it true that a face appeared in the film you shot last year?'

Akechi seemed to think that the reason that someone committed suicide the previous year, and people subsequently left the Film Club, was somehow connected to the summer outing. Takagi, however, didn't take the bait, and brushed his question away.

61

'Of course not. It was just a shadow cast by a piece of debris that looked like a face. The simulacra phenomenon.'

The simulacra phenomenon, also known as *pareidolia*, is the tendency to perceive a meaningful image in a random pattern—for example, recognising two dots and a line in a triangular layout as a human face. It's considered the biggest reason for so-called ghost pictures or other sightings of the supernatural.

'So there was no fuss made about it last year?'

'We just thought it might be a good idea to send it to a magazine about the occult. People who are scared of something like that are not cut out for the Film Club.'

So there was no relationship between the suicide and the film they made last year. Were the members who decided not to come along this year just overreacting, then? Or had something else occurred on last year's trip that had led to the suicide?

Suddenly a woman's cry resonated throughout the ruins. It had come from the room where the film crew had set up base. We ran over, to find Nabari hiding behind the smaller Shizuhara. She was obviously scared of something, but it was a rather surreal sight, as she was the one dressed as a blood-soaked ghost.

'Lizard! Lizard! Get it away!'

Nabari cried hysterically as she pointed to a corner where part of the wall had collapsed and fallen to the ground. Reluctantly, Shindō walked across, moved some of the debris with his shoe, and shook his head.

'There's nothing here.'

'Look more closely!' shrieked Nabari.

'It probably ran away.'

'Make absolutely sure! I'm the one who has to be standing in the room, and I'm not going to do it with a lizard present.'

When she had first mentioned her motion sickness in the car, I had already felt that Nabari was rather too sensitive. Shindō did not appear to be pleased either, and was about to say something to Nabari when he was interrupted.

'Well, allow us to assist. Finding animals is what detectives do.'

Akechi seemed eager to show what kind of detective he was.

'You?' Shindō turned to Akechi.

'It's all right. Hamura, you can help as well.'

'Yessir. Ah, Hiruko, you might hurt your feet, we'll do this.'

We turned the pieces of debris over and started looking for the lizard, to humour Nabari. We didn't find our prey, but I did notice something odd had been thrown away in one corner of the room. I picked it up. It was a small syringe.

'It looks as though other people had fun here, too.'

'Drugs? And they came all the way up into the mountains for that? Oh.'

Akechi found something else. Nearby, pieces of debris had been piled up in an obviously suspicious manner.We removed the debris and found a notebook with a black leather cover, which we flipped through quickly. Almost every page was covered with dense writing. It didn't appear to be a diary, but notes on something.

'What's that?'

Shigemoto had noticed our discovery and was peering over my shoulder to look at it. It was not particularly hot inside the building, but his shirt was sticking to his sweaty, bulky body. I quickly moved to one side.

'It was buried here amongst the rubble.'

He used his sweaty fingers to page through the notebook, as if he had some clue as to what it might be, but after a while he closed it and threw it into his own bag.

'You're going to take that?'

'Why not? It's not as if its owner is still around.'

'But it's wrong.'

I had inadvertently raised my voice, which attracted the attention of Takagi and the others. Shigemoto didn't take any notice, however, and was about to walk away until I grabbed him by the arm. The owner might be looking for it, and it might contain private information. Also, it might have been hidden in the rubble by someone other than the owner. I couldn't allow Shigemoto to just take it.

'Please put the notebook back.'

'Why? It's none of your business anyway.'

He brushed my hand away. We were about to struggle when Akechi stepped in.

'Hamura, let it go.'

'But…'

'I know. But forget it.'

Akechi looked intently at me and nodded his head slowly. I took a deep breath and apologised.

Shigemoto had already closed his bag and walked away. Nabari, who appeared to feel that she had been partially responsible for the sudden tense situation, said: 'Forget the lizard, I'm all right now.'

She had calmed down and was ready to start filming.

It took them three takes. They checked the footage on the laptop first, and when Shindō declared that was it for the day, the filming had officially ended. The time was half past four.

We cleaned up and carried everything back outside. It was still very sunny, but the wind brought some much-needed fresh air. Everyone let out a sigh of relief.

It was then that we heard the sounds of ambulance sirens, carried by the wind. There were many of them, and they started to overlap like singers in a roundelay.I guessed that there had been a number of heatstroke incidents at the nearby rock festival.

3

Our barbecue on the plaza in front of the Villa Violet had started at six o'clock. Two grills had been placed in the middle of the plaza, about twenty metres away from the parking lot. A nice fire was blazing in each of the grills. It was still bright outside.

I was a little apprehensive, because it would be the first time we would all be together with the three alumni. The trio had arranged for the grills and all the food, so it was not as if we could ask them to leave. I could only hope that their vulgar attitude would not make the women feel even worse than they had earlier in the day. Just the thought of what might happen was almost enough to upset my stomach. My worst fears did not materialise, however. It appeared that the older trio had reflected on their earlier behaviour. Nanamiya was genuinely acting like a respectable alumnus of the university and club.

'I'm pleased to welcome my juniors from Shinkō University again this year. I hope we can all become friends and have some nice summer memories together. Has everyone got a drink? Cheers, then!'

And so, with that dramatic speech, our barbecue began. An old-fashioned large radio cassette CD player, the kind you don't see around anymore, had been placed in the middle of the plaza, playing summer classics loudly. Ah, this is what a university club summer trip should be!

'Well, well, time to commence the questioning, then.'

The meat hadn't even been grilled, but Akechi was already holding a paper plate and a can of beer as he observed our surroundings.

'Questioning?'

'Well, we're not here to have fun. We're here to find out who sent that threatening note and for what reason. I want to know whether the note is related to the suicide. The three days will be over sooner than you think, so we have to act now.'

He went over to Kudamatsu and Shigemoto.I didn't feel much like going around asking questions, to be honest. A summer outing with only attractive women present, a club president with secrets, a trio of difficult alumni... I had the feeling that it would take very little to peel off the superficial surface, to reveal a truth that I would have been happier not knowing. Digging into a mystery and into a scandal were two very different things. Akechi would have to snoop around on his own, at least for today. As the youngest present, I was going to lie low for now and help out as best I could.

Shizuhara was the only other first-year student besides myself, and she was already turning the meat over on the grill with the tongs. I realised that I hadn't chatted with her yet. I had been curious about her. I got the impression that she wasn't all that keen on interacting with the others. She didn't really seem the type of person to have come on such a trip in the first place. I decided to tend to the food on the other grill. As the Guardian of the Grill, I wouldn't let a single piece of meat burn. I would wield the grill tongs and carefully make calculations based on each person's eating speed, the temperature of the grill and the cut of meat they wanted.

I didn't want my wristwatch to fog up in the smoke, so I took it off. The idea of having my watch move around in my pocket every time I took a step also bothered me, so I wrapped it in my handkerchief and placed it near the wall of the parking lot, on the ground directly beneath the light there.

Hoshikawa and Kudamatsu came over to chat with me whilst I was watching the food on the grill. Kudamatsu put a heap of meat on my plate, saying that boys should eat well. I liked her attentiveness. I suddenly thought of Kanno. Where was he? We were the only guests at the boarding house right now, so was he having a meal all alone? I looked up at the Villa Violet, one level above the plaza, but I couldn't make anyone out behind any of the windows.

'Thank you. Are you a first-year?'

I turned around to see a tall, tanned man. It was Tatsunami, the friend of the rich kid.

'It must be boring having to do all the work. Don't forget to serve yourself.'

He laughed as he spoke in a low, resonant voice. He was exactly what'd you expect from a thoughtful senior. Or perhaps he was just used to such events. I imagined that if we hadn't taken the grill tongs, he would probably have tended to the meat himself. It appeared as if he mistook me for one of the new members of the Film Club, so I decided to introduce myself.

'No, I don't belong to either the Film or Drama Club. I'm a last-minute addition because too few people signed up this year.'

'Last-minute addition? Why?' Tatsunami appeared unaware of the club's situation.

'There was a threatening note.'

It was the rich kid who spoke from behind Tatsunami. He was holding a plate in his hand. Lights had been placed around the plaza, but our spot was not well illuminated. Nanamiya's face looked pale in the light of the fire, strengthening my impression of him wearing a mask.

'A threatening note? Addressed to whom?'

'Who knows? Shindō claims it was just a prank.'

Whilst he was speaking, Nanamiya kept poking at his temple with his empty hand. He had done this when we first met today. Must be a tic of his.

Tatsunami thought for a moment before he turned back to me and asked: 'Huh. So then why are you here, exactly?'

A difficult question to answer. Especially by me. But then a familiar voice intervened.

'We're just plus twos.'

It was Akechi. I thought he had gone to question the other people, but here he was, suddenly joining in the conversation at the perfect moment. Had he been listening to us for a while? He explained to Nanamiya and Tatsunami that Hiruko had said she would only come if we could come along as well.

'Ah, you're the princess's escorts. I should thank you, then.'

Tatsunami still seemed to find our presence odd, but he smiled and opened a can of beer, which he handed to me. I was still a minor, but I couldn't refuse him now. I thanked him and took a sip. Akechi turned the discussion back to the earlier topic.

'I do think it's a bit of an overreaction that so many people decided not to come, merely because of a creepy note. I gather that the message on the note was rather curious,though.'

'Huh, what did it say?' Nanamiya sounded interested.

'Something like: "Who will bethe sacrifice this year?" Usually, you would expect that kind of note to say that they're going to kill you or put a curse on you, or that they'll be coming after you. Something to make the reader realise their life is in danger. But this note was hardly a threat. What do you think?'

'Probably just a bad joke, as Shindō said.'

Akechi paused theatrically for a moment, as if he were giving Nanamiya's comment careful consideration.

'But consider the following. What if the note wasn't addressed to all the members of the club, but only to some specific person or persons? The author knew that the message would be clear enough to them. "Sacrifice" might refer to something they wanted to keep secret, and the author was therefore threatening to make that something public.'

Tatsunami interrupted to make an observation: 'Shindō is the one who arranged everything, so he should know what the note actually means.'

'But he's not the only one. If the note is related to what happened last year on the same trip, then there are more people present who should have an idea.'

I was becoming very nervous as I listened to the three of them talk. Akechi was basically accusing them to their faces of having done something last year. He was so determined to get to the truth that he had no time for subtleties.

'I've no idea what you're driving at.' Nanamiya shook his head.

'Nothing that rings a bell?'

Tatsunami interrupted again. 'Akechi—that's your name, isn't it?— I believe your insinuation contradicts itself. If the goal of the note is to have the trip cancelled, then the author wouldn't be so vague and would simply reveal the secret. Then even more people would have changed their minds. So why did the author do such a half-baked job?'

A fantastic retort. One could interpret "sacrifice" in many ways. Could the fact that the author chose to use such a vague word mean that the note wasn't really serious?

'I personally think the note is more likely to be a prank in very bad taste, made by someone who paid too much attention to baseless rumours.'

Faced with Tatsunami's perfectly argued defence, all Akechi could do was smile and concede that he might be correct. In an attempt to smooth things over, I decided to offer them some of the meat that was done, but Nanamiya declined, saying, 'I don't like my meat charred black.'

He might be the son of the owner, but I didn't know how to react to such a rude remark.

'Don't mind him, he's always like that. He's obsessed with cleanliness,' Tatsunami whispered in my ear.

Nothing out of the ordinary occurred at the barbecue after that, but at one point Kudamatsu called out that her phone had no signal. I checked my own smartphone. I, too, had no reception, which was odd, because I'd been able to use it inside the building.

'Just try again later,' replied Shindō, so I didn't think much of the matter either.

But, thinking back to that moment later, I realised that things had already begun to spiral out of control.

4

With my appetite satisfied, I was enjoying the view when heavy low-frequency noises suddenly merged with the music from the radio cassette CD player. The noises were so loud they made the trees in the surrounding forest shake. I looked up at the clear blue sky that seemed like a reflection of the lake, and saw three helicopters in formation flying over us from the east. They looked like the helicopters of the Self-Defence Force,which are employed during crises, but I couldn't recall whether there was a base nearby. They started to descend on the other side of the mountains, near where the rock festival was being held.

'Penny for your thoughts.'

It was Hiruko who interrupted my thinking. She had been "entertained" by Tatsunami and the others with a fair amount of alcohol, but it didn't show on her face.

'Just enjoying a short rest.'

'I hope you don't mind me joining you, then.'

She suddenly plunged her hand down the front of her dress. To my great surprise, she withdrew a package of paper from beneath her clothes. It was the booklet.

'Why—why are you keeping that there?'

For a moment I had thought, or hoped, for something else.

'You never know when you'll need it. And it will also work as a shield, if somebody suddenly decides to stab me with a knife.'

I wasn't sure whether she was serious or not.

'These people are all so intriguing. Have you already memorised the names of everyone?'

'Probably. Just their surnames, though.'

I didn't have too much confidence. Having to remember eleven names in one day was a little too much for me. Whenever I read mystery novels, I always forget the names of the characters, and have to go back to the list on the front page.

'Really? I didn't have any trouble memorising everyone.'

Hiruko began to name everyone present.

'First there is the Film Club president, Ayumu Shindō.'

I remembered that Kudamatsu hadn't thought much of his mental skills, but I decided not to mention that.

'His girlfriend is Reika Hoshikawa from the Drama Club. A nice name for someone as attractive as she is. Though I do think she's out of her boyfriend's league....'

An astute observation. Hiruko couldn't know about the row the couple had had in Hoshikawa's room, but her thoughts were spot on. Shindō wasn't a bad sort, but he did act rather egotistically, keeping things secret and sucking up to the alumni.

'And the other girl from the Drama Club is Nabari. I forgot her given name, though,' I said.

'Sumie. The girl with motion sickness and a fear of lizards.'

'I'm impressed you remembered her name.'

'She seems rather neurotic and nervous. Nervy Nabari.'

She laughed loudly at her attempt at a funny nickname.

'Then there's Rin Takagi, the tall third-year student in the Film Club. And the silent smaller girl who's always with her is Mifuyu Shizuhara. I also had a chat with the two members who arrived here earlier. The boy who does all the equipment is Mitsuru Shigemoto. Second-year in the Science Faculty.'

That would be the geeky, short and overweight guy I fought with over the notebook.

'The girl is called Takako Kudamatsu. She seems like a strong-minded person.'

She was the woman who was participating in the hopes of securing a job.

'How did you memorise her name?'

'She's strong-minded and determined. Takako on the attack-o.'

Whatwas it with Hiruko and bad jokes!?

'And you probably remember the names of the other people. Yuito Kanno manages the boarding house, and Kanemitsu Nanamiya is the son of the owners. Haruya Tatsunami is the tall, handsome one. Tobio Deme has the face of a fish.'

I was impressed. I guess a great detective also needs to be able to memorise faces and names.But then Hiruko proceeded to speak more seriously.

'Have you noticed anything odd about this page?'

She had opened the booklet on the page with the room assignments. Although six rooms had been left empty originally, she had scribbled down the rooms the three alumni were staying in. She had probably asked Kanno for the information. I didn't see anything odd about it, though. At first sight, the assignments seemed completely random, not ordered by gender or what university year you were in. For example, Shindō's room was nowhere near his girlfriend Hoshikawa's room.

'I don't see anything strange.'

'It's not just the booklet. Look around you.'

Following her hint, I looked around. Suddenly I had to take another look at the booklet. People were sitting around everywhere and chatting, but I paid special attention to the three alumni. Tatsunami was having an amusing chat with Hoshikawa whilst holding a can of beer. Nanamiya and Kudamatsu were seated in the chairs near the grills, and as for Deme, he was accosting Nabari, who was leaning wearily against the wall of the parking lot. She seemed quite annoyed.

I looked back at the booklet. Tatsunami had room 204 next to Hoshikawa, Nanamiya had 301 next to Kudamatsu and Deme had 207 next to Nabari. They were all occupying rooms in different wings, so it couldn't be a coincidence. Did it mean that the alumni had chosen the rooms for everyone? That would explain why Takagi had been giving me those piercing stares throughout the day. She had been here last year as well,and therefore knew what was going on. She was on her guard for every man. Hiruko and I were still discussing her theory when Hoshikawa walked over to us.

'It's about time to wrap things up.'

We started cleaning up. I volunteered for dish washing. There was an outdoor sink next to the entrance of the Villa Violet, one level up from the plaza. I was washing the grill grates and grill plates beneath the one single light there, when I heard someone approaching me from behind. I thought it would be Hiruko or Akechi, but I was wrong.

'Did you enjoy today?'

It was Takagi. But why was she there?

'Yes, I was behind the grill, so I had plenty to eat.'

Takagi sighed loudly. She came to stand next to me, turned one of the grates around and started scrubbing it. She started speaking to me as the running water masked her voice.

'So, why are you and Akechi really here?'

She must have thought Akechi's behaviour in the abandoned hotel odd. If I didn't show my cards now, she'd probably become suspicious, not only of the two of us, but of Hiruko as well. I answered her question honestly.

'Do you know about the threatening note?'

'Yes, the one about the sacrifice.'

I explained how Akechi was very interested in staying in a boarding house because that sort of thing came straight out of a mystery story, how we learned about the threatening note and the suicide last year, and how we came along to accompany Hiruko.

'So that's it? I can't say that I get what goes on in that Akechi's mind though!' Takagi exclaimed, but then she looked at me and apologised. 'Sorry, I misunderstood you completely.'

What a sincere person, I thought. But given how those alumni behaved, it's no wonder she expected the worst of me.

'You'd better keep an eye on Kenzaki though,' she added.

'Ah, so the people here *were* chosen for a reason.'

'Probably. I'll bet Nanamiya put pressure on Shindō. That's why all the other women here are attractive, whilst on the other hand a guy like Shigemoto might as well not be here. It's not as if he's going to get lucky any time soon. And there's Kudamatsu, who's just hoping to land a job.'

Her remarks about Shigemoto were rather harsh.

'But why are you here then, if you know what's going on?'

As the water splashed around, she blurted out: 'How could I stand by and do nothing whilst the younger members are forced to join such a stupid event?'

'You mean Shizuhara?'

She nodded slightly.

'Shindō's dirty. Not sure if he's desperate for a job or anything, but he can't say no to those three, especially not to Nanamiya. He must have been in a panic when people started to withdraw after the threatening note appeared. The first person he used to fill in the openings was his own girlfriend.'

To be honest, I didn't want to know about all that. I would have been content just knowing him as a wishy-washy club president.

'But even he doesn't like someone hitting on his own girlfriend. So then the miserable guy started looking for other members he could bring along. That's how he settled on Mifuyu. He knew Mifuyu's personality, he knew she couldn't refuse him as her senior in the club.

By the time I learned about what he was doing, she was already on the list. I never wanted to return here, but I couldn't send her off to the slaughterhouse all alone.'

So Takagi had been a last-minute addition as well.I wanted to know more about the suicide that had occurred last year after the trip, but I didn't want to upset Takagi by raising that sensitive topic now, so I decided to ask her about something else.

'So the way these rooms are assigned….'

'You got it. I guess I should be relieved you turned out to be Mifuyu's neighbour.'

I was glad she trusted me. But I couldn't help asking. It was not beyond the realm of possibility that I would become interested in Shizuhara at some point.

'Suppose I were to have err, a moment of weakness?'

'Then I'll smash them.'

Takagi laughed loudly. She didn't specify what part of me she would smash.

5

The sky had turned dark long ago. A thick layer of clouds blocked the starlight. Takagi and I carried the grill grates and plates back down from the outdoor sink. Just as we passed in front of the entrance of the Villa Violet, I glimpsed the back of someone entering the elevator in the lobby. They were gone in a second, but I believed it was Deme.

'Is everything all wrapped up and done?' I wondered out loud.

'I think so.'

We reached the plaza. Everything had been cleaned up, and everyone was standing near the parking lot, but we immediately noticed the tense mood. The peaceful atmosphere had disappeared and everyone seemed on edge. I looked around. It was indeed Deme who was absent. Hoshikawa was standing next to Nabari, trying to comfort her.

'Has something happened?' I asked Akechi, who was standing nearby.

'I'm not sure, but I believe that Nabari, ahem, physically rejected Deme's passionate attempts at wooing her.'

He shrugged. Takagi clicked her tongue loudly. It was just as she had feared. Deme couldn't even wait on the first night.Tatsunami was trying to salvage the mood.

'I have to apologise to everyone,' he announced. 'Deme always becomes obnoxious when he's drunk, pestering women and not knowing where he should keep his hands. They always send him away, of course.'

Then don't give him anything to drink, I thought to myself.

'I'll tell him to cool down. And, as a penalty, I suggest he plays the ghost in the Trial of Courage we're going to do now. Are you okay with that, Nanamiya?'

'Yes, it suits him.'

Apparently, the power dynamics between those three weren't equal. Nanamiya and Tatsunami were the ones on top, and Deme was just their jester. Deme's attitude towards the others might come from a sense of inferiority.

Takagi, however, was against just continuing according to schedule.

'Can't we do the game tomorrow? A lot of us are tired this first day.'

She knew that Nabari was feeling awful, as were the other girls. Except for the ever-cheerful Kudamatsu, who ignored Takagi's suggestion and inched up to Nanamiya.

'Where are we going to hold our Trial of Courage? In that empty hotel?'

'No, it's in the other direction. There's an old shrine, fifteen minutes' walk from here. We go in pairs, and you have to bring back a charm to prove you've actually been there.'

They had no intention of changing plans. As Nanamiya was the one providing us with rooms, there was little we could say. The two alumni said they had things to prepare, so they told us to wait in our rooms until it was time, and left the plaza. We started climbing the stairs back to the Villa Violet.

'They're treating us as if we're just here to keep them entertained, whilst they do whatever they want.'

'Oh, just think of it as a stroll after supper.'

Shindō had his hands full appeasing his girlfriend, whose mood was growing worse by the minute.

Akechi, who had been staring at the sky, suddenly muttered: 'What's that?'

A brilliant aura behind the mountain had created a halo effect.

'Probably the Sabea Rock Festival. They are giving live performances in the park there. It's probably the light from the stages,' I suggested. It had been so bright during the day that we hadn't noticed it. Things must have been really lively over there, in contrast to the near silence where we were.

'Huh?' said a nasal voice behind me.

I turned around to find Shigemoto, who had been mostly invisible until now. He might as well not have been at the barbecue. He was busy tapping the smartphone he was holding, but he didn't explain himself further.

'What's wrong?' asked Shindō impatiently.

'I have no internet connection. I was trying to look up the festival.'

'Oh, it's been like that for some while now. I have no signal either,' said Kudamatsu.

'But I had a signal before the barbecue, I'm sure,' Shigemoto replied.

The others all took out their phones to check, and the reactions were all the same.

'Ah, you're right, no signal at all.'

'Eh, no way!'

We all had different models and carriers. It was obviously not just a simple connection problem.

'Even if there's a network failure, they still have a landline connection at the boarding house, and we can drive into town if necessary, so there's no need to worry.'

Shindō was right, of course. Still, I couldn't help but feel unsettled by the situation.I glanced at Akechi. He was usually sunny all day long, but even he appeared to be concerned.

'No connection to the outside world. That is exactly what a modern-day closed circle situation would look like.'

'But we can just drive down the mountain if we need to.'

'That's true. We could go at any time. And that's exactly the reason why we won't do it. And before we know it, it will be too late to get away.'

His words made me feel even more anxious. From habit, I raised my arm to check the time, but when I saw my naked wrist, I remembered I had taken my watch off during the barbecue.

I left the circle and went over to the parking lot light where I had left it, but it was no longer there. There was only my handkerchief, which I had used to wrap the watch in. It was now lying open, but there was no sign of the watch itself. It was unthinkable that the wind could have blown it away, as my handkerchief, which was of course lighter than the watch, was still lying here. Had someone accidentally kicked it away? Or had something else happened to it?

'What's the matter?'

Having noticed where I had gone, Hiruko called out to me from the circle.

'I can't find my watch, I left it here.'

'There was a watch there earlier,' said Nabari.'I was wondering why there was a handkerchief lying there, so I opened it and saw your watch.'

I returned back to the others to ask for more details.

'When was that?'

'Around the time we finished. Just before that creep Deme started to pester me.'

It was about twenty metres from the parking light to the barbecue party. I remembered seeing Nabari and Deme near the wall of the parking lot whilst Hiruko and I were talking about the rooms. So my watch was still there at that time? Akechi seemed to have caught the scent of a case, so he fired more questions at Nabari.

'Was there anyone who approached the watch while you were there?'

'No. I was looking for an excuse to get away from him, so I would have noticed if anyone had approached us.'

I don't know what they had been talking about, but she really didn't like Deme.

'And when the cleaning-up started, I thought it was my chance, so I tried to get away, but he suddenly put his arm around my shoulder. So I called out and pushed him away. I ran over to Reika, who was standing nearest to me, and that was it.'

So all that had happened whilst Takagi and I were washing the grill grates. Akechi continued his questions, which were now aimed at everyone.

'So after you called out, Deme was left behind at the wall where Hamura's watch was lying. Was there anyone else who approached the wall or the parking lot beforehand? Did anyone see someone doing so?'

A few people raised their hands. They had gone to the storage space inside the roofed parking lot to get the things they needed for the barbecue party. But that had all happened before I placed my watch there, so the information was of no consequence. Then Shizuhara raised her hand timidly.

'I kept an eye on Nabari and Mr. Deme when they were talking there. He seemed pushy, so I was worried about her. I'm sure nobody else went near the wall after they went there.'

Nabari confirmed her statement again, and nobody else had anything to add. Which prompted Akechi to declare: 'It seems only natural to assume that, whilst our attention was drawn to Nabari, Deme took the watch and left.'

'Ah, I remember now,' said Takagi sombrely. 'Something similar happened last year. Ebata drank too much and passed out, and someone took a ten-thousand-yen bill from his pocket. Do you remember, Shindō?'

Ebata was presumably one of the senior members of the Film Club.

'Err, I don't quite recall.'

'I'm sure of it. And it was Deme who was pushing him to drink. But he denied he had anything to do with it.'

When Tatsunami had mentioned earlier that Deme didn't know where to keep his hands, perhaps he meant that Deme had a tendency to steal. The others started to say they thought Deme was suspicious as well, and Takagi was already convinced he had taken my watch.

'Hamura, let's get it back. I'll go with you.'

'Just hold on. It's not as if there's any proof he took it,' protested Shindō. It was obvious he didn't want to start any trouble. Takagi was determined, however.

'We can just ask him if he took it. Or do you think someone else might have done it?'

Shindō went silent for a moment, but quickly retaliated.

'Well, ah, your reasoning is only based on what Nabari told us. But it's possible she's wrong.'

'So you're saying she's lying?' said Takagi, twisting his words. Nabari's eyebrows shot up.

'I don't mean that, but there's always the possibility she's just mistaken. Isn't that so, Akechi?'

Being thus addressed, a grave expression appeared on the face of the Holmes of Shinkō, and he nodded at Shindō's desperate attempt.

'If you consider the matter logically, everyone is a possible suspect if the watch had indeed been stolen before she walked over to the wall. But it's probably true that she did actually see the watch.'

'How can you tell?' asked Shindō.

Akechi didn't answer the question, but turned to me.

'Hamura, you said you had wrapped your watch in your handkerchief.'

'Yes... Oh!'

I instantly realised what he meant.

'Just now, Hamura mentioned he couldn't find his watch. Nabari immediately replied she had unwrapped the handkerchief and seen the watch inside. Hamura had not mentioned to us that he had actually wrapped it inside in his handkerchief. Normally, you would assume he had simply placed the watch on top of the handkerchief. But Nabari said it had been inside the handkerchief, which means she had actually seen it there.'

He was right. That meant that my watch had still been there when Nabari reached the wall.

'I see, so that means that either Deme or I stole Hamura's watch. You can search me all you want,' declared Nabari defiantly. Akechi added: 'Pure logic also suggests the possibility that she handed the watch to Hoshikawa when she came up to her.'

The only person to have approached Nabari after the business with Deme was Hoshikawa.

'Well, you can search me as well.'

Hoshikawa spread her arms out in front of Shindō, who was trying to protect Deme. Needless to say, there was no need to search either of them. It would have been obvious to everyone if they had been hiding a man's watch somewhere beneath their light summer outfits. They were also wearing metallic belts, which would have hit the watch and made a sound whenever they moved. One look was enough to know they couldn't be hiding it. Even so, Hiruko quickly patted them down to confirm it.

While logical reasoning had shown the possibility that either of them could have been the thief, if you don't have the goods, you're not the thief. Since neither of them had my watch, it became even more likely that Deme was the culprit. Even Shindō couldn't come up with any more excuses for him. As we all returned to our rooms, I decided to go to Deme to confront him. Akechi and Takagi were worried and thankfully joined me. But our visit was to no avail. We called out to him in his room, but he didn't answer.

'Oh, the three of them just came down in the elevator and went out,' replied Kanno when we asked him about Deme's whereabouts. We had taken the eastern stairs, so had missed them. They had probably gone to setup the Trial of Courage.

'Too late. What now?'

'I'll try again tomorrow.'

Takagi didn't seem too happy, and asked me if I was really okay with that. I nodded.

'He was just sent packing by Nabari in front of you all, remember? He might just have taken it in a fit of anger. The Trial of Courage is coming up, so I don't want to get him in an even worse mood.'

'I agree, he doesn't seem to be the type to say sorry if you present the logic pointing to him as the thief. He's more likely to snap. And we don't want him to take it out on the others, either.'

Akechi sighed as he agreed with me.

'Is it a valuable watch?'

'It's not an expensive watch, but it was a present from my younger sister, when I passed my high school entrance exams.'

She had given it to me shortly after the earthquake, when everything was still in a mess. She had worked hard to save up enough to buy it. To me, it was more valuable than any sum of money. So I had to wait for the right time to get it back.

6

We were called down with the announcement that preparations were finished, so we gathered once again at the plaza. Deme wasn't there. He was probably hiding somewhere, disguised as a ghost, to spook us somewhere during the Trial of Courage. Tatsunami was holding a paper bag.

'We're going to draw lots now to determine the pairs. The women can draw.'

I suspected there might be some trickery with the lots, but surprisingly, the couples were quite diverse. I formed a pair with Hiruko. Was it coincidence, or fate?

'How lucky. It must be fate!' she said.

Fate, huh?

There were six pairs. We would start as the fourth pair. The other pairs were Nanamiya and Kudamatsu, Shindō and Hoshikawa, Akechi and Shizuhara, Shigemoto and Takagi, and finally Tatsunami and Nabari. The idea was to take the lakeside road in an eastern direction. At one point, there would be a path up the mountain leading to the shrine. The mission was to bring back one of the charms left in the main building, to prove that the pair had actually been brave enough to enter the shrine.

It was nine o'clock. The first pair, Nanamiya and Kudamatsu, were about to leave. Sneaking a glance at me, Kudamatsu moved her lips silently so Nanamiya wouldn't hear her. She was saying 'Lucky me!' to me. Considering the room assignment and the way they chatted during the barbecue, Nanamiya had probably taken a liking to her. Both had ulterior motives, so I guess it was the best-case scenario for both of them.

'It's getting a bit chilly,' Hiruko whispered, rubbing her hands along her arms. She was still only wearing a one-piece dress. The heat of the afternoon had been dispersed by the cold breeze. Perhaps it was because we were at the lake now. I would have scored points if I'd been able to offer her my jacket, but unfortunately, I too was only wearing a t-shirt.

'Let's go up to the shrine and return as quickly as possible, then. Are you easily scared?' I asked.

'I'm average when it comes to being scared, and my endurance to cold is also average.'

That was more than enough. We could always cry out in fear together.

Five minutes or so later, the second pair left, and another five minutes later the third pair followed. Then it was our turn.

'Let's go,' I said.

The Trial of Courage had the cliché rule that pairs had to hold hands. Hiruko's hand was one size smaller than mine, and felt fragile. It took some time to arrive at a squeeze we both were comfortable with. Our hold was just tight enough for us to hold an egg without breaking it.

We followed the lakeside road for a while. There weren't many lights along the road, nor was there a proper sidewalk, so we walked by the side of the road, to avoid any cars. It was such a strange situation, now that I thought about it. I was holding hands and out on a walk with a senior student, even though we had only just met. I couldn't have imagined yesterday that I'd be doing such a thing.

I glanced at her. Hiruko was looking at the lake, and following my lead. She was a head shorter than I was, so I could look down her dress. She was surprisingly well developed.

'Hey.'

'Uh, yes?' My heart jumped.

'There was something I wanted to tell you.'

Tell me? Not Akechi?

'Yes?'

'It's about why I invited you two on this trip.'

Wasn't it part of the deal we wouldn't ask her about that? I turned to find her large eyes aimed at me.

'I invited you to this trip to make a pass at you.'

'… Huh?'

I froze at the startling confession. I would have found it more convincing if she had told me she was an alien.

'What do you mean?'

'You may have heard already, but I have been involved with many difficult incidents in the past. And I have reason to believe I will be involved with new cases in the future, too. And that's why....'

She suddenly pulled my hand towards her, and held it in both of hers.

'Let me put it straight to you. Become my assistant. I need you.'

How was I to interpret her words? Did she literally mean she wanted my assistance in her activities as a detective? Or was this her way to confess her love for me?

'Wait wait wait!'

It was all too sudden. Akechi did call me his assistant, but it was not as if I were managing his schedule or acting as his point of contact.

'I'm just a guy who likes to read books. I don't have specialist knowledge, nor do I come up with brilliant ideas.'

'That was true of Watson as well. All he did was say what was on his mind, no matter how commonplace it was. And if that helped solve the case, well, what could be better? I don't expect an answer right away. Think about it during the trip.'

It didn't sound as though she was pulling my leg. She really did want a detective's assistant.

'Why me?'

'… That's a secret.'

I sighed. I wasn't going to push the matter any further.

'Can I mention this to Akechi?'

'Please wait. I'm basically asking the two of you to break up. I'm sure he thinks of you as indispensable, too. I'll bring the matter up with him personally soon.'

Our conversation stopped there. If there was ever a moment in my life to want a ghost to show up, it was right now. I even felt strangely angry that no ghosts did appear.

Hiruko had solved many cases up until now, like the hero in detective stories. As a fan of mystery stories, it would be a bald-faced lie to claim I wasn't interested in such a life. If possible, I'd prefer to be the detective myself, but even being able to witness one from up close would be great. But to team up with someone other than Akechi to achieve such a dream: the weight of that decision was too much for me. If Akechi had not reached out to me, I'd still be wasting my time with those people from the Mystery Club. Because he was always driving hard, he needed me as his brakes. It was thanks to him I had met Hiruko, and that I was here on this trip.

The forest to our left opened up, and there was a small path that came down from the mountains. It was the path we were supposed to climb, but it was at that very moment that they came.

7

'Uuuuuaaaaa!'

I couldn't help shuddering instinctively when I heard the distant scream.It repeated two or three times, and then faded away.

'That was scary,' I said.

'It sounded as though they were really and truly terrified.'

Hiruko's voice was tense as well. The screams had sounded far more horrifying than you would expect from a simple game. It sounded like a man's voice, but I couldn't tell who it was. I couldn't imagine Akechi crying out like that, but perhaps something tricky had been set up to scare him.

I squinted and could just make out several figures descending the mountainside. At first, I thought it was the first pair returning, so I wanted to call out to them. But then I noticed something odd. There were three of them. Perhaps they were just locals?

'They don't look well, do they?'

As Hiruko pointed out, the three figures were all swaying from side to side, as if they were under the influence. Were they trying to scare us? But Deme was supposed to be playing the creepy part by himself. Had they hired extras? That sounded a bit unbelievable, even for Nanamiya. But then another unimaginable sight caught my eye.

'Hiruko, look!'

I pointed in the opposite direction from the mountain path, about three hundred metres away, to where the prefectural highway followed the curve of the land which protruded into the lake to our right. The lamp posts illuminated about a dozen swaying figures coming our way. They did not appear to be concerned that they were walking on a motorway and were occupying the whole width of the road.

'Look out!'

The figures from the mountainside were now at a distance from which they could reach us in a five-second sprint. They were moaning as they dragged their feet across the ground. The attempt to find a logical explanation clashed in my mind with the instinct which told me to run. Just a few more steps....

'Hamura!'

Hiruko pulled me by my arm just as the figures moaned again.

'Uuuhuuuh!'

The lamp posts illuminated their faces. Unfocused eyes. Slack mouths from which meaningless groans were escaping. Dark blood stains all over their faces and clothes. Some of them had torn clothes and were walking half-naked.And,worst of all, the smell! The pungent, rotten smell of blood, grease and more pierced our noses.

Instinct finally won. Run! I pulled Hiruko by the hand and ran back the way we had come. Not for a moment did I ever consider the possibility that the figures might be wounded or sick. As we ran, I looked back once. The number of figures descending the mountains was growing.

'Ah!'

We saw figures on the road ahead of us. We paused for a moment, but from their silhouettes we realised that they were the pair of Shigemoto and Takagi, who had left after us.

'Don't come this way. Go back!'

The two stopped in utter surprise as they heard us scream.

'What's the matter? Calm down, you two,' said Takagi.

'No! We have to get back. Some crazy people are coming.'

'Crazy?'

'I don't know what's up with them, but they're not normal.'

'They're here!' cried Hiruko.

At the sight of the countless number of figures moaning menacingly beneath the orange street lighting, Takagi jumped back.

'What are they!?'

'It must be an act,' mumbled Shigemoto a shaky voice. 'Those three went way too far with the game.'

I grabbed a stone and threw it as hard as I could at the advancing figures. It hit one of them, but they did not cry out, and kept approaching without any reaction.

'No way!'

'Did you see that!? We have to get away!'

We hurried down the road back to the Villa Violet. Tatsunami and Nabari, who had remained as the last pair on the plaza, were surprised to see the people who had just departed return in such a desperate frenzy.

'What's the matter? Did someone get hurt?'

How to explain what was happening? We all started shouting about the ghastly mob, but that only confused Tatsunami and Nabari even further.

'Anyway, we can't stay outside. We have to get inside and lock everything up.'

'No, we should get away from here.'

'But not everyone's back yet.'

'But those... things... might get here, too. We need weapons!'

'We have to tell Mr. Kanno first and find some weapons to defend ourselves with.'

We went up the steps to the boarding house. The staircase itself wasn't very wide, so the mob wouldn't be able to come up all at once.

'Oh man, what's going on?'

Tatsunami mumbled to himself, still not able to grasp the situation, whilst Nabari ran to Mr. Kanno. Suddenly someone pushed their way through the bushes behind the Villa Violet. Everyone froze, but the figure turned out to be a heavily-breathing Nanamiya.

'What are you doing there?'

'I bet he made his way back here straight through the forest from the shrine. There's no path, so it must have been hard.'

Tatsunami explained that the route straight through the forest wasn't one you'd take for fun. Twigs were hanging from and sticking through Nanamiya's clothes, which had been partly ripped off. There could only be one reason for someone with an obsession for cleanliness to go that far.

'On our way back... some freaks attacked us....'

I suddenly noticed that Nanamiya's partner wasn't with him.

'Where's Kudamatsu?'

A pale face looked back at us.

'Too late. They got her.'

Takagi exploded.

'You left her behind?!'

'There was nothing I could do! Did you see them? THEY EAT PEOPLE! The moment one of them grabbed her, they all went for her! They almost got me too!'

'Zombies,' muttered Shigemoto, who had seen the beings. 'They're real. But how?'

Nabari and Kanno came out from the lobby. Kanno was holding a spear. It was probably one of the weapons from the second-floor lounge.

'What happened? Are there suspicious people hanging around outside?'

'They're here!'

We aimed our flashlights at the group that was slowly entering the plaza below. An ear-splitting shriek escaped from Nabari's mouth as she saw the horrendous figures. The beings illuminated by the lights appeared human, but many parts of their bodies had been bitten off. It was a horrifying sight. The beings were completely covered in blood and kept on bellowing with their mouths wide open. They had lost all reason. Just as Shigemoto had said, they were exactly like the zombies from films and video games.

But Kanno, who had just come out of the boarding house, shouted that the people should be taken to the hospital, and started descending the stairs to approach the group. A young-looking zombie suddenly lunged forward to attack him.

'Get off him!'

It was Tatsunami who saved Kanno's life. He had gone after the manager to stop him from approaching the mob. He used his long legs to kick the zombie in the chest and it fell to the ground. But other zombies started to reach out to them.

'Run!'

The two ran for their lives back up the steps.

'We have to kill them!' shouted Shigemoto. 'It's all over if a zombie manages to bite you! They're not human. We have to kill them! If not, it is we who will be killed!'

The horrifying crowd of zombies had flooded the plaza and were now on the staircase. They seemed unable to climb steps, however. Some of them would slip, lose their balance and fall back down, so they moved very slowly up the stairs. Eliminating the zombie at the front of the mob would definitely buy us time. But Kanno didn't move. He hesitated to attack a being that had a human appearance.

'What are you doing? Give me that!'

Tatsunami took the spear from Kanno and roared as he plunged the weapon into a zombie whose head had come above the staircase. Whilst the head of the spear was blunt, the strength of a grown man was enough for the attack to pierce the zombie's chest. But blood did not come pouring out of the wound, and the zombie kept moving despite the spear in its chest.

'Damn it!'

Tatsunami pulled the spear out and stabbed the zombie a few more times, to no effect. Shigemoto shouted: 'Not the heart. You need to destroy the brain.'

'How the hell do I do that!?'

The human skull is quite thick. A blunt spear would not be able to pierce it.

'The eyes!' shouted Hiruko. 'Stab the spear through the eyes into the brain!'

Following her advice, Tatsunami took aim and thrust the spear a few times into the zombie's eye sockets. Eventually, it stopped moving and fell backwards, taking a few other zombies down the stairs with it.

'Oh... uuugh.'

Tatsunami vomited at the sight of the flesh stuck to the head of the spear. The zombies, however, kept ascending the staircase. Hiruko cried: 'We can't keep this up! We have to shut ourselves inside the house!'

'Perhaps we can get away on the other side?'

Nanamiya turned pale at Tatsunami's suggestion.

'Impossible! They chased me through the mountain forest. No, I actually think they came from the other side of the mountains.'

Where was Akechi? Was he under attack from the zombies as well? I had to help him. That thought crossed my mind for a moment, but then I realised it was already too late. Any attempt to make my way through the crowd of zombies to save Akechi would be pure suicide.

There was a sudden cry from the rear of the house. It was Shindō. He had probably pushed his way through the forest, just as Nanamiya had done. But his partner Hoshikawa wasn't with him. Shindō looked at us before he shouted: 'Where's Reika!? She should have returned before me!'

'Did you get separated?' asked Tatsunami as he wiped his mouth.

'I distracted those beings so she could make a run for it! Hasn't she made it back yet?'

Nobody had seen her, however. We were standing at the front entrance. We would have noticed it immediately if someone of our group had come back. When Shindō saw the anxious looks on our faces, he cried out 'No way!' and frantically ran inside the Villa Violet.

'Reika! Are you inside!? Reika!!'

The advancing waves of zombies weren't on his mind just at that moment. His only worry was the safety of his girlfriend.

'We'd better go inside as well. We have to shut ourselves in,' Tatsunami decided.

'But Mifuyu and the others are still outside,' Takagi protested.

'They may have found some safe place themselves already. If we don't move now, the rest of us will be in danger as well.'

It was only a matter of time before the zombies reached the front entrance. A painful look appeared on Takagi's face, but she didn't volunteer to go out and help the others all by herself. She and everyone else went into the building. On Kanno's directions, we started closing the shutters to protect the glass doors, when Shigemoto suddenly cried out and pointed outside.

'But that's...!'

The zombie which was about to reach the top of the stairs was suddenly pulled back and fell down the stairs. In its place appeared the familiar sight of the man with the glasses and the aloha shirt.

'Akechi!'

'Mifuyu!'

Akechi thrust the woman he had been protecting behind him, Shizuhara, towards us as he kicked the pursuers below him away. Out of breath and out of her wits, Shizuhara stumbled through the entrance, terrified. She fell exhausted on the floor, sobbing loudly. Fortunately, she didn't appear to have been hurt.

'Hurry up!' I screamed desperately to Akechi.

Had he heard me cry? He tried to follow Shizuhara up the steps when a hand grabbed his ankle from below, and a skinny female zombie ruthlessly sank her teeth into his calf.

'Aaaaah!'

His tall figure staggered and fell backwards. Our eyes met at that very moment, and his lips moved.

'...Things don't always go right.'

The indescribable expression of shock, the tearful smile that appeared on his face was burnt into my memory. Only a few metres in front of me, Akechi had fallen down the staircase into that hellish nightmare. He had disappeared in front of us.

'Noooo!'

Cries of despair escaped from all our lips. Yes, it was utter despair.I took a deep breath and forced back what I had wanted to scream out. It was already too late.

'Close the shutters,' I said. 'They're coming.'

And that is how I lost my Holmes.

8

Although the front doors had been closed, the house's defences were not reliable. The front side of the first-floor lobby consisted of a glass curtain wall. It was only a matter of time before the zombies made it through the fragile window and entered the building.

'We can't stay here!'

'We have to go upstairs! We have to barricade the stairs!'

We had barely evacuated upstairs via the eastern staircase, when the sound of glass breaking below us could be heard. They were inside!

We quickly carried the larger pieces of furniture, such as sofas and a cabinet, from the second-floor lounge. By placing them on the half-landing between the first and second floors, and the landing of the second floor, we were planning to create a two-tier barricade. As far as we could tell, the zombies already had trouble climbing normal staircases, so our barricades should hold them off. Shindō came running down from the third floor, apparently having just noticed the chaos below. The poor fellow had been wandering around the house in search of Hoshikawa.

'She isn't here. Reika isn't here. Reika, where are you!?'

He almost sounded delirious, and to our shock, he suddenly started to move the furniture we had started to pile up on the half-landing.

'What do you think you're doing!?' Tatsunami quickly grabbed Shindō by the shoulder.

'Let me go. I have to go find Reika.'

'You have to face reality. She's probably gone already.'

'No!' cried Shindō. 'She's still alive. She has to be. I have to find her. Let me go!'

'Damn it!' Shindō was floored by a blow from Tatsunami. He crumbled to the floor, crying out loud. I stood there with a cold look. My spirit had already been broken when I witnessed Akechi's death. We all wanted to believe that Hoshikawa was still alive, of course. But at this moment our first priority was to fend off the attack of the zombies. There was no time now to be bothering with Shindō.

Surprisingly, it was Shigemoto who was directing the construction of the barricades.

'We shouldn't just make a barricade to block them, we have to make it difficult for them to go up the steps in the first place. Like a slope. They'll probably slip on that.'

Following his suggestion, Kanno opened the empty room 208 with his master keycard. He and Shigemoto removed the slats from the bed and placed them on the steps. They also removed all the sheets from the linen room on the third floor and spread them on the stairs. It took six of us to rock the vending machine in the lounge left and right, in order to move it to the landing of the staircase, where it formed a wall together with the cabinet. When we were finally done, Nanamiya reminded us of the emergency staircase in the south wing, which we should block as well.

'The emergency exits leading out to the emergency staircase are made of steel, and because of security reasons they can only be opened from the inside. The doors swing outwards and can't be forced open that easily,' said Kanno.

'Oh no! The elevator!' Hiruko cried out suddenly.

We had completely forgotten about it! If any zombies were to get inside the elevator, they could easily make their way upstairs. We hurried back to the lounge. The elevator was still stopped on the first floor.

'What should we do? There might be zombies inside the cage already.'

'But if we leave it down here, we never know when it could come up. If there are a few inside now, we'll just have to kill them.'

Tatsunami, who had already finished off one of them, held his spear ready as he watched the elevator door. We followed his example and all grabbed weapons from the wall. Kanno pushed the elevator button, and the indicator above the door moved from 1F to 2F. We all held our breath as the doors opened. It was empty. We all felt relieved.

'Mr. Kanno, is it possible to switch off the elevator?' asked Hiruko.

'The power panel is downstairs at the reception desk. I fear those monsters are all over the place now.'

'But if they accidentally push the elevator button, they can call it downstairs again!' cried Takagi.

'Let's improvise for now, then,' said Hiruko, and she placed a nearby chair inside the elevator opening. 'That should stop it from moving.'

Aha. An elevator shouldn't be able to move if the doors don't shut completely, because of safety measures.

Nabari, who had been standing guard at the staircase barricade, called out to us: 'The zombies are coming!'

We grabbed our weapons again and ran to the stairs. We looked down between the gaps in the barricade. The number of zombies that had made their way into the boarding house seemed to have grown again. Innumerable zombie heads were slowly pushing up the narrow staircase like a rising tide.

But these zombies appeared to have badly-developed motor skills. Their speed of movement on the steps was much slower than on level ground, and they had trouble staying balanced. Any zombie that did somehow manage to make their way up found the barricades in their way, got their feet wrapped up in the sheets and tripped backwards, taking the zombies behind them with them in their fall. The process kept repeating itself.For the time being, Shigemoto's suggestions were working extremely well.

'But they might get through the barricade eventually. Are we going to stand guard here all the time?' Nanamiya asked the question we all had in mind.

'We have something for that.'

Takagi and Shizuhara both pulled out keychain personal alarms from their pockets.They were the type that would sound a loud alarm if you pulled the pin out. Tatsunami whistled, but a scowl appeared on Nanamiya's face when he saw what they were holding.

'Why do you have them on you?'

They had brought personal alarms on a trip with just a small number of members: it was clear they had been on their guard against the men. But Takagi didn't care about Nanamiya's reaction. Shizuhara had probably been told by Takagi to bring one along.

'Just to be safe. Nothing to be afraid of. Anyway, we can use them to make somekind of trap, so we'll know immediately if they manage to get through.'

Following Takagi's suggestion, Kanno brought some fishing line from the storage and made a trap at the back of the barricade. If the zombies broke through, the line would pull the pin out of the alarm and set it off, which meant that our defences were now complete.

'What should we do with this alarm?' asked Shizuhara, but Nanamiya suddenly grabbed it from her.

'Hey!' cried Takagi.

'This one goes on the emergency exit on the third floor. If we lose the third floor, it's all over.'

He was right. If the zombies managed to take over the floor above us, we'd be trapped. It was Nanamiya himself who had the room closest to the emergency exit there.

We gathered together in the second-floor lounge. It was half past ten in the evening. The world had changed completely in the ninety minutes since we started our game.

The surviving… no, the students present here now were myself, Hiruko, Shindō, Takagi, Shizuhara, Nabari and Shigemoto. Of the alumni, Nanamiya and Tatsunami were left. And there was the manager Kanno. Ten in total. We had lost four people already. Kanno prepared coffee for us all, but I didn't feel like taking it.

We switched the television on. Our phones still had no signal, so we had no idea what was going on.

'And Deme?' asked Tatsunami, but Nanamiya shook his head.

'They were feeding on him when we arrived at the shrine. They also got Kudamatsu.'

Kudamatsu had been so kind to me from the start, for example telling me to eat during the barbecue. I thought of her carefree smile. Her cheerfulness had been a saviour for me on the trip, but I had not been able to thank her once.

'Look!' Takagi pointed to the screen, which was showing a news programme. The words "Terrorist Attack?" were accompanied by footage of a large park. Takagi raised the volume.

"Around four o'clock this afternoon, the police and fire departments received calls about several attendees at an outdoor live event feeling unwell. The number of visitors to the Sabea Rock Festival—held at Sabea Park in S Prefecture—who felt ill kept on growing. The police decided to seal off the area due to the possibility of a bioterror attack. At this moment, they are working on the rescue operation and an investigation into the incident."

I found the news report very curious. Even though it was a possible terrorist attack, there were no interviews and no footage shot at the scene. They only showed part of a promotional video of Sabea Park. Even supposing the television crew wasn't able to send in their own cameras to the park, in this day and age, everyone at the festival should be reporting on it through Twitter and video sites.

Hiruko told Kanno: 'There is no signal on any of our phones. How about the landline?'

Kanno picked up the handset of the lounge phone and tried it a few times, then shook his head and replaced it.

'It isn't working. What could be causing it?'

'They may already have put extensive communication restrictions in place,' said Hiruko, nodding as she mumbled to herself.

'But the zombies?'

90

'They are the visitors who were feeling unwell, I fear. They were dressed like festival attendees, and came from that direction. There aren't many people living around here, so I thought it was curious that there were so many zombies. I can't say whether it's some kind of scientific or biological weapon, or some other biohazard at work, but I think we can safely assume that something happened at that festival that turned the attendees into those beings.'

Shigemoto looked scared.

'Oh man, there are about fifty thousand daily attendees of the Sabea Rock Festival. And if you're bitten by a zombie, you'll change into one of them. If the majority of those visitors have been infected....'

According to the news, the incident started around four o' clock in the afternoon. It was unclear whether that time was correct. But if it started in the afternoon, it had only taken a couple hours for it to snowball into the current situation. It was truly a crisis.

'But the authorities are already aware of what's going on. Surely they'll come to save us,' suggested Shizuhara timidly, but Hiruko mercilessly struck down her hopes.

'Given that we are under attack by those beings at this very moment, I think we should assume the authorities have not been able to control the situation. I think they have shut down any on-the-scene coverage in order to prevent the public from panicking. The government's first priority must be to prevent the calamity from spreading further. They have to make sure that none of those infected manages to escape the area around Lake Sabea. Saving the people inside is number two.'

I recalled that when we were doing the Trial of Courage, there had not been a single car on the road, meaning that everything had already been closed off. And what about the formation of helicopters I had seen flying by earlier? Why had they been sent?

'Anyway, I think we have to prepare for a long stay inside the building here.'

Nabari, who had been silent up to that point, suddenly exploded.

'Stay here? But how long do we have to stay locked inside before we are rescued?'

Nobody could give her an answer.

I once saw a film where the government wasn't able to contain the spread of an outbreak so they decided to bomb the whole city, with the survivors still there. Perhaps that was going too far, but this boarding house was basically like an island in the sea. If we didn't survive, that would only mean ten lives lost. It was quite possible that the government would decide to give up on us. But then Hiruko started to talk.

'Let's not be too pessimistic. If those zombies truly are moving corpses, in a few days the self-digestion and the decomposition processes will render any activity impossible for them. And we're in the middle of the summer, so their bodies will rot even faster. It won't even take a week.'

Shigemoto whispered unemotionally: 'In order to survive a siege, the priorities are food, water, electricity and weapons.'

'The water was still running when I made coffee,' said Kanno.

At the moment we also had electricity. The problem was food. The lounge had a water dispenser and a coffee maker, but I hadn't seen anything edible.

'The kitchen downstairs has enough food for several days, but....' sighed Kanno.

We decided to collect the food we were carrying ourselves. Kanno brought some emergency supplies down from the storage on the third floor. The region had earthquakes, but only rarely, so they only had the bare minimum prepared.The big surprise was that Shigemoto had brought a dozen 500ml bottles of cola. He said that was what he usually drank.

'What about the luggage of the people who died?'

Tatsunami felt uneasy asking the question, and I quickly replied: 'Let's leave them alone. It's not as though we are in desperate need of food for the moment.'

The thought of rummaging through the luggage of the others was uncomfortable to everyone, so nobody objected. Then Kanno handed out face masks he had kept for emergencies to everyone.

'I thought it might be wise to put these on if we need to fight the zombies.'

He was right. If we were dealing with some kind of infection, we couldn't be careful enough. Next we needed weapons for our defence. There were plenty of swords and spears, but their usefulness was doubtful. Not only had the blades been blunted, but they were much heavier than you might have imagined. Even a man would have trouble wielding them. Swords were the weapon of choice of Shindō, myself and, surprisingly, Shizuhara as well. The others each chose a spear. In terms of range, the spear was superior, but I had a feeling the sword would be easier to use in the narrow corridors.

'Is anyone here experienced in martial arts?'

Nabari looked anxiously at the group, but the men all shook their heads. I was not completely hopeless at sports, but I had never actually practiced any specific one. Shigemoto and Shindō were the indoor type, and Nanamiya was the lazy spoiled brat, so they were also out. Kanno only played tennis. Tatsunami, who seemed physically the most impressive of us all, had only practiced swimming until high school. But one of the women raised her hand.

'My parents made me practice the *naginata* (a pole weapon similar to the glaive) and *aikido* since I was a child.'

It was Hiruko. But the petite Hiruko seemed so far removed from the strong figure Nabari had been hoping for that she only nodded silently with an enigmatic expression.

According to Tatsunami, zombies didn't flinch, no matter how much you cut or hit them. So we should avoid close-quarters combat as much as possible. At the moment, the one effective move appeared to be to pierce the eye and destroy the brain from a distance, using a spear or something similar. But I doubted that I'd be able to pull that off smoothly. What would we do if a pack of zombies managed to swarm the cramped building? Our first move would be to flee, of course.

The other remaining problem was where we were going to spend the night. We only had the second and third floor left to us. There was also a staircase inside the storage room on the third floor, which led to the rooftop. The largest space where everyone could relax was the lounge. But if the zombies managed to break through the barricades, the first room the monsters would attack would be the lounge.

'We should all go upstairs to the third floor. We can make more barricades all the way up.'

'In the films, you know it all goes wrong the moment everyone splits up. We should stay together as a group.'

Takagi and Nabari both had the same thoughts, but Shindō demurred.

'You mean we'd have to stay cooped up in one room with five, ten people? I don't think so.'

Shigemoto agreed with him.

'I—I am against staying in one place with everyone. In the films, people only get killed off one by one because they carelessly enter the enemies' territory or because they don't realise who the enemy is.'

'What's your idea then?' Takagi glared at him.

'We are now basically... at war. The one thing we have to avoid is complete annihilation. If they manage to break through and overwhelm us, no one can escape if we're all packed together. But if we're divided amongst two floors, at least the other half can escape.'

'Huh. So the folks on the second floor are the bait?' said Nanamiya sarcastically, as he applied his eye drops. Perhaps doing it was a habit to calm himself down.

Kanno protested: 'It's not a given that they would attack the second floor first.'

He was right. There was always the possibility that, if the zombies broke through the barricades, they would just ignore the second-floor and climb the stairs up to the third floor. The outside emergency stairs in the south wing also led to the second and third floor, so it was also possible that the zombies would bypass the second-floor emergency exit and break through the door on the third floor.

'But still, the second floor is at the most risk. The zombies are slow at climbing stairs, so the people on the third floor would have enough time to run if the alarm went off, but that's not true for the people on this floor,' cried Nabari hysterically.

'But we can close the door between the east wing and the lounge.'

Kanno was referring to the doors dividing each wing.

'As you can see, the east and south wings can be closed off from the central wing with the emergency doors, but can only be locked and opened with this specific key, so if we lock them, we won't be able to use them in emergency situations. But if we lock the door dividing the central and east wing during the night, at least the rest of the second floor can remain protected, even if the zombies do manage to break through.'

I checked the booklet. Nabari in 206 and Deme in 207were the two occupants of the rooms in the east wing of the second floor. So the east wing door could be closed off if Nabari were to change rooms.

'And we don't know how many days we'll have to spend here. We should therefore try to protect the space available to us.'

If we gave up on the second floor right now, the only spot left to flee to would be the rooftop. If we managed to hold the lounge, we could at least go up and down to the third floor using the elevator.

Hiruko, who had not said anything in the last few minutes, asked Kanno a question:

'Are the elevator and the stairs the only ways to move between the floors?'

'No, there's one more way.'

He went over to the storage room and returned with an aluminium rope ladder for emergencies.

'If we hang this ladder from one of the balconies in the rooms upstairs, we can go up and down that way as well. Unfortunately, there's only one of them.'

'That's more than enough. How about this as a plan, then? We can each sleep in our own room tonight. If anyone hears them break in through the emergency exit, or if one of the alarms goes off, use the phone extension in your room to warn everyone, and remain inside. The doors in the building swing outwards, so they won't be able to break through them quickly. The people in the safe areas will then close off the doors between each wing to slow the zombies down, and use the rope ladder to save the people trapped inside their rooms.'

Hiruko's plan would prevent us from all getting eliminated in a sudden attack, but would also allow us to save anyone in trouble. Takagi and Nabari preferred everyone to stay together, but eventually they, too, reluctantly agreed to follow the plan. It was decided to place the rope ladder in front of the elevator on the third floor, so that anyone could use it.

Kanno then made an announcement: 'I will place the key to the wing doors on the television stand. Please use it if necessary. Ms. Nabari, you will have to change rooms, but, as I had no time to bring the keycards of the other rooms with me, you can use my master keycard.'

So Nabari would end up in the empty 205, and the east wing door would be closed. Even if the zombies managed to get through the barricade, we didn't have to worry that they would have a free run to the lounge.

'So then where will you stay, Mr. Kanno?' I asked. He would normally stay in the manager's room downstairs.

'I hate to ask, but I was hoping to use Ms. Hoshikawa's room. I want to stay near the lounge to keep guard.'

He looked at Shindō as he spoke. I had expected him to react angrily to Kanno using his girlfriend's room, but he just nodded meekly.

'Of course… But I want to keep her luggage.'

Hoshikawa's room 203 was opened with the master keycard and Shindō quickly carried her belongings out. After he had left, Hiruko asked Kanno: 'How are you going to shut this door, or activate the power? You just gave away the master keycard, so there are no more keycards left.'

The 203room keycard had been in Hoshikawa's possession, and had therefore been lost.

'I'll use the door guard as a doorstop to keep the door open when I'm not in my room, so that won't be a problem. And I can activate the power in the room by using Ms. Nabari's old keycard for 206.'

Takagi made a suggestion: 'You can also just put a driver's license or something in the holder to activate the power. I often used to do that in business hotels to keep the air conditioning in the room running while I was out.'

I had done the same myself as well. And in hotels which used a bar-shaped key holder, a toothbrush would do.

'The quality of the keycards used here is a bit better, so the power in a room won't go on unless the holder detects the magnetic strip on the rear of the keycard. So, although you can use keycards from other rooms to turn on the power, you can't use your driver's license.'

Tatsunami also had a question.

'What about the night watch? Shouldn't at least the men take turns and keep an eye on things during the night?'

Nabari shook her head.

'There's no need for that. Even if you noticed the zombies coming in, what would you do? Use your weapons to push them back? In the end, you'd have to flee to a room anyway.'

'And, during the night, everyone would be sleeping with their doors locked. So it would be the person on patrol who would have the bad luck to end up with no place to escape to,' added Hiruko.

The others, too, made worried comments. Because we had decided to split up for the night, any effect a night watch might have had been weakened.

Kanno addressed all of us.

'Please refrain from carelessly leaving your room during the night. I don't believe the zombies can scale walls, but don't forget to lock the doors to the balcony as well. And always carry a weapon with you, just in case. I will check the emergency exits and the barricades every hour.'

I felt bad leaving Kanno to do everything, but it was the safest option. Anyway, we had done all we could do now. It was already past eleven, but nobody showed any intention of returning to their room yet. Which was natural. In this situation, where we were surrounded by zombies, nobody wanted to be alone. But it was also true that the desperate tension that had been pushing us all this time was finally easing up, and we were starting to feel drowsy. Too much had happened to us in the span of just one day, and our brains needed some time to process all of it. We were exhausted. Please let us sleep. And let everything be a dream by the time we wake up.

'We should return to our rooms.'

I had been dozing off when Hiruko shook my shoulders. Shigemoto was standing in front of me with a trident. He reminded me of Zhu Bajie, the pig hero from *Journey to the West*.

'I'm going now.'

Following his example, the others slowly got up. The ones who had to go upstairs were Nanamiya, Shigemoto, Shindō, Shizuhara and myself. We couldn't all fit in the elevator, so I decided to take the eastern staircase. It was rather scary to get closer to the zombies, but I wanted to take another look at the barricade. I got up with my sword in my hand.

'I'm going this way. Could you lock the door behind me?' I asked Hiruko.

We had just agreed that the east wing door on the second floor had to be kept locked during the night. So I needed someone to lock it behind me after I left the lounge.

'I'll walk you to your room. I'll lock the door when I return.'

Hiruko was holding a spear. The sight of the two of us in our summer wear, whilst brandishing such impressive weapons, must have appeared ridiculous.

We went down the east corridor and arrived at the staircase landing. A pile of furniture and the rear of the vending machine were facing us. From the other side of the door came banging noises and a never-ending symphony of low growls. It seemed to be holding for now, but I felt physically sick just imagining what would happen if the monsters broke through and stormed the floor.

When we arrived upstairs, we immediately found ourselves in front of the door of my room 308. If the zombies broke through the barricade and proceeded to the third floor, my room would be the first to be surrounded by them. But it was no use worrying about that. Hiruko, for example, was in the room closest to the second-floor emergency exit, and poor Shizuhara was in the room right next to mine. I should be grateful I was on the third floor.

'If you hear something during the night, don't open your door carelessly. Make sure who's on the other side first.'

Hiruko acted as if she were my mother.

'You be careful yourself, too.'

I had unlocked the door and was about to go inside, when she called out to me.

'I was serious earlier. I want you to become my assistant. I'm terribly sorry for what happened to Akechi, but…'

'Don't say it,' I said, more bluntly than I had intended. 'This is not the time. I haven't even had time to think about what happened to him. How can you bring that up now?'

A stunned expression appeared on Hiruko's face, and she looked away nervously.

'You're right. I'm sorry, what was I thinking? Forget about it. Sleep well.'

Hiruko shut the door slowly and silently. I placed the keycard in the holder on the wall to turn the light on in my room. I made sure the door was locked. No problems there. I took off my shoes and lay down on the bed.

I hadn't been able to contain my anger just now. It was difficult to read what was going on in her mind, but at the very least I expected her to have some common sense. Her assistant? Was she still planning to play detective in such a situation? That was just plain idiotic.

I got up again, opened the French windows, and stepped out onto the balcony. The plaza below the thick layer of clouds was illuminated by several outdoor lights, but the lights were too weak for me to make everything out clearly. I could hear the groaning of the zombies below, like the rolling waves of the sea. The humid wind was also blowing the smell of death this way.

I had felt exactly like this after the earthquake. Feeling so powerless I almost forgot to breathe. The hopeless view, and just thinking of the important things I had lost in one single day, made me feel like the whole world had been swept away from under me.

Damn it. Villa Violet? It had turned into a villa of violence, a villa of death!

I took a deep breath. There was nothing I could do now. Whatever happened, happened.I calmed down a little. It was only then that it occurred to me that the infection might be airborne, so I hurried back inside to close the windows. All we could do now was await the morning. Fortunately, the zombies had trouble with the barricade and could barely climb steps. They were not as fearsome as in the films. As long as we stayed in our rooms, we would all be safe.

I could not have imagined that there would be a new victim that night.

CHAPTER FOUR
VICTIMS OF THE CALAMITY

1

It was a sign from heaven.The appearance of the walking dead, the idea that suddenly ran through my mind like lightning: all of this meant that something, good or evil, had chosen my side. The police wouldn't be able to come here any time soon. It was a golden opportunity.

I was being told to do it. That everything had been prepared for me. The place was ready. The method was ready. Those loathsome victims were ready. And my mind, my mind had been ready and prepared to take action long ago.

There was nothing to stop me now.I had been waiting for such a chance to exact my revenge. I had to go now. He was in his room.

A dark feeling of rejoicing burnt within me. I took a step forward. There was no going back now.

2

As soon as I woke up, my hand automatically started probing the nightstand. When my search turned up empty after two or three tries, I remembered I hadn't yet recovered my watch. I got up.

I took a look at the digital wall clock, which indicated six in the morning. Fortunately, nobody had been hammerin on my door, nor had there been any SOS calls from the others whilst I had been asleep. Despite the abnormal situation, I had been able to get a good night's rest. Yesterday had been exhausting, both physically and mentally.

But it felt too quiet. I took a look outside. It was drizzling. It seemed as though the crowd of zombies gathered beneath my window had grown, compared to when they first attacked us. They simply stood there, unprotected from the rain, looking up at the sky with their mouths open, as if they were repenting to heaven. It was a miserable sight.

Usually I would go back to sleep again at such an early hour, but considering the situation, I didn't feel like giving in to my lazy habit. I had a quick shower first, and then reached out for my sword. Whilst it was only a replica, it felt cold and heavy. To be safe, I first put the swing bar door guard on before I pushed the door ajar and peeked outside. I could see the staircase at the end of the empty corridor. Seeing there was nobody, I stepped carefully out of the room.

The first thing that came to mind was to make sure the barricade was still holding. Going down the stairs to the right of my room, I noticed some music coming from the direction of the lounge. I knew the lounge didn't have a stereo installation, so the music was probably coming from the radio cassette CD player we had used at the barbecue.

The barricade was still fully functional. The furniture had not been disturbed and the fishing line connected to the personal alarm was still stretched tight. Both security measures had fulfilled their tasks this first night. Beyond the barricade, I could make out the figures of the zombies who were still foolishly slamming their bodies against the barricade, tumbling and falling down the stairs again. It was like a commercial to show off the sturdiness of the furniture. Let's hope it was made in Japan.

I wanted to go to the lounge, but then I remembered the door to the central wing was locked. The key was kept on the television stand, so I couldn't open the door from this side. If there was somebody in the lounge already, I could knock on the door and have them open it, but if there was nobody, I'd just be wasting more time. After a moment, I decided I'd go back to the third floor and take the elevator down.

The elevator had been stopped on the third floor and a tissue box had been wedged between the doors. I assumed it had been left like that after the people on the third floor had come up in the elevator last night. I reached out to the tissue box, but then froze. Was it really all right if I went downstairs in the elevator now? Then Shizuhara, who occupied the room next to me, appeared in the elevator hall.

'Good morning.'

'Good morning. You're up early. Did I wake you?'

'No, I just got up by myself.'

Strangely enough, this was basically the first time Shizuhara and I had talked to each other. She looked upset, but otherwise still fine. She seemed puzzled at the sight of me standing there in front of the elevator.

'What's the matter?'

'If we take the elevator to the second floor, we'll have to block the doors to prevent it from going down to the first floor. But then the people here can't call the elevator back up.'

Shizuhara nodded. 'Oh, that's true. But the people on the third floor could always use the extension to call downstairs to ask them to remove the doorstop.'

If it was going to be that much trouble, we might as well just go down via the stairs. I used the phone in my room to call the lounge. Kanno was already up, it seemed, as he answered my call.

'Ah, you've called just at the right moment. We've found something curious. Could you please come down immediately?'

We hurried down the stairs and went into the lounge, where we found Kanno, as well as Tatsunami and Shigemoto. I remarked on how we were all up so early, and Shigemoto explained that he had been worried about the barricade. I assumed he had taken the eastern staircase down as well. The loud music had been coming from Tatsunami's room, which was connected to the lounge. At that moment, Hiruko appeared from the south wing. Whilst we were all wearing casual t-shirts and shorts, she looked classy as always, wearing a blue blouse with soft lines and a white skirt.

'What's the matter?' she asked.

Kanno showed her the sheet of paper he was holding in his hand.

'Mr. Shigemoto found this wedged between the door and frame of Mr. Shindō's room.'

The note had one simple line in a messy scrawl: "Thanks for the delicious meal."

'It could just be a prank.'

As I listened to Tatsunami's guess, I thought of the threatening note addressed to the Film Club, and I noticed that Shindō himself wasn't amongst those present.

'Shindō isn't answering any calls or knocks on his door.'

Shigemoto's eyes moved nervously. Kanno used the phone to call Shindō's room, but replaced the receiver with a worried look on his face.

'No answer.'

As the bad feeling we all shared started to grow, Hiruko made a suggestion: 'His room is on the third floor, 305, isn't it? We should wake up everyone on this floor and then check up on him together.'

Takagi and Nabari were quickly woken up, and we all went up to the third floor via the stairs. I was the only one armed. As I had guessed, spears were too large to carry around everywhere.

We knocked on Shindō's door, but there was no answer.

'Mr. Shindō, are you awake?'

'Shindō, answer us! Are you taking a bath?' Tatsunami yelled.

With no other options left, Kanno turned to Nabari and opened his hand.

'Could you lend me the master keycard I gave you last night?'

Nabari, her face pale, nodded.

Tatsunami volunteered to wake the absent Nanamiya, and left for the south wing. Kanno pushed the master keycard into the slot of the card reader. A beep followed as the door became unlocked. A nasty smell reached our noses.

'Uuugh.'

Kanno grunted as he peeked inside the room. We all stood behind him, but nobody had expected the sight that unfolded before our eyes.

Blood was spreading all over the floor, and had even been splattered on the ceiling. There were pieces of flesh lying everywhere. The French windows had been opened, and, lying halfway onto the balcony, was Shindō's body. Chunks had been gnawed out of it, and his lifeless remains were barely recognisable.

'What the devil?!'

Kanno was about to step inside the room.

'Watch out!' cried Hiruko. 'There might still be zombies inside!'

Kanno jumped backwards and I held my sword to the ready. Takagi shouted that she would get her weapon, and she and Shizuhara went down in the elevator together.

I pulled the face mask I had been given yesterday out of my pocket. The others who had them did the same, and the rest covered their faces with towels or handkerchiefs. I carefully observed the interior from the doorway. The room's keycard was in the holder on the wall. There was blood everywhere, but the room itself was not in disarray. Shindō's longsword was resting against the wall immediately to my left. The French windows had been opened wide. Had he attempted to flee via the balcony? Smudges of blood too vague to actually call footprints went out onto the balcony, and there was also blood on the railings.

'What happened... Aagh!'

Tatsunami, who had returned with Nanamiya, cried out as he saw the horrifying state of the room.

I was the only one with a sword, so I stepped slowly inside. There did not appear to be anyone in the room. I carefully opened the bathroom door, but inside was empty as well.

'It's okay, there's nobody here.'

Takagi and Shizuhara had returned with their weapons. They had a spear and sword, but the only ones who dared to follow me inside were Hiruko and Kanno, which was understandable, for Shindō's death had been truly horrible. It was not only his body that had parts bitten off. His head was lying sideways, and his face had been gnawed all over beyond recognition.

I was careful not to touch the body as I followed the blood tracks outside onto the balcony. I looked down. There was no rope or rope ladder hanging here. There were only the hordes of zombies swarming the ground below, moaning and groaning as usual. Meanwhile Hiruko had been examining the door, but had found nothing out of the ordinary.

'Oh, what a horrible fate....'

Kanno was about to crouch down beside Shindō's body when Shigemoto shouted a warning: 'No! Don't get too close to the body.'

'Why not?'

'We don't know how much time has passed since he was bitten and killed. He could rise as a zombie at any moment.'

We all stepped away from the corpse.

'Wait! Didn't he just move?' whisperedNanamiya.

'What?'

'His finger, it moved. I'm sure. He's still alive.'

No way. How could anyone survive such terrible injuries?

'He's not alive!' Shigemoto shouted again. 'Look at the colour of the blood from his wounds!'

The blood which had oozed out of the innumerable bite wounds all over Shindō's body had already turned a blackish colour, but in some spots, it had turned a greenish hue.

'The blood has dried! Nobody can survive lying like that for so long. He's not human anymore, he's turned into a zombie! We have to kill it before it attacks us!'

Shigemoto was shaking all over. Hiruko and Kanno, who were standing inside the room, were hesitant, as was I. I knew it couldn't be true, but we didn't want to abandon the possibility, no matter how small, that Shindō was still alive. If so, we needed to give him medical care immediately. But if he was turning into a zombie, we had to finish him off right then and there. Were we going to extend our hands to him, or thrust a spear into him? A pregnant silence hung over the room.

Then it happened. Someone suddenly stepped forward from behind me and resolutely plunged a spear through the right eye into the back of the head in a single blow. Shindō's body jumped once, and fell back motionless.

103

'Aaah!' Shigemoto let out a pathetic cry, even though he had been the one who had suggested we do it.

Heavy breathing.

'Rin...' Shizuhara whispered.

It had been Takagi. She had stabbed her club president without hesitation.

'There was no other way.'

Takagi twisted the head of the spear around twice before she pulled the weapon out. Sticking to the tip was the eyeball and some soft tissue, probably the brain.

'Mifuyu, it was too late for him. He had to be killed.'

Her grim determination didn't allow for any counterarguments.

Afterwards we moved Shindō's remains to a corner of the room and covered him with a bedsheet. His blood and flesh were all over the room. There was nothing more we could do, and we all wanted to leave the place as soon as possible.

'His body should start to decompose soon, given that it's summer. We should least keep the air conditioning on,' said Kanno as he used the remote control to activate it.

Shizuhara, who had been standing near the door, suddenly called out to us. 'What's this?'

A folded piece of paper had been lying in the room, right beside the door. We unfolded it and found the same messy scrawl we had seen earlier.

"Let's eat."

3

Hiruko pointed out that the zombie which had attacked Shindō could still be hiding somewhere, so we split up and searched every space, from the empty rooms on the second and third floors, all the way to the rooftop. We found no trace of the being anywhere. As the bloody tracks had suggested, the zombie had probably fallen off the balcony.

We gathered in the lounge once more. None of us seemed able to believe what had happened. All of us were completely mystified. The same question was in everyone's mind: Where had the zombie that had killed Shindō come from?

For a moment, there was a babble of voices as we each talked over the others, offering our guesses, but eventually one person silenced us all. It was Hiruko.

'Listen, everyone, we have to establish what happened to Shindō last night. At this moment, we don't know how or when the zombie managed to get inside. Let's ask everyone in turn to say if they noticed anything last night.'

'Are you going to playing detective at a time like this?' barked Nanamiya, as he applied his eye drops once again. He seemed very nervous, as he had been tapping his head and applying eye drops even more often than yesterday.

'Why not? We all want to know what happened. Let her handle it,' Tatsunami countered his friend. He was still calm. The seniors amongst us didn't seem to mind, so we all agreed to become the subject of Hiruko's questioning.

'Can something be done about the music first?'

Nabari was irritated by the cheerful music which had been going on constantly. Tatsunami shrugged and said that without the music it would be just like a sad funeral service, but he nevertheless returned to his room to switch the CD player off. There was a sudden silence in the lounge. Hiruko checked the room assignments as she began to speak.

'Let's start with the people nearest to Shindō, room 305.' She turned to Shigemoto. 'Could you tell us what you did after you returned to your room last night, and whether you noticed anything?'

Shigemoto, who was Shindō's neighbour in 304, looked up. He had a dark expression on his face.

'...Last night, Shindō, Shizuhara, Mr. Nanamiya and I went up to the third floor in the elevator and said goodbye there. I couldn't sleep, so I watched some DVDs I had brought with me. But I dozed off whilst I was watching the second one, probably just before one o' clock. I woke up at 05:50. It was still early, but I wanted to know whether we were still safe, so I left my room. That's when I noticed that piece of paper wedged between the door and the frame of Shindō's room....'

'It was wedged into the doorway?'

'Yes, like this.'

He took the piece of paper and folded it in three.

'It was made thick enough so it could be jammed between the door and the frame. At first, I thought it was a bad joke, so I knocked on the door, but there was no answer. He didn't answer the phone either, so I decided to take it with me to the lounge, as I wanted to check up on the barricade anyway.'

'So that piece of paper had been wedged into the doorway from outside the room?'

'Yes. Look at how neat it still looks. If the door had been firmly shut on it, there would have been more wrinkles in the paper. But I could pull it out without any problem.'

'But how could you not have noticed what had happened to Shindō, with only a wall between you?' snarled Nanamiya. Shigemoto shook his head. Kanno, however,was able to explain.

'The walls between the rooms are soundproof, so it's very difficult to hear anything from the adjacent room.'

Shigemoto protested: 'But I could hear Mr. Tatsunami's CD player last night. I couldn't get to sleep because it bothered me, and I could even hear it whilst I was watching my DVDs.'

I couldn't believe it. Had the music been playing continuously since last night?

'Oh, sorry about that,' said Tatsunami, who didn't seem at all sorry.

This new fact prompted me to ask Kanno: 'But if the walls are soundproof, doesn't that mean we won't be able to hear the alarm if the zombies break through the barricade?'

'No, I don't think we'll have to worry. The doors and ceilings are not soundproof, so you can still hear noise coming from the lounge and the corridors. From your room, you will definitely be able to hear the alarm in the staircase. You just won't hear any noise from the room next door.'

And with that, Shigemoto's turn was over. It didn't seem as though he had mentioned anything of importance. The next in line was Nabari, who occupied 205, the room right beneath Shindō.

'It was an awful night. Usually, I take sleeping pills, but I couldn't very well take them now, not knowing when those zombies could make it up here. So I was awake all night. All you see outside are those monsters, so I was slowly going mad. That's when I decided to get a glass of water. I know we agreed we shouldn't leave our rooms at night, but the pantry is close to my room. That's when I saw Mr. Kanno, who was doing his rounds. Remind me what time we met.'

'It was my second round, so I believe it was around two o' clock.'

'Yes, that would be about right. I returned to my room about ten minutes later and then I just curled up in my comforter. I kept hearing them groaning. I was afraid the morning would never come.'

'Did you notice anything else?'asked Hiruko, and Nabari seemed to recall something.

'I don't remember when, exactly, but I think I heard a loud thud coming from above me. Perhaps that's when....'

It could have been the time Shindō was killed.

'Could you try to pinpoint when it was?' persisted Hiruko.

'Not exactly, but it happened after I had my glass of water, so around half past two, perhaps later. But I didn't hear any cries.'

'Aha, considering how the blood reached all the way up to the ceiling, the zombie might have gone for the throat first. Shindō wouldn't have had any chance to cry after that first attack.'Hiruko nodded at her own suggestion.

'Mr. Kanno, could I ask you for your account, as you were mentioned just now?'

Kanno seemed nervous as he started to speak.

'After seeing you all off last night, I checked the emergency exits and the barricade again. That's when I saw you, returning from the third floor. After cleaning up and checking everything, I withdrew to my room before midnight. I had decided I'd make my rounds every hour. I've held all kinds of jobs before, so I'm used to irregular sleeping. I had a short rest and I got up at one for my first round. That was when I met Mr. Shindō in the lounge. He had taken the elevator down and it had stopped at the second floor.'

'Why had he come downstairs?'

'I believe he wanted a drink, too. He said he couldn't sleep because of what had happened to Ms. Hoshikawa.'

There was a short pause.

'But...and perhaps I only have this feeling now I know what happened, but he seemed to be acting strangely. He appeared quite alarmed upon seeing me. He quickly took the elevator back upstairs.'

'Alarmed, you say?'

'Yes. For a moment, I thought he might have been planning to meet someone.'

'But you had not heard anyone talking in the lounge, correct?'

'No. It was just a guess of mine, I'm sorry.'

Kanno apologised politely.

'On my second round, I saw Ms. Shizuhara. I did not see anyone else during my other rounds.'

'Did you hear the thud Nabari mentioned?'

Kanno shook his head.

'And you noticed nothing out of the ordinary about the entrances during your rounds?'

'Not a single problem. The emergency exits and the barricade, the east wing door, and the elevator were all as they should be.'

'And what about that piece of paper wedged into Shindō's doorframe?'

Kanno appeared distressed and started looking for the right words.

'Up until my third round, which was around three o'clock, I'm quite certain it was not there. But I can't be so sure about what happened after that. I did pass by his room, but by that time I had become used to the routine, and the emergency exits and the barricade were my only worries, so I didn't pay much attention to the guest rooms.'

The lights inside the building were all on, allowing for a clear view everywhere, but it was still possible to simply overlook something. I myself had not paid any attention to the other rooms on my way back to my own room last night.

The questioning continued for some time, but there was nobody who could offer any valuable information about the attack on Shindō. The people on the second floor, of course, had no way of knowing what had been going on in Shindō's room. Shizuhara and I were in the east wing on the third floor, and Nanamiya in the south wing, so it was unlikely we would have heard anything happening in the central wing. None of us had heard the thud Nabari had mentioned. When we were all done, Hiruko bowed and thanked us all.

'For the moment, we have learned three facts that pertain to the murder. First, that Shindō was still alive at one o' clock, then the thud Nabari heard around half past two, and third, the piece of paper that was probably left after three o' clock. But those facts cannot explain what happened.'

It was then that I noticed a contradiction.

'Wait a second. If Shindō was killed around half past two, isn't it strange that the note hadn't yet been wedged in the door by the three o' clock round? What was the killer doing after the murder?'

Hiruko, however, did not give much weight to my point.

'There's no way to know if the noise Nabari heard occurred at the time of the murder, and the time frame is also vague. We don't need to pay too much attention to it.'

It was at that moment that Takagi asked the question that had been on everyone's mind.

'But... was it a human who killed Shindō? Or a zombie?'

'Did it look as if anything but a zombie could've done that? The teeth marks were still visible! He was bitten to death! The zombie probably fell off the balcony after killing Shindō.' Shigemoto rattled off the points.

'But where did the zombie come from? We know the emergency exits and the barricade are all intact. If zombies could get in so easily, we'd all be looking like them by now,' retorted Tatsunami.

It did seem unlikely that our defences had been penetrated. I took a look at the elevator doors. The elevator was now stopped on the third floor. But it made me think of one other possibility.

'What about the elevator? According to Mr. Kanno, Shindō had taken the elevator down to the lounge around one o' clock. What if the elevator had accidentally gone downstairs and a zombie had got in?'

Hiruko immediately rejected that possibility, however.

'Then he would have been murdered inside the elevator, which has not a single bloodstain inside. I'm convinced he was killed inside his room.'

'Ah, I guess you're right.'

It had been just a guess on my part, so I quickly folded. Shigemoto, however, seemed to be holding on to the idea that a zombie was the killer, and suggested a different possibility.

'What if a zombie had been hiding inside before we made the barricade?'

Tatsunami seemed unconvinced.

'You mean a zombie somehow got up here without us knowing? I don't think there was any opportunity for it to do so.'

'Yes,there was!' exclaimed Takagi.'After we fled back here, Mr. Kanno descended down to the plaza with a spear, which means there was nobody inside the building at that moment.'

'But only Mr. Kanno and Mr. Tatsunami went down to the plaza. The rest of us all were standing in front of the entrance, so we would have known right away if any zombie had attempted to go inside. In the same way that we noticed immediately when Mr. Nanamiya and Shindō arrived from the rear of the building,' countered Nabari.

'Then they got in through the back entrance.'

Shigemoto wasn't about to give up. There was a terrace which also functioned as a smoking area on the first floor, and there was a door there that connected to the outside. Kanno denied the possibility that a zombie could have entered via the back entrance, however.

'That's not possible. After you left for your Trial of Courage, I made sure to lock up everything on the first floor. I locked the terrace exit and the windows in the corridors, all of which have stoppers which prevent them from opening wide. A head wouldn't even fit through the windows below. I was sitting at the reception desk all the time until Ms. Nabari came to notify me. I also have monitors there, connected to the security cameras at the front entrance, so I would have noticed anything trying to enter the premises.'

'I also tried to get in through the terrace entrance at first, but the door was locked so I had to go round to the front,' added Nanamiya.

'And do you really think a zombie which had managed to get inside would just play hide and seek and wait patiently until we had gone to bed? We were all running around the place whilst we were building the barricade, but none of us saw a monster strolling around. But most importantly, just think about those notes we found in the room. Do you think a zombie could have written those?'

Tatsunami's relentless arguments had weakened Shigemoto's position. Backed into a corner, he asked: 'If it wasn't a zombie, who did it, then!?'

'A living human. I don't know who, but someone who hated Shindō's guts killed him.'

'Mr. Kanno just said nobody could have got in from the outside. You can't mean....'

'That's right. I think one of us is the killer.'

We could all feel the tension arising from Tatsunami's accusation. Shigemoto snorted in disbelief.

'I can't believe it. What about those wounds all over Shindō's body? They weren't made by a blade or anything. Something gnawed him!'

Tatsunami's reply was shocking.

'That's right. But is there a rule that says zombies are the only ones who can bite a person to death?'

'...Huh?'

'A human could just as well bite someone to death. Then, if we can be made to believe it was a zombie, no suspicion falls on the killer.'

Aha, he had a point. There was no way to prove that those bite marks had been made by a zombie. Takagi had killed Shindō for sure, but we could not be certain that he had indeed been infected. Perhaps the murderer had counted on us killing him, just to be on the safe side. Maybe that had been part of the real killer's plan.

Hiruko shook her head at the suggestion.

'It's an interesting line of reasoning, but it's not one I can wholeheartedly agree with.'

110

'Huh.'

Tatsunami could not be expected to have known about her background, but did seem impressed by her calm behaviour.

'Would you care to explain yourself?'

'Of course. It's very simple. We all saw those wounds. There were dozens of bite marks all over his body, some penetrating his clothes and some wounds even going as deep as the bone. If they had all been the work of a single human being, it would have been extremely painful for their own teeth and jaws. They would be bleeding from their own mouths, too. But as far as I can see, none of us here has hurt their mouth.'

Everyone shot glances at those around them, but everyone appeared normal. I was impressed by her keen powers of observation. Whilst we had been averting our eyes from the atrocious appearance of Shindō's remains, she had already been considering the possibility.

'Furthermore, you suggested that the murderer was trying to divert suspicion to a zombie, but that doesn't explain the messages left at the scene. In fact, it would have been better not to have left any notes.'

Although Tatsunami's theory had been shot to pieces, he still appeared calm.

'I agree you do have a point there. But if you're right, that would mean that a zombie did it. So where did they come from? Did they scale the wall and climb in through the windows?'

'No, I think that's very unlikely. As we saw yesterday, zombies can't even climb a flight of stairs without difficulty. Actions such as climbing walls or using a ladder would require too much dexterity from them. There is one thing I want to confirm before I go on, though. Is there anyone here who will admit to leaving those messages? Someone who simply wanted to pull a prank on Shindō, but had nothing to do with his death? If that's the case, I ask that person to honestly admit that now.'

Everyone looked at the notes placed on the table. Two messages. "Let's eat" and "Thanks for the delicious meal." Based on the paper and pen used, it was probably safe to assume they came from the same person. But no one admitted writing them.

'Nobody? We can therefore conclude they were written by the killer, which in turn means the killer is a human being. According to Shigemoto, one of the notes was wedged between the door and the frame from the outside, which means that the murderer left the room after the murder, wedged the piece of paper in the doorway, and is therefore still inside the building.'

But if she was right, then the murderer had to be one of us, who had brought a zombie inside from somewhere. Which brought us back to the problem of how the zombie had got inside.

'Uggh, I just don't get it.'

Tatsunami put a cigarette in his mouth and lit it. He looked up at the ceiling as he puffed out a cloud of smoke.Everyone in the lounge shared his sentiments.

'Tatsunami, piss off with your cigarettes!' screamed Nanamiya, kicking the table.'It's the same as that threatening note! Those messages are meant for us!!'

'Nanamiya, calm down.'

'If it's not a zombie or a human, then there's only one answer! It's a zombie which has retained its mind and is trying to get revenge on us....'

'Control yourself!!'

After Tatsunami's warning, Nanamiya tapped his cheek restlessly a few times, then cursed and started grabbing emergency rations and bottles of water from the cabinet.

'What are you doing?' asked Tatsunami.

'I'm going to stay in my room! Don't even try to come near until the rescuers are here!'

With that, he quickly left the lounge. Nobody tried to stop him.

'Don't mind him. The kid can't take it if things don't go his way.' Tatsunami shrugged.

'But we didn't have much food in the first place,' muttered Takagi. She was more worried about the food than Nanamiya.

After that, we decided it was time for a simple breakfast. Needless to say, none of us had much of an appetite, having begun the morning by witnessing the remains of one of us. Most of us only had the soup from the emergency rations. After that, we gathered around the television with the volume up, but there were no new developments.

Nobody said it out loud, but the fact that one of us had been killed inside his own locked room worried all of us. But for the hand of fate, any of us could have been the one to have been eaten by a zombie and have their brain pierced by a blade by the one of the others. After some time, Tatsunami made a suggestion.

'I was just thinking, isn't it better to keep the doors of all the unused rooms open? We can keep them ajar by using the door guard as a doorstop. That way the automatic lock won't work.'

'That's right, but why?' Kanno frowned.

'Suppose you're not in your room when they break through the barricade. You'd want to run inside the nearest room, but if all the rooms are kept locked, the only room you can flee to is your own. That's no good.'

'I think that's a good idea,' said Hiruko. 'There shouldn't be any problems if we do it with the unoccupied rooms.'

For the moment, it appeared as though Hiruko, Tatsunami and Kanno were the ones taking the initiative in our discussions. There was nobody against the idea, so except for the room with Shindō's remains, all the other unoccupied rooms, including those of Akechi and Kudamatsu, were kept open, using the swingbar door guard as a doorstop.

4

It was past nine o'clock. We had all had enough of sitting all together in the lounge by now, so we started going our own ways.Tatsunami switched the radio cassette CD player in his room on again. Western rock music reverberated throughout the lounge, lightening the sombre atmosphere. Shigemoto disappeared sluggishly to his own room. Kanno said he was going to check the storage on the third floor once more, to see if he could find anything that might be useful. Tatsunami and Hiruko joined him. Nabari had not slept last night, so she said she was going to rest for a while, and retreated to her room. Perhaps it was just the loud music that annoyed her.

I, too, had returned to my room, but I didn't feel like resting again. Whilst the life-threatening situation we were in obviously scared me, I couldn't get the completely inexplicable circumstances of Shindō's death off my mind. Akechi would never have remained still, faced with such a mystery. I decided to have another look in Shindō's room. Fortunately, the door was open. There was somebody in there already.

'Oh, Hiruko, you're here.'

I hadn't really had time to think about it since the morning, with all that had happened, but we had said goodnight under awkward circumstances, and that was still bothering me. I felt strangely tense as I called out to her.The air conditioning had been kept on to preserve the body, so it was cold in the room, much colder than you'd expect from a summer day. The stench of death still permeated the room, however, and I put my mask on.

'Oh, err, it's you.'

She looked nervously away when she saw me. Gone was the imperturbable woman who had led the discussion in the lounge. Whilst she appeared cool-headed, she was actually quite bad at hiding her true feelings.

'I—I'm really sorry for what I said last night. It was really inappropriate. I hope you can accept my apologies.'

Hearing her apologise to me like that made me feel bad as well.

'It's okay, I shouldn't have snapped either. Let's both forget what happened.'

A weight seemed to fall from her shoulders. I changed the subject.

'This case doesn't make any sense.'

'I agree.'

'The Villa Violet itself is surrounded by zombies and the doors of the rooms lock automatically, which means that the murder took place in a double-layered locked room. So how did the killer manage to get inside and kill Shindō?'

'Huh?'

'Eh?'

Hiruko had reacted in such surprise, I thought I had said something odd.

'Err, I was wondering how the murderer managed to kill Shindō in his room.'

'Oh, that. So you're one of those types who start from there.' She clapped her hands together, as if it all made sense to her now.

'From there? From where?'

'You see, I don't worry too much about the method.'

I was baffled by her confession. Considering that she had been involved with so many puzzling cases, I had assumed Hiruko loved locked room murders, fabricated alibis and suchlike. She pulled a strand of her beautiful black hair and played with it in front of her mouth.

'Whether it was a locked room murder or not, the fact of the matter is that Shindō was killed. So it's no use crying that it was impossible or unbelievable. All that means is that there was some clever method of accomplishing the murder.'

'So then what's bothering you?'

'The culprit's intention.'

'You mean motive?'

'Not exactly. I mean, I can't begin to imagine how many reasons people have for killing others. The police might start their investigations focusing on the motive, but that's only to narrow down

114

the number of suspects, from an unspecified large number to a manageable list. Anything could be a motive, from a lust to murder to some kind of heavenly mission. What I mean is: why did the culprit choose this particular method, and why did it have to be done at this particular time?'

'So basically, the whydunnit.'

'Whydunnit?'

I explained the terms whodunnit, howdunnit, and whydunnit to her. Each put the spotlight on a different aspect of a mystery: a whodunnit focuses on the identity of the culprit, the howdunnit on the method used, and the whydunnit on the reason the crime was committed.

'Ah, yes, I see.'

Hiruko nodded after I was done with my explanation and started to walk around the room. She carefully avoided the bloodstains on the carpet and the pieces of flesh lying around as she spoke.

'I don't know much about mystery novels. But at real crime scenes, there's always an abundance of evidence pointing towards the aims and intentions of the culprit. Apparently, I'm just sensitive to those kinds of clues.'

It was a sensation I was not familiar with, as the only crime scenes I knew were fictional inventions in novels and television dramas.

'Most real murders are committed on an impulse, spurred on by emotions of hostility and hatred. Because the main goal is simply to rob the victim of their life, the attempts to cover up the crime afterwards are usually quite naïve. Which means that the probability of the culprit leaving evidence at the crime scene, to serve as a major clue, is therefore very high. That's why they slip up easily once the police start scrutinising them. Then you have murders that are committed to gain an advantage from the victim's death, for example through an inheritance or life insurance. In those cases, you can sense the intention to make a death seem like anything but murder--for example, an accident or death by natural causes.

'That is why, in my eyes, a locked room murder is the least logical way to commit a murder. If you're fabricating a locked room murder anyway, you might as well make it appear a suicide. I can't see the point of making it look like murder by a third party.'

I interrupted her.

'But suppose you wanted to direct suspicion towards the person in possession of the key to a locked room?'

'Inconceivable. There's no reason why someone with the key would purposely lock the crime scene themselves.'

She was right. A person with the privilege to enter a specific space would be the first one to be suspected if they didn't leave it accessible to anyone after the crime.

'Furthermore, it takes a lot of courage to try and fool the police with a locked room murder, in this day and age. In novels and on television they like talking about the perfect crime, but if you ask me, the crime is already half-way solved by the time the body is discovered. The murder method, time of death, motive... a body is like a treasure box full of information. The true perfect crime isn't one which makes the police give up, it's a crime which is never recognised as such. It's killing someone without anyone noticing, it's getting rid of the body without anyone noticing, and it's returning to normal life afterwards without anyone noticing.

'Let's get back to what we were talking about. Basically, I am really not interested in meticulously thought-out trickery. What I'm interested in, is the reason why the culprit decided to kill Shindō now. Because, right at this very moment, we're all in big trouble, surrounded by zombies. We're trapped in a situation we don't know whether we'll survive or not, so why was it necessary to kill Shindō inside a locked room?'

I slowly started to grasp the point Hiruko was trying to make. No matter how much the culprit might hate Shindō, he was still important, as we needed everyone to survive the zombie attack. What could be the purpose of killing him right away, despite the fact we were in a life-threatening situation?

'So, you're of the opinion he was not killed by a zombie, but by a human?'

'Yes. I only mentioned the bite marks earlier so we wouldn't start fighting amongst each other.'

If the killer was a human, as she suspected, who could that person be?

'Perhaps it was someone who hated Shindō so much they wanted to kill him themselves.'

'That's the most likely reason. But then consider the crime scene. That would mean you had a killer who wanted to kill Shindō themselves, but who nevertheless used a zombie to commit the actual murder. That doesn't make any sense.'

She was right. That would mean the killer had arranged for a zombie to murder Shindō, even though the reason they decided to kill Shindō now was because they didn't want him to be killed by the zombies. That was clearly a discrepancy.

'Earlier on, we talked about whether the murderer was trying to divert suspicion to the zombies, remember?' I said.

'Yes. But that wouldn't explain why those messages were left. They were clearly meant to tell us that the crime was committed by a human.'

But for those notes, we would all have believed that a zombie had committed the murder. Hiruko continued playing with her hair as she whispered: 'Perhaps the crime was committed exactly because we're in our current situation.'

'What do you mean?'

'Given the extreme circumstances, if the murder eventually goes to trial, the culprit might get away with it by claiming they were not of sound mind during the crime.'

'So it could just be a ruse to get a lighter sentence?'

I had not thought of that. It was, of course, impossible to remain completely calm whilst those monsters were threatening our lives, so it was difficult to predict how the crime would be viewed afterwards. Perhaps the murderer would be considered legally insane and get away with a "not guilty" sentence. Leaving those messages might be a way to make it seem as if they were out of their mind. But then Hiruko groaned, as she was not satisfied with her own idea.

'Even so, I don't see why the murderer would go to all the trouble of making us believe a zombie attacked the victim.'

The problem was becoming more confusing by the minute. It appeared that the murder hadn't been committed out of hatred; nor had it been committed in such a way as to divert suspicion to the zombies; nor had it been made to appear a suicide. As Hiruko had pointed out, at this point it was completely incomprehensible as to why the murderer had killed Shindō in his room at that moment. I was lost in thought when somebody called out to me from the corridor.

'I thought you might be here, when I couldn't find you.' Takagi was peering through the doorway. 'Playing detective? I just shudder at the thought of going into that horrible room.'

'Sorry. We were just wondering about the murder.'

'I'm not angry at you. I just came here because I couldn't stand the atmosphere in the lounge anymore. But I really, really don't want to step into the room. Do you mind coming out here? Did you stumble on anything?'

I explained to Takagi what Hiruko and I had been discussing. Then Hiruko made a suggestion.

117

'I don't think we're getting anywhere with my approach. You've been thinking about the locked room aspects. I don't know much about mystery fiction, so could you share your thoughts on the locked room with us?'

'I'd just be repeating what I learned from fiction.'

'That doesn't matter.'

Urged on by Hiruko, I unveiled all the knowledge regarding locked room mysteries that I had accumulated by reading detective stories. Fortunately, I often had discussions on locked room mysteries with Akechi, so it wasn't too difficult.

'A locked, closed, or sealed room refers to a space that appears impossible for anyone to enter or leave. Shindō's room might have been difficult to enter from the outside, but it's simple to leave, due to the doors here, which lock automatically when closed. So, let's call it a semi-locked room. At the same time, it's also impossible for someone from the outside to enter or leave the building itself, because of the barricade and all the zombies roaming around on the first floor. Therefore, this whole boarding house can also be considered a giant locked room, so we're facing a double-layered locked room situation.

'A locked room murder, as the term suggests, refers to a murder committed inside a locked room. To be exact, however, in mystery fiction, most of the time it's a murder that's made to look as though it occurred in a locked room.'

'You mean the room was not truly sealed?'

'Correct. The examples are endless, but take, for example, the situation where the body is discovered inside a locked room, which is what happened here. What often happens is that the person inside the room is killed by someone outside at the time. For example, the victim is shot, or poisonous gas is used, and there are also examples where some object is used to strangle the victim. So, even though the culprit might not have entered the room themselves, they could have used a small opening to commit the murder.'

'But, based on the bite marks on the body and all the blood, it's clear Shindō was killed by someone inside his room, isn't it? He wasn't attacked from outside,' replied Takagi, as she looked up at the bloodstains on the ceiling. I agreed with her, of course.

'Then there's the situation where the victim is fatally wounded outside the room, flees inside and passes away there. The culprit never sets foot in the room. But that possibility is also ruled out, for the same reason you just mentioned. It's clear as day that Shindō was attacked inside the room.'

118

'Next is the situation where the death appears to be murder, but is actually suicide,' I continued. 'A suicide made to look like murder. That, too, is quite unlikely in our case.'

'Not unless there are people who can bite their own faces off,' observed Takagi dryly.

Hiruko interrupted.

'Wait. What if this was a semi-suicide?'

'A semi-suicide?'

'What if Shindō himself brought a zombie to his room, and had it attack him?'

As a fan of detective stories, this was the type of solution I liked, but that still did not resolve everything.

'Murder with consent of the victim? It would certainly explain how the zombie got into the locked room, and how Shindō died, but it doesn't explain the note wedged in the door. I can't imagine the zombie going out into the corridor after the murder to put it there. And it doesn't explain how Shindō had managed to get the zombie in, and how the zombie got out again. It would have been too difficult for Shindō to move the barricade out of the way all on his own, so that would mean he'd have to have used the emergency exits or the elevator.'

Hiruko then realised there was yet another problem.

'Anyway, he would have needed to somehow bring only one single zombie into the room, or at most a very small number, whereas there was a whole mob of them roaming around. That would have been just too risky and completely inconceivable.'

Going down in the elevator to bring one zombie back up? Opening the emergency exit and closing the door behind it, once one got in? Whatever the case, Shindō would have been attacked by the zombies on the spot and, if he was going to try something risky like that anyway, he might as well have made an attempt to escape from the building. The hypothesis was innovative, but had to be rejected. So then what if it hadn't been a zombie that had got in from the outside, but a human?

'What if an outsider committed the murder? Suppose the murderer was already hiding inside before the room was locked,' I suggested.

Hiruko looked at Takagi. 'That was the idea you and the others talked about in the lounge, earlier. Every entrance was watched by us from the moment the zombies appeared, but someone could have got inside before that, for example when Mr. Kanno was on his rounds making sure everything was locked up.'

119

Takagi nodded vigorously.

'If that person happened to know where the keycardswere kept behind the reception desk, they could have found an empty room to hide in.'

That could explain how the "outer" sealed area had been penetrated. However, we didn't find anyone when we searched the premises that morning.

'If the culprit was someone from the outside, that would mean that, after killing Shindō, they left the note outside the door and then just went up in smoke, vanishing from the house. I hate to say this, but....' I hesitated to continue.

'It raises fewer questions if we simply assume the culprit is one of us, doesn't it?'

Hiruko had finished what I had wanted to say. We could forget about zombies or outsiders. If the killer was one of us, the problem of the house itself being the "outer" sealed room wasn't relevant in the first place. I continued with my locked room lecture.

'Next up is trickery with the help of some kind of mechanism or tool. Situations which seem ridiculous at first, but are actually possible. Someone scaling the walls outside, throwing a rope up at the balcony and climbing up or perhaps removing the door entirely from its frame, ideas like that. Or a secret passage.'

'Huh. But there's no end to it once you start imagining those possibilities,' said Hiruko as she went back into the room. She checked the railing of the balcony for marks that something had been hooked there and looked around the room for hidden passages, but could not find a single indication that any such method had been utilised. The building had not been designed by the architect Seiji Nakamura from YukitoAyatsuji's *House* series.

'The paint on this railing comes off more easily than you might think. If a rope ladder or a rope had been attached here, there would definitely be traces.'

I had also considered the possibility of attaching some kind of thin wire to the balcony railing to use as a hook, to which a rope could be attached, but that seemed unlikely, too. There were no natural footholds on the wall which would allow someone to climb up. After seeing that possibility rejected as well, I felt a bit sorry.

'Err, I didn't mention this earlier because I was explaining what a locked room was....'

'What, you're still not done?' said Takagi in surprise.

'There's a way to open this kind of lock from the outside without resorting to the methods I mentioned earlier.'

'Huh?'

'Oh, that's right,' Hiruko nodded.

'You're aware of the trick?'

'It's a method often used in hotel thefts.'

'Hey, don't leave me in the dark!' said Takagi.

'First you need an L-shaped metal wire, about the length from the floor up to the door handle. The end needs to be twisted, like a hook. You push it into the room through the gap between the floor and the door. Then you turn it around so that the wire points upwards, and, using the twisted hook at the end, you grab the door handle and simply pull it down. That way, you can open a hotel door without the key. You can find this method on video-sharing sites too. Once you've unlocked the door and can set it ajar, you can use rubber bands or strings to unlock the doorguard or door chain if necessary.'

Takagi stared at me, flabbergasted.

'Wait a second! You just showed that, as long they had the right tool, anyone could have got into the room. So what was all that previous twaddle about locked room methods all about!?'

It was just as she had said. In fact, it could have been done even more easily, by simply making up an excuse and asking Shindō to open the door for them. But then who would consider such a banal situation a locked room mystery? There was one more thing I needed to mention, however.

'There's something else I didn't mention, because it doesn't qualify as a mystery. Yesterday, Nabari was given the master keycard, so she could have easily entered the room any time she wanted.'

Hiruko nodded in agreement, but Takagi seemed even more frustrated. She came up close to me and planted her fist in my stomach.

'Get straight to the point next time.'

All my locked room lecture had shown was that anyone for whom the "outer" sealed room was irrelevant (meaning any one of us) could have found some way of entering Shindō's room. It would have been especially easy for Nabari. Nevertheless, Hiruko seemed quite pleased with my conclusions.

'Honestly, thanks to you, I've been able to organise my thoughts on the matter. Just as I thought, this is an unprecedented locked room murder.'

'How can that be? Apparently it's as easy as pie to get through the door. So, to me, all the preceding discussion was a complete waste of time. Or am I missing something?' protested Takagi.

'There's no need to make things too complicated. All the methods we talked about earlier were about how to get into a locked room, but to actually commit the murder, the killer has to fulfill one more condition.'

'Which is?'

Hiruko became serious: 'Only a human could have used the methods we discussed to enter the room. Thanks to Hamura's lecture, I'm now convinced that the possibility of a zombie penetrating the double-layered locked room, by accident or coincidence, is zero. But there was nobody amongst us who showed signs of having bitten Shindō to death. That means any of us could have got into his room, but we couldn't have killed him. But likewise, a zombie could have killed him, but wouldn't have been able to enter his room. Those are two separate problems: the way access into the room was gained, and the way the murder was committed. This is a locked room murder where the killer has to satisfy both conditions.'

Takagi started rubbing her head vigorously.

'...Doesn't that mean nobody could have committed the crime? Isn't there some other angle from which we could tackle this?'

'Earlier I rejected the idea, but a human could indeed have brought a zombie inside via one of the emergency exits. That would have posed an enormous risk to the killer, however,' replied Hiruko.

'What about the suggestion that Nanamiya made earlier, a zombie who has retained human-like intellect?'

I myself didn't think this was likely, even though I was the one mentioning the idea. It would mean that the zombies were far more advanced than we were assuming at this moment. If it were true, then it would be impossible to even guess what they were capable of. It would be like the menu-guessing game Akechi and I were always playing. Just as my mind started to run into a dead end again, Hiruko clapped her hands together.

'I suggest we change our approach. We need to learn much more about these unknown quantities, the zombies.'

Hiruko knocked on Shigemoto's door. He was Shindō's neighbour. The door opened, and Shigemoto's grim face peered back at us.

'You need me?'

It was gloomy behind him. The lights in the room were off, and the curtains were closed. The pale light reflecting off the walls was probably the television.

'I'm sorry to trouble you. We wanted to know what you could tell us about those horrible zombies.'

'Why me?' The eyes behind the glasses blinked.

'Yesterday, you realised right away that those monsters couldn't be stopped unless their brains were destroyed, even though none of us had ever encountered such a being. This morning you were also the first person to point out the possibility Shindō could rise as a zombie. So I'm assuming you're knowledgeable about such beings.'

Hiruko smiled at him as she spoke. I couldn't tell whether it was a calculated act, or her natural self, but no man alive could resist being praised by someone so attractive. Shigemotowas no exception.The moment he spoke, it was clear his initial caution had disappeared.

'Actually, I'm not really all that knowledgeable about them. But come inside. I can only offer you cola, though.'

The air conditioner was working hard, but the room was not as cold as Shindō's. Even so, it was chilly here with just a t-shirt on. I could hear the music from Tatsunami's room immediately below. Shigemoto didn't appear to be the tidy type. Even though only one night had passed, his bed sheets were rumpled and there was a half-empty bottle of cola on the nightstand and five empty ones next to his waste bin. The cola addict got a new bottle out of his refrigerator and put it on the table.

'Feel free to pour a glass for yourself.'

A small DVD player had been connected to the television which was part of the room furniture. The film had been paused. I recognised the foreign actress on the screen. Sand and dust covered the beautiful face of the blonde with short hair. She was holding two guns in her hands.

'Isn't that *Resident Evil*?'

Shigemoto nodded. It was the live action film adaptation of the well-known zombie video game series. I couldn't care less whether someone was watching a DVD or playing a game, but I honestly didn't know what to say about someone who could even think of watching a zombie film under the current circumstances. Takagi, obviously feeling the same way, muttered: 'He's nuts....'

Shigemoto sat down on the carpet, and we formed a ring around him: Hiruko and I on the bed, and Takagi straddling the chair.

'Do you usually watch that kind of film?' asked Hiruko.

'Yeah, I mostly watch what people call zombie films. Of course, although they're all about zombies, each story has a different kind of zombie. Nowadays they even publish survival guides for when the zombies attack. I've read them, but there's only so much you can do in a country where you can't buy guns.'

He spoke very rapidly. He took out more DVDs and related books from a bag, and lined them up on the carpet. He was a much bigger fan of this stuff than I had imagined. Hiruko interrupted him and got straight to the point.

'We were talking about the circumstances under which Shindō was killed, but then we realised that we simply didn't know enough about these monsters. About their physical capabilities, whether they possess enough intellect to fool us humans, things like that. That's why we hope you can give us some advice. What more can you tell us about them?'

Shigemoto's expression became even grimmer. He got up and went to the desk, where he picked up several sheets of paper covered in sloppy handwriting. The question "What is a zombie?" in the centre had been circled in black several times. It appeared as though our resident zombie fan had stayed up all night to organise his thoughts.

'In order to discuss these creatures—let's refer to them as zombies for now—the first thing we need to make clear is how they became zombies. I've been giving this a lot of thought from several different angles.

'First of all, judging by how the zombies came to attack us, and the clothes they are wearing, it appears they were attendees of the Sabea Rock Festival. So it's clear that the incident on the news, where many people fell ill, was instrumental in creating them. The news even suggested it might have been a bioterror attack.

'Secondly, as far as I can see, all the zombies have been wounded, and have attacked our friends by biting them. If we connect that to what we learnt from the news, I think the possibility that one becomes a zombie through such wounds is very high. We can consider zombies as people infected with some kind of virus or bacteria, just as in the films.

'Thirdly, although we still don't know much about the exact method of transmission, the main source of infection is probably through direct contact, such as being bitten by a carrier. Considering that we're all still okay, I doubt there's an airborne transmission route, but I can't say anything about infection through droplets. Anyway, it's best we avoid direct contact with blood or other bodily fluids. Next is vector transmission.'

'What's that?' asked Hiruko.

'Getting infected through animals or insects. Don't forget this is the mosquito season.'

'They do say that mosquitos kill the most people, besides humans themselves. What if you're bitten by a mosquito full of zombie blood?'

'It's quite possible that the mosquito would die the moment it drank the zombie's blood. Even so, it wouldn't hurt to wear long-sleeved clothes.'

Said the man who was wearing a t-shirt.

'If it's an infection, isn't there some way it can be treated?'

Shigemoto shook his head in answer to Hiruko's question. He pulled a book out of the bag, and opened it at a specific page.

'According to *The Zombie Survival Guide*, a zombie virus is carried through the bloodstream to the brain. There it reproduces and effectively kills the host by destroying the frontal lobe and stopping heart activity. Then the virus transforms the internal organs at a cellular level, bringing the infected individual back to life as a being that surpasses the original human in certain ways. I think some points made in this book also apply to our real-life zombies.'

He pulled the camcorder we had used the day before out of the bag and connected it to the television. What he showed us was not the scary film we had shot at the ruins, but footage of the zombies roaming everywhere around the boarding house. When had he filmed them?

He had zoomed in as much as possible, catching the appearance of the infected non-humans in detail. It was not a pleasant sight. Takagi became annoyed and snapped at Shigemoto.

'Enough of the gory video. Just tell us what you know.'

'It's just my interpretation, and I'd like to hear your thoughts as well. As you can see for yourselves, the zombies aren't bleeding, no matter how serious their wounds are. I suppose part of the reason is that enough time has passed for the blood to start clotting, but you can also see spots where the blood has hardened and turned a greenish colour. They may well have lost a lot of blood, but I also suspect that their blood has transformed, losing its liquidity. Remember when Mr. Tatsunami killed that zombie yesterday? He kept stabbing it, but no blood came spraying out.'

'But what does that mean?' asked Takagi.

'Don't you see? The blood inside them isn't circulating. That means they don't need oxygen. That's why they can still move, even if you destroy their hearts. They're literally walking corpses.'

Shigemoto chose his words carefully.

'But, because their muscles have become rigid, their agility and walking speed are simply not as good as when they were alive. The brain is probably still controlling the body, but because of the lack of oxygen being circulated, it has trouble coordinating the movements of the limbs. I also doubt that their brains are capable of handling complex matters. Basically, the virus has taken over and they are only following simple orders.'

'What simple orders?' I asked.

'Survival and reproduction. That's all the zombies have on their minds. They're not attacking us because they want to kill us. We're just a means of reproduction.'

I honestly didn't know how to react to Shigemoto's theory. Hiruko nodded, however, and seemed impressed by his analysis.

'I thought it was strange the zombies didn't attack other zombies. If they were hungry, it would be easier to start eating each other, rather than chase a handful of humans. But that would be explained if their goal is to reproduce.'

'Exactly!'

Shigemoto seemed pleased that someone agreed with him. He leant forward as he continued his enthusiastic analysis.

'And so the expression "eat" we used to describe their actions is incorrect. If they were really attacking humans because they were hungry, all that would be left of their victims would be the bones, just as if they were eating fried chicken. But if you look carefully, you can see none of them have been chewed down to the skeleton. So their bites are nothing more but a method of transmitting the virus. I can't imagine how, but they can sense which people haven't been infected yet and attack them.'

I recalled an article I once read. It was about some kind of ant in Brazil or thereabouts. Carpenter ants had had their brains taken over by some kind of new bacteria and been turned into zombies, which had been controlled to find the perfect place to spread the bacterial spores. Controlling a different creature's mind in order to reproduce is

126

something which really does occur in the real world. That would explain why the zombies didn't attack each other.

With so much new information to process, I asked Shigemoto for a sheet of paper, so I could make notes of the most convincing points he had made.

'...If there is no blood circulation, then naturally their digestive organs don't function either. That's why parts of Shindō's body were lying around the room. The zombie wasn't eating him. Does that mean that, if we can hold on for a few days, we'll be saved because their bodies will rot?'

Shigemoto, who had been quite excited until now, turned grim again at Hiruko's question.

'No... it might even become worse. According to one of my books, there are microorganisms normally involved in the decomposition process of a corpse. If the zombies' bodies are transformed in such a way that they can kill those microorganisms, or simply keep them away, I'm afraid their bodies will keep for much longer than we might hope. I didn't want to mention this to everyone earlier, but we might be talking weeks in the worst-case scenario.'

'Microorganisms? I hadn't thought of that....'

Hiruko seemed to accept the new revelation, but Takagi, irritated as she was, fired another question at Shigemoto.

'Then tell me this. Why are all those zombies here? They had to cross a mountain to come here from the rock festival. Why would they come all the way here?'

'Don't take it out on me! Supposedly, there were about fifty thousand attendees at the festival per day. Suppose there was some kind of terrorist attack and only ten percent were infected. That would still mean five thousand zombies. As far as I can tell by looking outside, there are less than five hundred of them around the building, in fact just a fraction of that. Nevertheless, they left the busy rock festival to come all the way to the Villa Violet. They must have some kind of ability beyond the normal five senses to detect humans. If not, they wouldn't have surrounded us as they did.'

'Do you think only humans can be infected?'

'...I can't say. Different films say different things. But there are plenty of viruses and bacteria that can only harm certain beings, so it wouldn't be surprising to find that the zombie virus specifically targets humans.'

I wondered what the zombies were capable of exactly, so I asked Shigemoto about that.

'If their brains don't function normally, I assume it would be impossible for them to use tools, unlock a door or concoct an elaborate lie to deceive Shindō?'

Shigemoto's response was firm.

'Impossible. Or else they wouldn't have so much trouble with our barricade. You saw them yourself. They walked right into the cabinet, lost their balance because of that, and fell back down the stairs. And they kept doing so over and over again. They don't even have the learning ability of a child. Their brain only seems capable of sending simple orders, and the coordination of their limbs is so bad they can't even run. Their one advantage is that they have unlimited stamina. The zombies in the films possess more dexterity.'

'I wonder how long it takes to turn into a zombie,once you're bitten,' asked Hiruko.

'It's hard to say. Where you got bitten, the severity of the wound, and the physique of the victim are all factors to be considered. I suppose the government will be providing a detailed report on the subject, but whether we'll still be alive by the time they publish it is another matter.'

Shigemoto didn't sound optimistic. There was a hissing noise as he opened the plastic bottle.

'So that just brings us back to the conclusion that a zombie couldn't have got into Shindō's room,' said Takagi, frustrated by the realisation that our visit might not have been very fruitful.

6

We gave a collective sigh on leaving Shigemoto's room. It was as if we had been trapped in a haunted house.

The notes I made were as follows:

1. Cause of zombies is likely virus or bacteria. If bitten, you become infected and will turn into a zombie. Details on the time it takes to change and the exact transmission methods still unknown.
2. Zombies do not need oxygen and can continue activity unless the brain is destroyed. Thus they have unlimited stamina. However, their learning and athletic abilities are underdeveloped.
3. They bite people not to feed, but to reproduce. They move on once the target has been infected to a certain level.

4. Extremely sensitive to living people.

A look at this list made it clear the zombies were a horrifying opponent, but as they had underdeveloped learning and athletic abilities, it wasn't an impossible fight.

At that moment, Tatsunami appeared from the south corridor, holding a spear in his hands.

'Yo, Detective Club. Find anything out?'

It didn't sound as though he was making fun of us, he really just wanted to know. I shook my head.

'No, if anything, we keep stumbling on new questions.'

'Things just seem complicated because a human is involved in this somewhere. Someone is trying to spook us by making it appear that a zombie did it,' said Tatsunami.

'Perhaps. At the moment, that seems to make the most sense,' agreed Hiruko. The culprit had left clues that suggested the murder had not been committed out of hate, but also that they had not tried to implicate the zombies. Because of that, we were now facing both fear and confusion. If that had been the goal of the culprit, then the mastermind behind the crime had to be a human being.

I remembered that Nanamiya occupied room 301 in the south wing, and Tatsunami had just come from there.

'Did you try to talk to Mr. Nanamiya?'

'Yes, I suspected he might be lonely. But the louse wouldn't even open the door. What a coward. I'll bet he's shaking like this right now,' he said, and he mimicked how Nanamiya would tap his temples. It was a tic that really bothered me.

'He always taps his head like that. Why is it?' I asked.

'He says he's been having headaches since last month. He takes a lot of medicine for it, too.'

Takagi, who had been listening to us, said dryly: 'Perhaps it's his contact lenses.'

'His lenses?'

'He's using eye drops all the time, did you notice? I've seen Mifuyu use the same drops as well. They're eye drops for contact lenses. Mifuyu told me that if you have overcorrected lenses, lenses that are too strong, it causes eyestrain and is bad for the blood flow. Eventually, the stress caused will even affect the hormones in your body and could lead to headaches or nausea.'

'Huh, Shizuhara wears lenses?' I hadn't noticed.

Takagi's explanation seemed to ring a bell with Tatsunami.

'I think he did mention that he bought some contact lenses somewhere online.'

The four of us went down to the second floor in the elevator. It was cramped inside, and we all touched shoulders.

'Shigemoto counts for three in here, ha ha.'

As Tatsunami was joking, I was worrying that he might accidentally push the button for the first floor. One false move and we would descend into zombie hell. Fortunately, he pushed the correct button and the elevator brought us safely to the second floor. We didn't forget to use a chair to keep the elevator door open.

Shizuhara was in the lounge. Loud rock music was coming out of Tatsunami's room. I noticed that he had kept his door ajar, using the door guard as a doorstop. He seemed not at all worried about his own safety or security, despite the circumstances.

It was past noon. A whole day had passed since the incident at the Sabea Rock Festival, and the television news had started reporting on new developments. They still did not report on the number of victims, or the scale of the crisis, but they did hint strongly at a biohazard caused by human hand.

"Although no abnormalities have been detected in the water of Lake Sabea, the water supply from the lake has been temporarily suspended. People in the Lake Sabea region are warned to not drink water from the lake under any circumstances. Anyone whose eyes have come in contact with the lake water is advised to wash them with fresh water. Attendees of yesterday's Sabea Rock Festival are asked to call the number below or to contact the police immediately. We ask you not to touch the injuries of the wounded directly and to follow the instructions of the local authorities."

'They stopped the water supply!' Takagi cried out in a panic.

Just then Kanno appeared in the lounge, and explained that there was a water storage tank on the rooftop, so we wouldn't be out of water right away.

'Even if we were completely booked, we would have enough water to last for half a day, and we also have bottled water, so we should have enough for the next two or three days. But, knowing that we won't have water for the time being, it's best to be careful about how much we use.'

'It's just as if we're on a small island in the middle of nowhere...,' sighed Takagi out loud, and others joined her in lamenting our current situation.

'I assume that means we'll have to skip the shower for the moment,' I said. To my surprise, Hiruko seemed to take offence. She grabbed a lock of her hair and started sniffing it like a puppy.

'Does what I said upset you?'

'If my hair starts bothering you, feel free to tell me. I am a lady, after all.'

'She's counting on you,' laughed Tatsunami.

I didn't even remember what I'd said. Shizuhara, who had not spoken until then, interrupted us.

'Would it be possible to reach the parking lot somehow? If we could get in a car, the zombies wouldn't be able to get to us.'

'The parking lot...' Takagi frowned as she looked at the others.

The building was surrounded by zombies. Despite that, Shizuhara continued.

'The zombies are all focused on the second and third floor. The plaza and the parking lot should be relatively empty. If we could somehow break through their lines somewhere....'

'We could get in a car and just run them over and get away, huh? Mr. Kanno, do you have the key to the van with you?' Tatsunami asked.

'I left it at the reception desk, I'm afraid.'

'So we'd have to use the remaining two cars. Wouldn't that be great? I'd love to see Nanamiya's face when his beloved GT-R is covered in zombie blood.'

'It would suit the red paint job.'

Shizuhara was capable of rather scary comments.

'But how would we get outside? We could jump out of the windows, but we can't jump over those mobs.'

'Fire! I once saw a film where they used a torch to keep the zombies away. If necessary, we could set the whole building on fire and....'

Her ideas were becoming scarier by the minute.

'That won't work.'

Shizuhara's heated suggestion was interrupted by the zombie fan, who had come down from the third floor.

'I wanted to know what their weak point was myself, so I threw some of the fireworks that we had originally brought for this evening right into the middle of them. But it was no use. They noticed the noise, but they didn't seem scared of the fire or the heat, and didn't run away.'

That was all he said. He grabbed a cereal bar from the emergency rations and went back to his room.

'Thus spoke the professor. So let's forget about burning the place down.'

Tatsunami shrugged. Shizuhara, disappointed, fell silent.

We had an emergency ration lunch and then hung around in the lounge, but people came and went all the time. When Nabari, who had been cooped up in her room, finally came out, Shizuhara said she was going to her room, and left for the eastern staircase. Takagi walked her to her room. After a while, Hiruko, too, said she needed some rest, and returned to her room. With nothing else to do, I started playing with the wooden puzzle in the lounge, one of those where you have to use all the parts to make a particular shape. After a while Takagi returned and started to meddle with it. At that point Tatsunami got up, but instead of heading for his room, he went up to the third floor in the elevator.

'Where is he going?' I wondered, but Kanno had an idea.

'I think he's gone to the rooftop to smoke. I've unlocked the door to the storage room upstairs and you can use the staircase inside to get out on the rooftop. It's not pleasant to have to stay inside all the time.'

'A smoke, huh?' muttered Takagi, as she tried to attach the puzzle piece in her hand to the corner piece. It was clearly the wrong piece, so she removed it and looked for a different one. But the piece she then picked was obviously not going to fit either. She clearly had no intention of completing the puzzle, and was just toying with me.

'Do you smoke, too?' I asked her.

'Stopped. Mifuyu didn't like it.' A scowl appeared on her face.

'You're good friends?'

'I've been teaching her make-up and other things ever since she joined the club. She doesn't talk much, but she really looks after my health. She's in Nursing Studies.'

'So why did she join the Film Club if she's in the medical department?'

There was no direct bus connection between Shinkō University's main campus for general studies and the medical campus. The distance was about thirty minutes by bicycle. It was rather inconvenient for medical students to join clubs located on the main campus.

'She's a first year, so she still has a lot of general courses and lectures at the main campus. I don't know what she'll do starting next year, though.'

As we chatted on about majors, we found out we had an unexpected connection. Takagi and I were both taking Economics.

Nabari had been playing with the television's remote control for some time, but then mumbled she was going crazy and got up and left. At first, I thought she was talking about our predicament, but the scowl she directed at the half-open door made it clear her comment was aimed at the music coming out of Tatsunami's room. Kanno left the lounge at that point as well, leaving only Takagi and myself. I decided to make use of the opportunity to ask Takagi some questions.

'Regarding the threatening note and the messages we found earlier, you saw how strangely frightened Nanamiya's reaction was. I think that the sacrifice mentioned in the threatening note wasn't about some cursed film you shot last year. It has to be about something that occurred on this same trip last year.'

'...I knew it.'

Takagi looked regretful as she turned her head away.

'I was on the trip last year as well, but you have a pretty good idea of what kind of person I am. So I had a pretty easy time, as none of those three set their targets on me. I think it was on the second day. There was an odd mood when we met that morning. I tried asking the people in the senior years what was wrong, but they hardly told me anything. It turned out that that night, Deme had sneaked into the room of one of the girls to... you know.'

I couldn't believe it. He had done such an awful thing last time and now tried to hit on Nabari this year?

'But that wasn't even the biggest issue. He failed, you see.'

'So you mean... the other two succeeded?'

That would be Nanamiya and Tatsunami.

'Well, both of them did keep on seeing their girls after the trip. But both couples broke up soon after the summer. Actually, it wasn't really breaking up. From what I heard, the girls were literally dumped. The girl who was dating Tatsunami left university and returned back home, and I haven't been able to get in contact with her since. He must have been horrible to her.'

'And the one who dated Nanamiya?'

'She committed suicide.'

Takagi's fingers flicked one of the wrong wooden parts away.

'She took an overdose of sleeping drugs. Megumi, she was a senior in the club and always helped me out. I heard she even wrote a suicide note.'

So Megumi was the woman who had committed suicide after the trip.

'But the members of the Film Club don't know the details about the affair?'

'Nanamiya's lawyer probably made sure everything was hushed up through settlements.'

Herewas a possible motive for Shindō's death.

'...Shindō knew about this, didn't he? So why did he organise this year's trip?'

'All the senior members in the club are aware that Nanamiya has been very persistent in putting pressure on each new club president over the last few years. Just as with other clubs, the president basically changes each year, as the previous president resigns to prepare for their graduation year. Shindō might have appeared to be a sincere guy, but he still recruited all these girls for this trip, knowing very well it meant offering them as sacrifices to those three. They say you shouldn't speak ill of the dead, but if you ask me, he's better off dead.'

7

I left the half-finished puzzle up to Takagi and went up the staircase to the third floor. At first I was planning to return to my room, but when I saw the door to the storage room was open, I became curious and decided to take my first look inside.The concrete walls were bare, and the room was slightly more spacious than our own. Double-column cabinets had been placed at one metre intervals. They were filled with spare foldable chairs and tables, an industrial vacuum cleaner and other materials, such as paint and brushes. The staircase leading to the rooftop was in the rear. Next to it were a snowboard and fishing equipment, probably belonging to the owner or Nanamiya.

I climbed up and pushed the steel door leading to the roof open, to be greeted by a dull and cloudy sky. The rain had mostly stopped, but you could still feel the remaining droplets carried by the wind. Tatsunami stood smoking amidst the fine drizzle. I myself don't smoke, but I thought it surprising that cigarette didn't get wet.

'It feels great here! Come on!' Tatsunami called out to me when he noticed my presence.

The wind on the rooftop was a bit strong, but that felt good. As long as you didn't look down at the zombies below, and admired the great misty Lake Sabea beyond the woods, you could almost remember that it was summer holiday.

'Want one?'

Tatsunami offered me a cigarette, but I politely declined. A line of smokedrifted upwards. It reminded me of incense. My late grandfather once told me that that the smoke of incense served as a bridge between this world and the world beyond. The thought made me feel miserable. Just dozens of metres below us were hundreds of beings who weren't able to go the world beyond, roaming aimlessly around. We couldn't even light some incense for them. And it was they themselves who prevented us from doing so.

From the western side of the rooftop, I could look down on the emergency exits on each floor, leading to the emergency stairs outside. Zombies had managed to climb the stairs and were now crowded within its steel railings. The sounds of their attempts at breaking through the emergency exits could be heard, even from the rooftop.

A few zombies halfway up the stairs noticed my presence and, as they looked up, our eyes met. I felt threatened by their dull gaze. A middle-aged zombie on the outer edge of the mob kept glaring at me, and then started to climb over the railing.

I wasn't even able to cry out. The middle-aged zombie lost his balance, fell through the air and crashed onto the crowd of zombies on the ground below. To my surprise, other zombies on the staircase noticed my presence as well, and they, too, climbed over the railing and fell to the ground. I felt sick watching them.

'Just like lemmings.'

Tatsunami had joined me.

'Lemmings?'

'It's a video game. Never played it? Lemmings—they're like mice—keep falling down on the stage, and you have to give them directions to lead them to the goal. But there are cliffs and sunken parts at various points on the stage and, if the player doesn't give them the right orders, the lemmings will just keep on falling to their death or getting stuck in the sunken parts. Just like those things down there.'

I retreated to a spot where the zombies couldn't see me. They may be zombies, but the notion that I had caused several of them to take such a fall made my heart jump. It was a very different kind of horror from simple fear.

'Don't think too much about it. They don't have the brains to understand anything that's happening any more.'

He puffed out one final line of smoke in memoriam. A moment of silence passed between us.I felt bad that I had made him do all the talking, but it's not as if a gloomy guy like me, who could only boast about being a fan of detective stories, can come up with witty conversational topics. After some thought, I decided to try something easy.

'Do you like rock music?'

I was thinking of the music coming from the CD player.

'I like loud, powerful music. No need to think about anything then. But I do like the artist playing now.'

'Who's that?'

'Bruce Springsteen.'

Nope, never heard of him.

'He's a singer-songwriter who debuted in the seventies. One of the best-known rock singers from the United States. He's in his sixties now, but still performing. I happened to hear one of his songs long ago in a shop somewhere, and became a fan of his lyrics. But that's not really interesting, is it?'

Tatsunami let the wind carry away the remainder of his cigarette. The living dead watched it fly away with open mouths.

'Do you think we can get out of this alive?' he asked, as he lit another one.

'... I don't know. Chances are fifty-fifty, I'd say.'

'Shouldn't you say we should help each other and get out of this together?'

I suppose he was right. What was he going to do with my dry probability analysis? I apologised, but he laughed.

'Ha, I like you. Your answer is much better than just looking at things from the bright side or denying reality. Lip service isn't of much use when you're dealing with zombies, after all. I have to say, you're rather composed. Nanamiya must appear like a complete idiot to you, with that terrified act of his. Crying and locking himself up in his room.'

'Not really...' I didn't want to say what I really thought, so I just kept on talking. 'I've experienced something similar in the past.'

As soon as the words were out of my mouth, I regretted them. Now it was as if I were trying to sound mysterious.Tatsunami didn't seem to mind, however, and asked me if I could tell him about that experience, if that was okay.

'It happened when I was in middle school. An earthquake. I was standing like this, on a rooftop looking down at a view that felt so unreal. I thought it was all over. It's a lot like how I feel now. I don't know how to put it. It's a feeling of fear, of course. I don't want to die, and I want to help everyone. But when confronted with such an incredible force, there's nothing you can do, no matter how much you panic or cry.'

What could ten people do if all the zombies crawling around below came swarming in all at once? Ever since what had happened to me, my imperturbability had become merely resignation to fate. Tatsunami simply nodded at my story and remained silent. But then he caught me off-guard.

'So, are you dating Kenzaki?'

I felt my heart jump. It wasn't just the idea of myself together with someone as attractive as Hiruko that made me blush, but also the fact Tatsunami had suddenly brought up the topic of women. I replied, "Not really." But his reaction to that was another surprise.

'She likes you.'

He mentioned it as if he was talking about the weather.

'Hiruko?'

No way.

'You ever been in a relationship before?'

I shook my head. He grinned.

'Ah, so both of you are beginners. That's when you enjoy each other the most.'

'She might be experienced.'

'It's just a hunch, but I'm sure I'm right. If not, there's no way she'd be so obvious around you.'

I could see what he was talking about. But I couldn't help but try another angle.

'Perhaps she's just frank and is friendly with everyone.'

'That's possible. The first time we met, I honestly considered trying my luck with her. She's a fast thinker, and how often are you going to meet a knockout like her? But nope, she's not for me. She looks as though she's playing a part, but she's really pure like that. I can't handle girls like her anymore. They don't understand that when it's over, it's over. They're more trouble than pleasure.'

I had not expected him to start lamenting about women like that.

'Sorry for putting it like this, but I was under the impression you weren't that picky when it came to women.'

'I've had my fair share of experiences. But all that remains are memories I want to forget. At the beginning, when you start dating, there's nothing more fun than that. But the more you learn about the other, the less clear it becomes that you're truly in love. Then you start doubting the other. And when it's all over, it's as though everything had been nothing but a deception.'

'If you're thinking like that, I doubt I'll ever get it.'

Tatsunami's large feet stepped on the cigarette butt, which he had dropped on the dark, damp concrete rooftop.

'If you ask me, it's like an illness.'

Even though the fire had been put out already, he kept crushing the butt with his shoe.

'You're talking about romance?'

'Love. It's just like the zombies. Look at them. They don't realise they're sick. Same with love. Everyone in this world is infected by it and merrily dancing to its tune. I'm the only one who didn't turn into a zombie. I'm still normal, but pretend to be one of them. I mimic their expressions, I mimic their actions, I mimic how they sound. I just pretend to be one of them as we share the pleasures of the flesh together, but then I can't take it anymore and knock the zombie next to me away as I flee.'

Did the zombies which had overrun this building look to him like people blindly lusting for love? There was no way for me to tell whether he was really feeling like that. Perhaps he just liked sounding profound and had got carried away. If what Takagi told me earlier was true, he had a very guilty conscience. Still, I had a feeling it had been our desperate situation that had prised the confession out of him.

But to my regret, there was nothing I could say that could give him comfort.The only thing I could do was pry even further, as the boor that I was.

'What do you think was the reason for killing Shindō?'

Tatsunami was not fazed by the question at all.

'I wonder. Nanamiya seems absolutely terrified, but I guess everyone has done something that earned the hatred of someone else. Some will invoke the name of God and say thou shalt not kill, while others will go out murdering people and claiming it's God's will. There's no telling what drives people to their actions. The only thing we should worry about is whether we'll survive this or not.'

Tatsunami rolled up his shirt. He was carrying a knife tucked into his belt. The knife was not one of the decorative weapons from the lounge and was probably his own. He probably knew that, even under normal circumstances, there were people out there who didn't like him.

'You'd better stay close to Kenzaki.'

Tatsunami was about to light another cigarette, when a new visitor appeared on the rooftop: Nabari, who had gone to her room earlier. When she saw me, she said she had come for a breath of fresh air, but when she noticed Tatsunami's back, she frowned and walked to the other side of the rooftop. I said goodbye to Tatsunami, and left.

8

I returned to my room. A look at the clock told me it was half past four. After drying my hair, which had become wet in the drizzle, I fell onto the bed and dozed off.

I woke up after a ninety-minute sleep. My smartphone still had no signal. I decided to go to Hiruko's room. Partly because she had been on my mind, following my talk with Tatsunami, but also because I had a feeling she might have made progress with our mysteries since this morning.

She occupied room 201. It was the room at the back of the south wing of the second floor, closest to the emergency exit. I made sure to bring my sword. I hadn't ventured into this part of the building since the initial zombie attack, but I was shocked at the scene there. The steel emergency door certainly looked very sturdy, much more reliable than the barricade we had had to improvise. But even now you could hear the relentless sound of the zombies trying to break through from the other side.

BAM! BAM! BAM! BAM!

Each time, the steel frame of the door would creak. The door had been subject to such attacks for more than half a day, building up damage. The zombies weren't slamming their bodies against the door. It was something much harder than flesh, yet not something metal. It sounded as if they were swinging a wooden bat against the door.

Could it be their heads? The image of the uncontrollable zombies battering the door with their own heads, as pieces of flesh flew around, made me shudder.

Perhaps I had been wrong. I had assumed that our weak point was the improvised barricade and that the steel emergency exits would hold, but it was actually here that the zombies were able to make best use of their strength. The reason was probably the footing. When at the barricade, they could only stand on a cramped staircase, but here there was a fairly sizeable landing on the other side of the door. That meant the zombies could stand firmly and concentrate on their attacks.

You must definitely be able to hear the constant banging noise from Hiruko's room. It must be causing her incredible stress, and not allowing her a moment of rest.

I knocked on her door, and she called back.

'It's me. Do you have some time now?'

'Wah! Wai—wait just a minute!'

I could hear a lot going on on the other side of the door. After three or four minutes, the door opened.

'Sorry for the wait.'

'What's the matter?'

Hiruko's face turned red, and she said she had been changing her clothes. But as far I could see, she was wearing the same outfit as when I last saw her.

'I had changed into something more relaxing for my nap.'

She was worried about her bedhead apparently, because she kept patting her hair. I was reminded of my impression of her yesterday. She seems rather mindful about how she appears in front of others, probably because she grew up in a rather prominent family.

'Were you sleeping in your underwear or naked?'

'Of course not!! Just a casual shirt and shorts.'

'I wouldn't have minded you answering the door if you had been.'

'I—I would have minded!!'

She turned even redder. I suddenly had to think of what Tatsunami said earlier. I couldn't look straight at her.

'I just wanted to have a talk.'

'You came at the perfect time. I was just thinking about finding someone to talk to.'

She invited me inside and offered me the chair.

'Who'll start?' she asked.

After a short pause, I decided I'd go first.

'You see, I was still thinking of the matter of howdunnit, the trickery that has been used. But if you go first and your ideas poke holes in my theory, I won't get my turn.'

She nodded, so I started.

'I'll continue my locked room lecture of this morning. I talked about several variations of the locked room mystery then, but people have been claiming that the gold mine that is the locked room mystery has been considerably depleted for a long time now.'

'What a pity. What about all the books that need to be sold?'

'In reality, though, detective stories are still being written and there are still those that focus on locked room mysteries. One of the characteristics of modern locked room mysteries is that they make situations more complex by combining several patterns together.

'Suppose there are only five variations of tricks. If you combine two of them together, that would make ten variations possible. Even if each individual trick might be simple on its own, it's possible to make the mystery more complex by combining multiple elements.

'And so I tried mixing several tricks together to see how they could apply to Shindō's murder.'

'That sounds interesting.'

I regretted having raised her expectations, but it was already too late. I started explaining what I had come up with.

'First, suppose the bite marks on the body were not made by a zombie, but a human.'

'So a human bit him all over, in order to kill him?'

'Yes. But as you pointed out earlier, nobody in our group could have done that. That means a third party entered Shindō's room.'

'That would take us to the problem of the double-layered locked room, the Villa Violet itself, and Shindō's room, which locks automatically.'

'Indeed, but the inner locked room could be entered simply by Shindō himself inviting the culprit into the room.'

'A murder with the victim's own consent? But how did the culprit enter the outer locked room: the Villa Violet itself?'

'That person... let's call them X. Suppose X had been inside the building before the zombies arrived. Mr. Kanno drove all the way to the station yesterday to pick us up, remember? X could have slipped inside during that time. I don't know why, but Shindō may have schemed to let X inside the Villa Violet without us knowing.'

'But X couldn't have "borrowed" one of the keycards from the reception desk.'

Hiruko had a sharp eye and a great memory. She remembered that the reception desk had to be unlocked before Kanno could hand us our keycards.

'That's right. So X was not hiding in one of the rooms, but somewhere on the first floor. But whilst X was still hiding, it turned to night, and then the zombies started surrounding the building.'

'That's the scenario that the killer had been inside from the start which you mentioned earlier, isn't it? So X had been hiding downstairs. Next?'

'After it became night and everyone had gone to sleep, X went up to the second floor. It was probably Shindō who guided them upstairs.'

'How? Our phones don't work.'

'There's the extension. X and Shindō had been working together from the start, so X would obviously know where Shindō's room was. X used one of the phones downstairs to contact Shindō, and they discussed how and at what time X would go upstairs.

'Kanno said he had seen Shindō last night around one o' clock. If he had been out of his room at that time in order to save X, he might have used the elevator to go down.'

'I think the elevator would have been too dangerous to use. If a zombie had managed to get inside, it wouldn't merely have messed up their plan. We all would have been in danger.'

'How about the ventilation ducts, then? As in the films,' I tried.

'Hah, the secret passage! But considering that X did disappear after the murder, that does sound more likely than the elevator.'

'After being invited inside his room, X then attacked Shindō, biting him until he died. X then left the notes and returned downstairs.'

After I was done with my theory, Hiruko pulled at a strand of hair and started patting her cheeks with it, as if it were a makeup brush.

Was my deduction so perfect she couldn't find any counter-arguments? Of course not. It was more likely there was so much to pick apart she didn't know where to begin. But she was kind enough not to crush my theory to pieces immediately.

'Well, if X is a human, why did they do such a thorough job of biting Shindō all over? Why not just kill him and be done with it?'

'True, but what about this? What if it was X who was murdered, and Shindō was the culprit? That was why the body's face was completely mutilated, to hide the fact it was actually X. And that was why it was made to seem as if he were killed by a zombie. It's the old trick of swapping the bodies.'

'But that doesn't explain why those notes were left behind. It would also mean that Shindō is still hiding downstairs....'

Hiruko seemed to struggle with what to say. I apologised mentally. That's what happens if you just throw random knowledge of mystery fiction at the problem and see what sticks!

'Oh, don't take me too seriously! Eventhough the body's face was barely recognisable, I'm pretty sure it was Shindō, based on his hair and everything else. I only wanted to point out a different possibility if you ignore the whydunnit angle. I'm actually more interested in what you have to say.'

Her fingers finally let go of her hair.

'What I have isn't really a deduction. It's more like a complaint. I have considered several possibilities, but I have the feeling that it's those two notes which make everything so frustrating. We have to twist and turn our theories around only because those messages saying, "Let's eat" and "Thanks for the delicious meal" exist. Because of them, we have to consider the possibilities that a human was involved in the murder of Shindō, and that the murderer is still inside the building.'

That was exactly right. The Shindō murder scene obviously indicated it had been the work of a zombie, but that was contradicted by the notes.

'Perhaps they were left simply to confuse us. It's curious that the killer left any notes in the first place. If they wanted to make us know a human was involved in the murder, they could have just left the "Let's eat" note inside the room. If they wanted to make us think the murderer was one of us,the note wedged between the door and the frame saying "Thanks for the delicious meal" would have been enough. The reason why those messages were left at two separate places might be the crux of the mystery.'

I remembered something which had puzzled me when Shizuhara first found the note saying, "Let's eat."

'Don't you think the note with "Let's eat" was lying in a rather random spot, given that the note with "Thanks for the delicious meal" had been so carefully wedged between the door and frame? It would have made more sense if the "Let's eat" note had been lying closer to the body. So that got me thinking. Even though that note was found lying near the door, I don't think any of us noticed it at first.'

Hiruko instantly understood what I was driving at.

'You mean it was placed there only after we had entered the room.'

'Exactly. And any one of us could have done that.'

'That would mean that both those notes had been outside the room at first. By writing two connected notes that say "Let's eat" and "Thanks for the delicious meal," the killer made us assume that it wasn't a zombie, but a human who had got into the room.'

'Whereas in fact, the human never entered the room.'

We kept building on this idea.

'That's possible. But does that mean that the person who left the notes was not directly involved with the murder of Shindō...?'

The mystery still wasn't solved.

143

Afterwards we learnt from Kanno that the building's ventilation ducts were very narrow, and that they were blocked in several places by ventilation dampers, making it impossible for a human to pass through them. And with that, my Mystery Trick Special was shot down.

9

Half past seven in the evening. Last night at this time, we were enjoying a barbecue, but that was a distant memory now.

Nanamiya was the only one not present at supper. Kanno said he'd take him something later. The meal consisted mainly of emergency supplies, so I couldn't help but laugh at the canned Danish pastries that had been sliced diagonally like a baguette and served in a fancy manner. When I asked about them, I learnt that Shizuhara had done her best to lighten the mood at the dining table. There is actually quite a great variety of emergency supplies available nowadays, with even stew dishes and rice you can eat at room temperature. It's amazing how much the mood at the dining table can be improved, just by putting a little effort into the presentation.

During dinner, Hiruko and Tatsunami chatted a lot, and I also tried to join in the conversation. If not, the mood would surely have become gloomier.Nabari looked even paler than during the afternoon. Misery had completely taken over her small, finely-chiselled features and made her look as pale as a ghost. She had been the distressed type from the start, and the current extreme situation was taking its toll on her mind and body. Shizuhara would answer yes or no whenever her neighbour Takagi spoke to her, but remained silent otherwise, just ripping her bread apart and eating the pieces. Shigemoto had a bottle of his beloved cola next to him and only had eyes for the television. The reason why so many of us had become silent was the fact that it was now night.

'Someone!'

I didn't immediately recognise the voice that had spoken. To my surprise it was Shizuhara who had decided to open her mouth.

'Those monsters. Someone must have created them. So, who?'

It was a fundamental question, even though none of us had asked it before. From what we had learnt from the news, we could assume that the outbreak had started amongst the attendees of the Sabea Rock Festival, and that the infection had spread from there. The news did

144

not say so out loud, but it hinted at a terrorist attack. But nothing had been said about the people behind it....

'It was Madarame.'

It was Shigemoto who spoke. Everyone was puzzled by the name nobody had heard of before.

'What's that?'

'I don't know. But I believe it's the name of an organisation or institute, not a person.'

'Did they talk about them on the news?'

Takagi frowned.She had spent most of the afternoon in the lounge. Every time the news mentioned Lake Sabea, she had immediately rushed to the television in the hope of hearing new developments. As all the wireless devices were still down, it would have been impossible for Shigemoto to have obtained information the rest of us didn't have.

'It was in the notebook I picked up yesterday.'

'Notebook? The one from the abandoned hotel?'

He had read the notebook, even though it was the private property of someone else. I frowned at his confession, but Shigemoto didn't notice and just nodded in response to my question.

'I don't know if it was done on purpose, but there are parts written in different foreign languages, all mixed up. I was curious, so I decided to use the dictionary on my smartphone and try to translate it. It's not really one body of text, more like random memos. So it's really difficult to understand, and there are also many specialist terms, so I haven't got very far yet.'

'So, what is Madarame, then?' asked Takagi.

'The only word that appears in the notebook that seems to be of Japanese origin is "MADARAME." There are also segments that say "MADARAME org," so I guess that its full name is the Madarame Organisation, but there are no details in the book. The notes seem to be talking about some kind of virus. There were also terms like "eternal youth" and "the dead" in there. If only we had an internet connection, we could read the whole thing easily.'

'But that isn't enough to connect it to what's happening now....'

'There's more. The last page in the notebook is dated yesterday, together with the word "pandemic".'

There was a silence, then Hiruko observed: 'There were signs people had been staying in that abandoned hotel, and there were syringes lying around. The terrorists may have been hiding there before they commenced their action.'

145

'How low can they get!? They must be crazy, going about creating zombies!' cried Nabari. Shigemoto did not agree with her.

'No, you're wrong. They may have created the virus, but it's the people on this earth who have wished for the creation of zombies.'

'I never wished for anything like that. Who do you say did?'

During the entire trip, Shigemoto had not seemed as alive as he was now.

'We automatically started calling those monsters "zombies," but zombies actually refer to the slaves created by the shamans in voodoo religion. In Haiti, they use some kind of neurotoxin to put people in an apparent state of death, so they can bury them once and then revive them again. But voodoo seemed so mysterious to Caucasians when they first encountered the religion, they started imagining it to be much more than it actually was. That's how the zombie became a monster. *White Zombie* in 1932 was the first film to feature a zombie, but their portrayal was still close to the zombies in voodoo religions, who didn't attack and feed on people. In fact, zombies were portrayed in that film as poor victims of necromancy.

'The current image of the zombie which attacks people and won't stop until its brain is destroyed, and where victims who are bitten also transform into zombies, was created by *Night of the Living Dead*, a 1968 film by George A. Romero.'

'I saw that once,' said Tatsunami. He seemed very impressed by Shigemoto's enthusiastic lecture.

'The image of the zombie which that film imprinted in people's minds was so stunning, it became a staple of the horror genre. Everyone started to think of zombies as monsters that attack people and which gradually grow in numbers. But if you ask me, there was already a basis which allowed those characteristics to be attributed to zombies.'

'What basis?' asked Tatsunami.

'The undead. Rising from the grave to attack people. Turning their victims into monsters by biting them. There was already a popular monster that did those exact same things.'

'… The vampire?'

Shigemoto nodded. He started speaking even more freely.

'In the period when zombies were still portrayed as slaves in the voodoo religion, vampires and Frankenstein's Monster were infinitely more popular horror characters. The Romero-type zombie took its characteristics from them, becoming The Modern Zombie. From that point on, more and more films with the modern zombie were produced, while the number of vampire films started to dwindle.'

Hiruko, who was sitting next to me, whispered in my ear: 'What is he talking about again?' but I could only shrug. Just let him talk for now.

'Many kinds of zombie films were made before the first zombie boom ended in the nineties. King Romero came up with his own sequel *Dawn of the Dead*, *The Evil Dead* led to the splatter boom, and *The Return of the Living Dead* added a comedic touch. Then the psycho killer took over the main role in horror films for a while, but they were brought back to life again in the 2000s with the hit *Resident Evil,* followed by *28 Days Later,* and a remake of *Dawn of the Dead*. Romero himself created new works like *Land of the Dead* and *Diary of the Dead*. There was a lot of diversity, such as the comedy masterpiece *Shaun of the Dead* or the Spanish film *Rec*, which was filmed in the camera POV style.

'But what I wanted to draw attention to is the fact that zombie films aren't just horror stories. They also act as social commentary on modern society, reflecting the changing sentiments within us. *Dawn of the Dead* showed the irony of consumerism, for example, with the protagonists cooped up in a shopping mall and living a fancy life, thanks to all the consumer goods around them, whilst still being surrounded by zombies. *Diary of the Dead*'s theme revolved around the merits and demerits of the information society and the media. What's especially fascinating is that, following the release of *Resident Evil*, which came out a year after 9/11, the main cause for zombies has been a pandemic due to a new virus. In the past, they weren't explained. Zombies just crawled slowly out of their graves or there'd be some kind of radiation which caused them to rise. Zombies are not simply grotesque, horrifying monsters anymore. They are beings that can be used to cast a light on so many themes: the sin of man, economic class differences, the strong and the weak, or the tragedy of how friends and family can turn into enemies in the blink of an eye. Zombies are projections of our own egos and minds.'

It was an outstanding lecture. He wasn't merely a zombie fan; he was a zombie master. And I had a question for the zombie master.

'So, what kind of ego created our zombies?'

'Just take a look at modern medicine and biological science. Artificial reproduction, gene manipulation, cloned animals... Mankind is committing a sin. It can't be a surprise that within this process zombies are created as a by-product. Scientists say that

147

technology itself is not unethical, that there's no problem as long as it's used wisely. But there's no being less suitable to make the right decision than humankind. And the punishment for our hubris is this. That's what I think.'

Shigemoto sighed.

According to him, the creation of the zombies was inevitable. If it hadn't been here, a handful of people with twisted ideas would have caused the exact same incident somewhere else in the world. It had just been my bad luck to be here. Just as with the earthquake.

10

The dial in the upper-left corner of the television screen indicated ten o' clock in the evening. In the end, we had not managed to learn anything about Shindō's killer, or about how it had been done. None of us could be sure that they would be safe from the murderer that night.

Takagi was telling Shizuhara to be very careful about locking her room, when Tatsunami observed: 'You're all so careful about locking your rooms, but if you ask me, it's completely nuts to keep your room locked when you're not inside.'

'I don't see what you mean,' said Takagi.

Tatsunami then started to explain what he meant, so thoroughly that it almost sounded sarcastic.

'What I mean is that it's senseless to keep on clinging to your usual notions regarding safety, given that we can't get out of the building. The most important matter is how fast you can get away, once the zombies get in. Having to unlock a door whilst the zombies are right behind you takes precious time. It could even be fatal. That's why it's better to keep your door open with the door guard, as we've been doing with the empty rooms. You can lock your room when you're inside.'

I realised that Tatsunami's idea made absolute sense. He had indeed kept his own room open all day. But the women didn't seem to like his suggestion.

'No way.' Takagi immediately shot the idea down.

'Because of you, we've been listening to that nasty music all day. I almost feel brainwashed,' complained Nabari.

'I agree it's the sensible thing to do in an emergency, but I balk at the idea of making my private lifestyle public for everyone to see.'

Hiruko turned the suggestion down firmly as well. It's at such times that women form a united front.

'Well, with all the ladies being this careful, I doubt the killer will have an easy time tonight,' laughed the handsome man, but Takagi gave him a warning.

'According to our great detective, the doors of our rooms can be unlocked rather easily from the outside anyway.'

'Really?'

As all eyes were now on me, I repeated my conversation with Takagi this morning, about how you could open the door with a metal wire.

'Aha. So even those automatic locks aren't fool proof.'

I felt sorry, as this only seemed to fuel the anxiety of everyone, but thankfully, Tatsunami managed to divert attention elsewhere.

'This morning, we concluded that the person who attacked Shindō couldn't be one of us, correct?'

'Err, yes.'

It was unthinkable that the mouth of anyone who had gnawed Shindō's body like that could have remained unharmed.

'Then for the moment, we only need to worry about outsiders getting in. The person who killed Shindō must be covered all over in blood. But there was not a single drop of blood outside in the corridor. As the bloody tracks indicated, they must have got outside via the balcony.'

When Hiruko and I were discussing the case earlier, we had arrived at the same conclusion. And we assumed that someone else had left those messages.

'So what you mean is that we should be more careful of our windows, and not the door?' asked Shigemoto.

'Bingo. It's not likely, of course, but what if the murderer is a firefighter? They could just use their ladder to climb in via the balcony.'

'That's one dynamic murderer,' I had to interject.

'If you like the idea, you can use it in a book. Anyway, make sure to lock your windows.'

Kanno tapped his chest and tried to assure us.

'I'll try to patrol as much as possible.'

'But you must hardly have slept last night. Please take care of yourself as well.'

Shizuhara thanked Kanno for his work, and Nabari echoed her for some reason.

'Yes, you don't have to take on so much responsibility, just because you're the manager.'

'Thank you. But for the moment, I want to do whatever I can.'

Subsequently the discussion turned to what Kanno had done before he came to work at the Villa Violet. He used to work at a company in Tōkyō, but after the firm folded, he wandered around a bit until an acquaintance introduced him to Nanamiya's father, and that was how he got the job of manager. Takagi asked him about his family.

'I'm all alone. My parents died early, and my sister recently passed away in an accident,' he said vaguely.

After dinner Kanno poured some coffee, just as on the previous night. We talked a bit more after that, but around eleven Tatsunami said he was sleepy and was the first to get up.

'I'm going to sleep. I hope I'll see all of you again tomorrow.'

He swung his half-opened door fully open. Shigemoto shouted after him.

'Please switch off the music tonight before you go to sleep!!'

Just before the door closed, Tatsunami raised his hand up in reply, and a few moments later the music stopped. But strangely enough, the silence soon became unbearable and that was the sign to call it a night. Hiruko turned to me and said she'd see me to my room. She got up to walk with me, as she had done the night before, but she looked sleepy.

'This time, I'll see you to your room.'

'Why?'

'Because the wing where your room is located is creepier than mine. If you like, we could swap rooms.'

'Oh, you're talking about the emergency exit? You don't hear much noise inside the room actually, because the air conditioning drowns it out. But if you want to see me safe, let's go on our short date, then.'

Was I a fool for feeling my heart jump because of such a simple word? Hiruko tried to suppress a yawn as she mumbled: 'I couldn't think of anything.'

She was talking about the Shindō murder.

'There's nothing you could have done, there simply aren't enough clues. There's nobody suspicious lurking around, nobody has an alibi, we don't even know the exact time of the murder, or how it was done... We can't find the murderer like that.'

'Hmmm, that's not what I mea.... Oh, well.'

Her suggestive line was followed by a loud yawn. When we arrived at her room, she inserted her keycard into the slot of the card reader on her door.

'Good night. Make sure to lock everything. Don't forget the windows, and place your sword somewhere close by.'

Just before she closed the door, she waved to me. I turned around to return to my own room, when I ran into Takagi, who had the room next to Hiruko. She, too, looked exhausted and could hardly keep her eyes open.

'Oh, it's you. Mifuyu is helping Kannoto clean up the lounge. Would you mind walking her to her room?'

I was surprised by her request. I had seen Takagi accompany Shizuhara to her room several times now. It wasn't like her to leave it up to a man. Takagi seemed to read my mind, and explained.

'She has something to discuss with you. So lend her an ear as well.'

She tried inserting her keycard in the slot while she said that, but she had trouble opening her door.

'You're holding the keycard in reverse.'

She was almost asleep already. I flipped her keycard around and the door opened. She thanked me and disappeared inside. I returned to the lounge to find Kanno and Shizuhara, cleaning up after supper.

'I'll do the rest, so please go and get some rest. Good night,' said Kanno.

And so Shizuhara and I decided to return to our rooms. I looked at the elevator, but the display light indicated the third floor. Shigemoto had probably gone up in the elevator. We couldn't call the elevator back down now, so Kanno saw us off from the lounge whilst rubbing his drowsy eyes. As we walked along the third floor corridor, Shizuhara was looking down at the floor, but when we arrived in front of my room, she finally opened her mouth.

'I really should have apologised to you earlier.'

Her whispering voice reminded me of old recordings.

'Apologise?'

'I'm only alive now because of Akechi.'

So that's what she wanted to talk to me about. I had only lost Akechi yesterday, but it felt as though I hadn't heard his name in ages. Tears came into my eyes.

'During the Trial of Courage, when we were surrounded by zombies, he grabbed me by the hand and pulled me to safety. We hadn't even met before yesterday.'

I nodded.

'Yes. He was like that.'

'If he hadn't been there with me, I would have given up on the spot. But when we finally made it to the top of the staircase, with the Villa

Violet just in front of us... I was so relieved... I forgot about him for a second. And the zombies got him. I didn't try to save him, but just ran away.'

I relived that moment in my mind. Akechi slowly falling backwards down the stairs. His stunned face. His long legs in the air.I took a deep breath to return to the present.

'I am so sorry. It's my fault your friend is dead. I know it can't be forgiven by a mere apology, so if there's any way I can make up for what I did, please tell me. Money, my body, anything.'

Shizuhara bowed deeply. Did she fully realise what she was saying?

I felt honoured in a way. Here in front of me stood a person who remembered how recklessly brave Akechi had been.

Even Sherlock Holmes was once thought to have died in a waterfall after a fatal confrontation with his nemesis. It wasn't only the Watson in the stories who mourned his death: fans around the world grieved. But hadn't Holmes made a miraculous return afterwards?

I had not seen Akechi's body with my own eyes. He would always brazenly stick his head into cases. Wouldn't he, too, make a triumphant return? How disappointed he would be if he could see his Watson depressed like this.

I told Shizuhara to look up.

'You don't have to apologise. Akechi doesn't resent you. Keep your head up, and live your life the way you want. That's all I wish for.'

Shizuhara bit her lip and bowed again deeply.She made sure I got safely inside my room. After I closed the door behind me, I opened the curtains to look out of the window.

Zombie figures floated in the darkness, only illuminated by the light from the boarding house. I tried to look at them carefully, but could not see any familiar faces. I felt relieved, but I also imagined our missing friends might be stuck somewhere, calling out for help.

Then I noticed a faint light coming from the window of the room diagonally to my right. It was Shindō's room. It appeared that a light had been left on. Oh, probably because of the location of the switch. The ceiling lights and the nightstand lamp could be operated together, using the switches built into the nightstand. But the desk lamp could only be turned on and off using the switch beneath the mirror. Somebody had forgotten to turn it off.

Oh well, who cares? Let's sleep.

At that time, I couldn't have known that the culprit's murderous hands were reaching out towards their second target.

CHAPTER FIVE
INVASION

1

Some people in this world are nothing but scum.

Wicked people, who don't think twice about doing inhuman things just to satisfy their own urges.

He was one of them. He was the same as those wretched people.

That's why I did it. I had to do it now.

And I succeeded.

But I do feel sorry for her.

I shall have to lie to her, despite her desperate efforts to solve the case.

2

Night had not yet turned into morning. After getting up, I had been going through the bag lying beside the bed, when I suddenly looked up and listened carefully. Wasn't that a faint cry coming from outside the room?

At first I thought it was a cry from them, so I held my breath, but I was wrong. The voice screamed again a few seconds later, this time much closer. It was a man's voice. It was Kanno. I looked at the timepiece. It was just before half -past four in the morning.

'The zombies! They've broken through the second-floor emergency exit!'

The voice moved away again.

The second-floor emergency exit! Hiruko's face flashed through my mind. My hand reached out for the door handle, but then I remembered to wait for a second. I put the door guard on before opening the door to make sure there were no zombies in the corridor. For a moment, the lights in the corridor blinded me.

At the same time the neighbouring door opened slightly to reveal a scared-looking Shizuhara peering through the small opening. She looked at me, horrified, and I looked silently back at her. We both understood we were in trouble.

Kanno had gone to the south wing of the third floor. That's where Nanamiya's room was.

'Please open the door! The room beneath yours is in danger!!'

When Shizuhara and I arrived there, it was clear that Kanno had lost his usual composure. He was banging loudly on the door of Nanamiya's room. When I noticed the rope ladder in his hands, I immediately understood what was going on.

The zombies had broken through the emergency exit below and swarmed the corridor, so that Hiruko and Takagi were now trapped in their rooms in the south wing. Their doors might swing outwards, but they were infinitely weaker than the steel door of the emergency exit and would not take hours of relentless attacks by the zombies to give way. We had to get the two of them out of there immediately. Nanamiya's door opened at the same time Shigemoto appeared.

'They got in below? Damn!'

Nanamiya apparently slept in his underwear, because his appearance was curious: he was only wearing his briefs, as well as an eye mask on his head. Kanno led the way inside the room and attached the metal hooks of the rope ladder to the railing of the balcony. I leant across the railing and looked down. Someone on the balcony below was looking up at me.

'Hiruko!'

She waved back when she heard me, to signal she was all right, and started climbing the ladder which had been lowered down to her. The railing started to creak.

'Hey, isn't the railing making a lot of noise?' cried Nanamiya.

'It can hold the weight of one person, I believe?' I asked Kanno.

'I don't know! We've never used it before!'

Kanno, Nanamiya and I all went out onto the cramped balcony to support the railing. Shigemoto and Shizuhara looked breathlessly at us. Hiruko's weight seemed to pull the railing outwards slightly, but for the moment it held. With each step she took, the ladder swayed dramatically. I held on desperately whilst I urged Hiruko to take it slowly and be careful not to fall.

Eventually her upper body came within reach, and Kanno and I pulled her up.

'… I haven't used a ladder like this before, so it took me a while.'

Hiruko sighed in relief as she leant on me. Before I knew it, I was giving her a strong hug.

'Now to save Ms. Takagi.'

Kanno ran out of the room with the rope ladder in his hands. The room right above Takagi's was 302, which had been used by Kudamatsu earlier, but which was now empty. With the first rescue mission a success, I finally had some time to look around.

Nanamiya's room was reasonably tidy, considering he had been hiding in his room all day yesterday. I recalled he had a thing for cleanliness. Separately packed eye masks, emergency rations and unopened bottles of water, some generic painkillers, and the eye drops for his contact lenses, were all placed neatly on the table.

'I hope Takagi is okay,' I said.

'Yes, I just saw her on the balcony below,' replied Hiruko, as she frowned at the white paint from the railing that had stuck to her hands. We hurried to 302, but Takagi had already quickly scaled the rope ladder. Thankfully, she had made it out as well.

'What about the others?'

'I closed and locked the south wing door below, so the zombies are stuck there. For the time being, they have not reached the lounge, but...'

Kanno paused for a moment, as if he didn't know what to say. I had a bad feeling about what he might say next.

'Where are Mr. Tatsunami and Nabari?' asked Shigemoto, regarding the two people not present.

'I have not gone to Ms. Nabari's room yet. You see... Mr. Tatsunami has been killed in the lounge.'

Nanamiya sank to the floor upon hearing the news.

3

Tatsunami's body was in similar—no, even worse—shape than Shindō's.He had been found lying inside the elevator on the second floor, his upper body protruding out of the elevator cage and sprawled on the lounge floor. He had probably been murdered inside the elevator, as there was a sea of blood inside. Drops of blood had fallen through the gap between the elevator and the lounge floor and into the darkness. There were marks indicating that the body had been dragged across the elevator floor and blood had sprayed on the walls. But what attracted the most attention were the injuries all across Tatsunami's body. Just as in Shindō's case, he had horrible bite marks all over him. But that was not all.

It was impossible to recognise what had once been Tatsunami's head. It had been smashed so severely that bone fragments and hair had been embedded deep into his brain. Not an inch remained of the handsome mask he wore in life. Next to the body lay what was probably the murder weapon: a mace. Flesh was still sticking to it. A mace is a weapon with a shaft of some seventy to eighty centimetres, and a metal head. If you bludgeoned someone with a mace with all your force, it would probably be far more powerful than a metal baseball bat.

Tatsunami was a miserable corpse now, so we didn't have to worry about him turning into a zombie. A piece of paper had been placed inside his skull.

"One more to go. I'll be sure to devour you."

It had been wise of Kanno not to call Nabari. She was already almost at her limit last night. If she learnt what a horrible tragedy had occurred just outside her room, she might pass out. But Kanno had made one mistake. No, it wasn't just him. Everyone here, including myself, had unconsciously been putting too much faith in one woman.

'Hey, Kenzaki!'

Takagi cried out from behind me. I turned around to find Hiruko collapsing in her arms. She had fainted upon seeing Tatsunami's body.

BANG! BANG!

The relentless banging noises that reverberated through the lounge felt like direct attacks on our hearts.

Hiruko had been brought to Kanno's room 203 because it was near the lounge. She regained consciousness after about fifteen minutes. She looked incredibly pale. When she noticed I had been watching over her all the time, a brave smile appeared on her face, and she started talking as if nothing had happened.

'Oh, gosh. I took a look at the body just as I let my guard down. Made me feel a bit lightheaded. But I'm okay now. I'll have a look at the scene right away.'

'No. You need to rest first.'

I tried to make her sleep, but her cold hands brushed me away.

'The zombies could take over the second floor at any moment. I have to investigate the scene before that happens.'

Kanno and the others were busy moving our main base from the lounge to the third floor. The circumstances had been explained to Nabarias well, and now they were moving food and drinking water upstairs. The zombies were contained in the south wing of the second floor for now, but the doors that separate each wing are far weaker than the emergency exits, so they wouldn't hold for very long.

156

Still, I hesitated to have Hiruko face that horrible sight once again. She might have felt it was her duty to solve the mystery and catch the killer, because she had already solved numerous cases before. But here we had no police, no forensics. We didn't even have handcuffs or anywhere to hold someone, even if we caught the murderer. So, what could she accomplish alone? This wasn't a detective story. This was reality. I couldn't let her push herself so hard.

'Hiruko, listen to me.'

I held her cold hands tight and looked her straight in the eye.

'I agree this is an inhuman case. But right at this moment, we need to focus on staying alive. You're under no obligation to solve the case. So why do you need to push yourself like this? Is it because you can't ignore criminals? Is it because you can't close your eyes to unsolved mysteries? Right now, you have to think about your own safety. You are just one woman. And if anyone has a gripe, I'll personally kick their ass.'

Hiruko looked surprised as her large eyes blinked, but then she giggled.

'Hahaha, I thought you were under the wrong impression before, and now I know I was right. You really thought I solved all those cases before out of some kind of sense of duty, or in the interests of justice?'

'…What do you mean?'

'Heh, I'm not that cool. Heheh.'

She kept laughing at me for a while, as I looked at her in confusion. Then she took a deep breath.

'Don't look at me like that, it makes me blush. You see, I'm not the Great Detective you imagine me to be.'

'But I heard you solved a lot of cases before.'

'It is true that suggestions from me have helped solve some cases,and so a lot of people in the police know me by now. But I don't like the role one little bit. If anything, there are few things I hate more than cases like that.'

'So then why do you get involved with them all the time? You were awarded a commendation by the police for your assistance, and people call you a great detective.'

'You're under the wrong impression. Not once in my whole life have I become involved in a case because someone asked me to, or of my own free will. That is just how I naturally am. It's my idiosyncrasy. You can call it the fate with which I was born. It's like a curse. I attract dangerous and freakish incidents. In that sense, I'm

157

fundamentally different from the detectives you so admire. I am never hired, it's not my curiosity that's being piqued, not a sense of indignation towards criminals, not a feeling of duty to uphold the law, nor a desire to learn the truth. I just happen to get involved in cases and do everything to solve them, because I want to survive.'

There was nothing I could say. She never got involved with cases of her own accord. She only tried to get away from whatever calamity happened to cross her path.

'They call me the cursed child.'

Hiruko told me that ever since she was born, there had always been incidents involving her family, other relatives and the family business. At one time, Public Security even kept an eye on her because she became involved with the police too often. In time, rumours started that misfortune would occur wherever Hiruko went. At first her parents didn't take them seriously, but by the time she went to middle school, they moved her out of their home. Apparently it was for the safety of her two older brothers, who would become the next family leaders. But because her family was wealthy, she was well-provided for, even though she lived all by herself.

'The first time I got involved with a murder was when I was fourteen. We were on a school trip. Two people got killed at our destination, and the killer turned out to be my homeroom teacher. From then on, I started running into murders two or three times a year, and now I come across a body once every three months. And the more incidents I encounter, the more vicious they become. Multiple victims over the course of one single case. And frequently I find myself in mortal danger.

'I'm scared out of my wits. Unlike the detectives in the mystery stories you like so much, I don't get a special, safe VIP seat. One false step and I could get myself killed. I could accidentally witness a crime and become the next unfortunate victim, because I get in the way of the killer. That is why I need to find the killer, before I myself am murdered.'

Hiruko's confession had been spoken harshly, but then she suddenly adopted a gentler tone.

'But then I started hearing stories at campus about the Holmes of Shinkō, about Akechi. At first I just thought that it takes all kinds to make a world. I could not comprehend how anyone would want to look for cases of their own free will. But there was more to the rumours. They said Akechi had an assistant. It was an eye-opener. Why hadn't I thought of something as simple as that? There was no need to take on everything by myself. If there was someone by my side to support me, I could survive longer than on my own. I'd been stupid, and that's the secret you wanted to know. I know I've only caused trouble for you, but you see, I hoped you would accept this fate of mine, considering that you like detective stories. But now all of this has happened. I'm sorry. I'm really, really sorry.'

Her humbling confession hit me harder than any mace could have done. I had foolishly assumed that Hiruko was like those superhuman detectives from the mystery stories. I thought she had the gift Akechi and I had always dreamed of. She seemed such a brilliant person— somewhere in my heart I was even jealous of her—and that's why I thought it so insensitive when she tried to scout me as her assistant.

Even though the last two days had shown me clearly enough she was not that kind of person. Sometimes she could be as innocent as a child, sometimes she would try to hide her true feelings clumsily, sometimes she'd be embarrassed about the smallest things and sometimes she'd be more attractive than any woman of her age. I knew all of that.

Akechi and I must have seemed so comical to her. Mystery stories. Detectives. Locked rooms. Tricks. How stupid we were. How thoughtless we were. Throughout her cases, Hiruko had been confronted by her own fleeting life.Even now, she was only taking on the mystery to survive our current ordeal.

'Let me go. We don't have much time left.'

But still... I didn't want her to overdo it.After some thought, I proposed a compromise.

'Let's hear what everyone has to say first, and get a clear picture of what happened last night. It will only muddy things if we check out the scene first. Let's prioritise getting to understand the circumstances first, so we know what to look for.'

After a short pause, Hiruko nodded.

'I guess you really are the Watson of Shinkō. You're absolutely right; let's listen to what the others have to say first.'

I felt relieved that I had managed to change her mind, but at the same time, I had an uneasy feeling.

For I'm no Watson.

We assembled in the elevator hall on the third floor, which had been empty until yesterday, but was now furnished with a simple table and some foldable chairs.

It was only a matter of time before the zombies took over the second floor. All that remained were the third floor and the rooftop. If the zombies managed to break through the barricade on the eastern staircase, or through the third-floor emergency exit, the only remaining option would be to escape to the rooftop through the storage room, which is why our new base had been set up close by.

Now that Tatsunami was dead, it was Hiruko who led the discussions. She had left her room in her sleepwear earlier, but was now wearing a coat she had borrowed from Shizuhara.

'There's one thing I want to have confirmed first, before we listen to everyone's individual stories. Last night, right around the time we returned to our rooms, I was overcome by an intense drowsiness and literally fell on my bed to sleep. And I was still fast asleep when the zombies broke through the emergency exit and swarmed the corridor. I noticed nothing. When I got up, my hands felt weak and I staggered around. Thinking back, that now seems very curious. Did any of you have the same experience?'

One after another, the others confirmed her suspicions.

'Yes, my hands were so weak, I was afraid I'd fall off the ladder.' Takagi was the first to speak, followed by Kanno.

'Yes. I had intended to make my rounds every hour, just as I did last night. I was planning to take forty winks, but fell into a deep sleep and didn't hear the alarm on my phone go off....'

Shizuhara and the insomniac Nabari had had similar experiences.

'Do you mean...?'

'Yes. We were drugged.'

Everyone looked nervous. It clearly meant that the culprit was one of us.

'It's all become clear to me now! I was in my room all the time, and nothing happened to me. That means someone drugged the food you all ate last night. One of you is a killer!'

Nanamiya's blood-shot eyes, scared and furious, glared at all of us.

'Don't make things up!' Nabari snapped back.

'Errr, I have something to say. You see, I felt fine, too,' said Shigemoto timidly.

Takagi frowned.

'Huh? Does that mean some of the food wasn't drugged?'

Shigemoto shook his head.

'No, there was one thing I didn't have yesterday. The coffee after the meal. I only ever drink cola, so I didn't have any coffee last night.'

I had something to add as well.

'I didn't have coffee either. And I didn't feel particularly strange waking up this morning.'

Nanamiya shot me a suspicious look.

'You're telling me there were two people amongst you who didn't have any coffee after supper?'

'I have a coffee allergy.'

'Coffee allergy? What's that?'

It was Shizuhara, from Nursing Studies, who helped me out.

'I've heard about that. It's a delayed-type allergy. A few hours, or in some cases a few days, after drinking coffee, the body will start to show symptoms. The symptoms are similar to those of caffeinism, so it's hard to tell the difference between them.'

'In my case, I can handle green tea and black tea. I can prove my allergy to you, but it's not a pretty sight.'

'That won't be necessary. The first time we met at the café, I recall that Akechi had ordered a coffee, but that you had a cream soda.'

Hiruko had remembered even such a small detail as that.

'Anyway, that makes it plausible that it was the coffee which was drugged. If I recall correctly, you also poured coffee for us on the first evening, correct?' Hiruko asked Kanno.

'Yes, I did.'

'Which means that it was reasonable to predict that you would also pour coffee for us yesterday. Even if you hadn't offered, the killer could have suggested that they wanted some, which you would then have made. The coffee maker works by injecting hot water from the water container through special capsules. So all one needs to do is to introduce some sleeping medicine into the water in the container in advance. Any one of us would have had an opportunity to tamper with the coffee maker during the day. Something like the water dispenser might not be used by everyone, so the choice of coffee was very cunning.'

Which meant that preparations for the murder had already been made before supper. But what was most troubling was that it was now undeniable that the culprit was amongst us.

161

'Anyway, with a few exceptions, someone managed to drug us, and thus restrict our nightly activities. Let's get a clear picture of what happened after everyone returned to their rooms. I'll startwith myself.'

Hiruko spoke with authority, discouraging any comments. Nanamiya was fidgeting nervously and tapping his temples again. Kanno nodded to himself a few times, as if he were going over his own movements in his mind. Nabari was holding her head, as if she were trying to escape reality.

'Last night, Hamura saw me to my room. I was very sleepy and it could not even have been half past eleven when I went to bed. I remained sound asleep until I was awakened by my phone ringing.'

'Your phone?' I repeated.

'The extension in my room. I don't know where the call came from, because there's no display on the phones. Anyway, I'm sure it had been ringing for a long time. When I finally picked up the receiver there was a strange voice on the other end of the line.'

Everyone looked bewildered.

'It sounded like the groaning of a zombie. It went on for about ten seconds and then they hung up. I couldn't make out whether it was male or female. At first I assumed it was just a very bad joke, but then I finally realised something had been banging on my door. It wasn't a knock, but more random, as if some drunk kept collapsing against it. I put my ear to the door and I knew instantly there were a lot of them roaming the corridor. When I realised the zombies had broken down the emergency exit, I immediately called Mr. Kanno in 203. That was when I looked at the clock for the first time. It was twenty-five past four. But Mr. Kanno must have been drugged heavily as well, because it took him quite a while to answer the phone.'

Kanno looked apologetically at us.

'Yes, I was fast asleep and it took me some time to realise the phone was ringing.'

'Mr. Kanno answered the call after about thirty seconds. I told him the zombies had entered the south wing and asked him to check the rest of the building. If the zombies had already reached the lounge, even Mr. Kanno wouldn't be able to leave his own room. I also asked him to lower the rope ladder down from the floor above if possible, and that was it. The call took about two minutes, I think.'

Apparently Hiruko had been the first to wake up, not counting the culprit.

'Then I rang Takagi in the room next door, because I was afraid she might accidentally go out into the corridor. I think she answered my call in about ten seconds.'

'I was sleeping soundly as well. I hadn't noticed anything of what had been going on outside,' said Takagi.

'Soon after explaining to her what was happening, Mr. Kanno lowered the rope ladder down from the room above, and that's how I got out. That's all I have to say about what occurred,' Hiruko concluded.

Kanno was next in line.

'I was the last person to stay in the lounge last evening. After seeing Mr. Hamura and Ms. Shizuhara leave via the eastern corridor, I made my usual rounds of the second and third floors and locked the door to the east wing. The elevator had been stopped on the third floor. I then returned to my room, set the alarm on my phone, just as I had done the previous night, and lay down on the bed. But, as Ms. Kenzaki mentioned earlier, I was fast asleep until she called me. When I finally realised the phone was ringing, I was absolutely shocked that I had been sleeping for so long. Yes, she called me at twenty-five past four, and it changed to twenty-six during our call. After hanging up, I left my room cautiously, because I knew the zombies could be there too. I didn't find any zombies in the lounge, but Mr. Tatsunami was lying there in that horrible manner. Though utterly stupefied by what had happened, I did check whether he was still alive, and had a look at the surroundings. It was then that I noticed that the door to the east wing was open, even though I had shut it. Meanwhile, the south wing door, which should have been left open, had been closed.'

Earlier we had agreed to keep the east wing door closed during the night, as it was closest to the barricade.

'So it wasn't you who shut the south wing door to stop the zombies?' asked Hiruko.

'It was already closed when I left my room. But it was only closed, not locked. Anyone could have opened it just by turning the handle.'

'Where was the key to the wing doors?'

'In its place on the television stand. When I saw it, I hurried to get to it in order to lock the door. We are lucky the zombies aren't smart enough to open a door, but we were this close to having them flooding the lounge. Then all of us would have been stuck in our rooms.'

I was very puzzled by the strange turn of events, and listened attentively to what else he had to say.

'I had to decide what to do next. I had no choice but to set the matter of Mr. Tatsunami aside for the time being. My first priority was to rescue Ms. Kenzaki and Ms. Takagi, who were trapped in the south wing. I feared Ms. Nabari would be greatly upset by the gruesome state of the body, so I decided not to wake her, and ran up to the third floor. There wasn't time to wake everyone up one by one, so I shouted out about what was happening. I picked the rope ladder up in the elevator hall and went straight to Mr. Nanamiya's room.'

So it was indeed Kanno's shouts I had heard.

'Afterwards we all gathered together. As far as I know, Ms. Kenzaki was the only person who called me in my room. I was asleep so I can't be absolutely certain, but I don't thinkI received any anonymous calls.'

Takagi was next, but she basically just confirmed what the previous two had said. One aspect of her story did stand out, however.

'After leaving Mr. Kanno and Mifuyu in the lounge yesterday, I had a short chat with Hamura in the corridor and then went into my room. I was really sleepy then and had trouble using my keycard. I think I fell asleep just after eleven. I didn't wake up until Kenzaki called me. But I have the feeling that my phone did ring for a long time before she called. And it wasn'tjust for ten or twenty seconds, more like a minute or more. But my head felt so foggy, I simply couldn't manage to answer. The ringing stopped, but then immediately started again, and that finally got me out of my sleep. That second time was Kenzaki. Did you try to call me several times?'

'No, I only tried once.'

'Huh. Anyway, her call woke me up, and when I checked the clock, it was twenty-eight minutes past four. She warned me not leave my room, but hearing them banging on my door was enough to keep me inside anyway. After that, I was saved. There's nothing else I remember.'

After the three most important actors in this morning's drama had finished their stories, Hiruko looked at the others one by one and finally turned to me.

'As mentioned earlier, I first walked Hiruko to her room and also helped Takagi get to her room. I then met up with Shizuhara in the lounge and we went upstairs together. We had a short talk and said goodnight in front of my room. It appears I wasn't drugged, so I was awake until relatively late last night. It wasn't as if I had anything to do, so I was just rolling around in bed and I don't know when exactly I fell asleep. I guess around one o' clock, perhaps half past. After I got up this morning, I heard Mr. Kanno shouting. He said the emergency exit on the second floor had been broken through. It was just before half past four.'

I looked at Kanno, who nodded back.

'Startled by his cries, I peered out into the corridor with the door guard on. Shizuhara had done the exact same thing as I and had been peering outside from the room next door, so we looked at each other. We then followed Mr. Kanno together. I didn't get any calls.'

'So the culprit only called me and Takagi.'

As was her habit, Hiruko placed a strand of hair against her lips whilst she was thinking. Then she asked Shizuhara to tell her story. Shizuhara's account was more or less the same as mine. She had basically drifted off immediately, due to the sleeping drugs, but Kanno's cries had awakened her. She didn't remember the exact time. Nabari, Shigemoto and Nanamiya's accounts followed, but there were no new discoveries. Nabari had been sound asleep in her room until everything was over. Like Shizuhara and myself, Shigemoto and Nanamiya hadn't noticed any of what had been going on below until Kanno came to warn us. They didn't get any phone calls either.

When everyone was done, Hiruko announced she was going to have another look at the crime scene.

'It's possible we won't be able to go to the lounge later.'

'I'll join you. What if the zombies manage to break through the door there too....'

Kanno gripped the sword in his hand tightly.

'I'll go too.'

'Well, me as well.'

'...Sure.'

To my surprise, everyone decided to go along, save for Takagi and Shizuhara. Perhaps because everyone had had enough of not knowing who the murderer was.

5

Arriving in the lounge, Kanno took up a position in front of the south wing door, prepared for any zombie attack. We could still hear them slamming their bodies against the door from the other side.

Hiruko put her face mask on and headed straight for the body of Tatsunami, which was still lying in the elevator opening. The horribly damaged head had been covered with a piece of cloth, but I stood close to Hiruko, fearing that she might faint again.

'How horrible, his head has been completely smashed. But it's odd actually. The killer wasn't this thorough with Shindō.'

She had a point there. Why had the killer gone so far this time? What if it hadn't been a zombie who had attacked Shindō, and there had been no need to make sure he was dead?

'Look there.'

Hiruko pointed to some bruise marks around Tatsunami's wrists.

'His hands must have been tied with a rope or something. You can see the same marks around his mouth, so he was probably gagged as well.'

Only yesterday, Tatsunami had been talking to me about love on the rooftop. He had told me to stay byHiruko's side. He had hoped to see all of us this morning, but he had been turned into this thing within just a few hours.He may have had women problems, but I didn't dislike him.

'He must've been attacked whilst he was asleep,' I suggested.

'Yes. And that means…'

Hiruko proceeded to examine the door to Tatsunami's room. It had been opened with the master keycard already, and kept open with the door guard. Tatsunami must have been fast asleep due to the drugs, so the killer had managed to gain entry into the room without his help. But how? Hiruko, who had been kneeling down, called out. A tissue box had been stuck inside the door, immediately below the door handle.

'Was this his countermeasure to the trick with the metal wire you were talking about?'

'Yes, and it's pretty clever. You can't catch the wire hook on the door handle because the box will be in the way.'

Which meant that my trick was not applicable here.

'Could you bring that chair over?'

She examined the top of the door.

'The dust here has been disturbed in an unnatural manner. Could you take a look?'

She was correct. The top of a door is seldom clean, so there was naturally a thin layer of dust there, but some of the dust had been swept away over a distance of ten centimetres, measured from the corner.

'What do you think it means?' asked Hiruko.

'It shows that someone unlocked the door somehow, then used the gap they had created to pull a wire or string around the door guard. The two ends of the wire were then pulled over the top of the door and the door was closed again. The door guard was unlocked by pulling the wire sideways.'

'Which means we can be sure that the killer entered the room through the door.'

We then examined the door and the surrounding floor inch by inch, but found nothing that attracted our attention. We also took a look inside the room, but there were no signs of a struggle. Tatsunami had probably been attacked and rendered helpless whilst he was fast asleep. To the rear of the room on the left, hidden behind his bed, stood his beloved radio cassette CD player, still connected to the power outlet.

Nabari, who had been watching us from outside the room, made a timid suggestion.

'Once the killer restrained Mr. Tatsunami, wouldn't only a man have been able to drag his body all the way to the elevator? He was the tallest amongst us, and even though he was slim, he must have weighed at least seventy kilograms.'

It was a very practical observation. Detective stories tend to gloss over the fact, but it requires a lot of strength to move a dead body on your own. The carpet in the lounge further prevented anything from sliding smoothly across the floor, so pulling the body to the elevator must have been a difficult task. Hiruko's reply, however, was surprisingly dismissive.

'Oh, that's no problem, I think.'

She turned to me and pointed to the floor.

'You weigh well over sixty kilos, at a guess. Can you sit here with your legs extended?'

I obliged and she went behind me.

'You see, there's a trick to lifting a person.'

The petite Hiruko grabbed hold of me by my sides and tried to lift me up, but she lacked the strength.

'Most people would try to lift someone by their sides like this, or by carrying them in their arms. But that's very difficult. That's because the centres of gravity of yourself and the other person are just too far apart and because you try to lift from your back. But the trick is....'

Suddenly Hiruko's chest was planted against my back. Hiruko! How come you're so small and have *those*!

'...To stick your own body as close as you can to them, so as to get your centres of gravity as close as possible.'

She breathed in my ear. My heart was racing, but she obviously couldn't tell. She wrapped her arms around my sides, with each hand

167

firmly grasping the opposite upper arm. She moved even closer, sliding her legs around me.

'And here we go.'

In one smooth move, Hirukoand I were suddenly standing upright. It was as if I had been lifted by a crane.

'There, I did it. The trick is not to lift with your back, but to use the strength of your legs to lift yourself up. It's a method often used in old martial arts and by nurses. The smallest of us is Shizuhara, who has the same build as I do, so either of us could have lifted Tatsunami this way.'

Which was great, of course, but basically proved that any one of us could have committed the crime. And, although she hadn't meant anything by it, it had also been a great demonstration of her innocent naivety. You normally don't get so close to someone else!

Nanamiya, who had been watching it all, suddenly burst out.

'Just think! It's obvious who killed them! There's only one of us who had the master keycard, both now and yesterday with Shindō. She could have entered any room easily. Isn't that right, Nabari?'

Nabari gave him a frightened look.

'Do you think I did this?'

'Yes, I do. I remember what you said yesterday morning. You said you usually take sleeping pills. You used your drugs to drug the coffee, didn't you?'

The victims of both murders had been bitten all over, so these were not simple crimes where all the murderer needed to do was gain entry into the rooms, but Nanamiya had lost his nerve and was overlooking such basic facts. Nabari looked down at the floor, and her shoulders started to shake. I thought she was shaking out of humiliation or anger, but I was wrong. Her hair flew back as she raised her head again and started laughing uproariously.

'Hahahahaha! Hahahahaaa!'

It was a bloodcurdling laugh, as if she were playing the role of a madwoman. Nanamiya, too, was taken aback by her reaction, and held his breath. Nabari stopped laughing and turned to Kanno, addressing him calmly.

'You see? This is exactly what I was afraid of. I knew some idiot would put the blame on me just because of the master keycard.'

The poor manager looked apologetic as he turned to the rest of us to explain.

'I'm terribly sorry. I feel bad about hiding this from you until now....'

'What is she talking about?'

'Last night, after everyone had left the lounge, Ms. Nabari came to me and exchanged her master keycard for my keycard.'

It wasn't only Nanamiya who was shocked. We all were. Kanno had been carrying Nabari's old keycard, which belonged to the now empty room 206. Nabari pulled her keycard from her pocket, which indeed had 206 printed on it.

'He's not to blame. I asked him to keep it a secret from you.'

She had raised her voice now as she refuted the accusation against her.

'I knew the moment Shindō was murdered that if another murder happened, the first person to be suspected would be the one with the master keycard. And it's not as if I would have had an alibi for the middle of the night. Once suspicion falls on you, it's impossible to shake it off. That's why I returned the master keycard to Mr. Kanno, without letting any of you know.'

Which meant that Nabari couldn't have entered Tatsunami's room last night. Hiruko interrupted her.

'Could you perhaps check on your sleeping drugs?'

'Of course.'

Kanno opened room 205 with the master keycard and Nabari soon returned with her pills. Hiruko had a look at them and nodded to herself.

'These aren't the pills which were used last night.'

'How the hell can you tell!' barked Nanamiya.

'I've been involved with an incident where sleeping pills were used,' replied Hiruko nonchalantly.

'Sleeping and sleep-inducing drugs are very similar, but the ones you use to fall asleep immediately, and which don't take a long time to start working, are actually sleep-inducing drugs. They vary in effectiveness, but the ones Nabari uses are called "ultrashort-acting," and are usually prescribed for people suffering from light insomnia. It doesn't take long for them to start working after you take them, but their effect doesn't last long either. They simply ease you into falling asleep. They wouldn't cause the sense of weakness or trouble standing up straight, as we experienced when we woke up.'

'Then Kanno's the murderer! He has the master keycard!'

Nanamiya was just lashing out now, but Nabari countered this accusation as well.

'It was my own decision to return the master keycard to him. How could he have predicted I would do that? And I returned the master keycard because I didn't want to be suspected, so would he be so stupid as to use that very same master keycard to commit a murder? You've been spouting these cheap accusations, but this building is owned by your parents, so I wouldn't be surprised if you had one or two master keycards of your own. I heard you amused yourself here last year.'

She, too, had known about the rumours. As everything was turned back on him, Nanamiya's face turned red and then blue. The next moment he exploded, shrieking like some monstrous bird.

'Damn it! I'm not staying here with you killers!'

He ran over to the crossbow hanging on the lounge wall. Everyone felt their heart jump.

'What are you doing!?'

'Don't even come near my room! Anyone who approaches me will get shot. Don't say I didn't warn you!'

So saying, he rushed up to the third floor, crossbow in hand.

6

An awkward silence hung over the room, which was only interrupted by Kanno's soft "My apologies." Hiruko said she would continue her investigation because there wasn't much time. Shigemoto shrugged and started making fun of Nanamiya.

'He only has one arrow, so just let him use it. Only amateurs pick projectile weapons.'

Nabari's pallor had improved.

'I hope he doesn't do anything to Takagi and Shizuhara. I'll go and check,' she said, and went upstairs as well. Hiruko stepped out of the room into the lounge and walked around the table for a while in search of clues, but didn't seem to find anything significant. She turned to Kanno.

'Have you noticed anything out of the ordinary here?'

'I can't say I have... But wait....'

Kanno went over to the nine bronze statues surrounding the television set. The scale statues of King Arthur, David and the other Nine Worthies reached up to my waist.

'I think they are facing just slightly the wrong way.'

'The wrong way?'

'Their order is the same as usual, but their faces seem to be looking in a slightly different direction. Usually they are lined up so as to look straight at the table, but the two at the right end are turned away.'

We hadn't noticed anything wrong with the statues, but Kanno cleaned them regularly, so he would know.

'Someone might just have moved them accidentally. There's nothing to indicate that the murderer moved them.'

I stepped up to one of the bronze statues to check its weight. It was pretty heavy. The statue was barely a metre high, but it probably weighed around forty or fifty kilograms. I could lift it, but not even a man could have wielded it as a weapon. I told Hiruko, who nodded and returned to Tatsunami's body.

'What puzzles me as well are the bite marks. It's the same as we saw with Shindō. The fabric of his clothes has been torn and, in some places, the injuries reach the bone.'

'So the killer is a zombie!' cried Shigemoto excitedly.

'You're saying a zombie drugged us?' I asked, unconvinced.

'Just because most of them are dumb, doesn't mean all of them are. In *Land of the Dead* one zombie learned to use a pistol and commanded other zombies to fight humans. And if the cause of these zombies is bacteria or some kind of virus, it's possible that some people have better resistance or adaptability.'

Kanno frowned at the zombie master's suggestion.

'Are you seriously suggesting there are zombies with human-like intelligence?'

'Mr. Kanno, you shouldn't forget that they used to be humans! The killer zombie must have entered the building through the emergency exit together with the other zombies. The zombie killed Mr. Tatsunami and then left through the south wing door. That's why that door wasn't locked.'

'But who called Ms. Kenzaki and Ms. Takagi?'

'The zombie, of course!'

The zombie master was on a roll. His theory had gone well beyond common sense, but if he were actually correct, it would explain how the murder had been committed. Hiruko, however, refuted Shigemoto's theory by first allowing the possibility.

'The possibility can't be denied, but even if it were true, there would still be contradictions surrounding this second murder. If the murderer is a zombie who came in through the emergency exit, as you suppose, then that same zombie couldn't have drugged us.'

The zombie master was silent.She had a point.We had been the only people inside the boarding house since yesterday morning. If the coffee maker had already been tampered with by that time, then each time one of us had coffee, someone would have fallen asleep. But

171

nobody had fallen asleep unnaturally. Which meant that the sleeping drugs had only been administered just before supper, and that one of us had to have done it.

Blast! We were in the same situation as with Shindō's murder. We had, at one and the same time, actions that only a human could have taken and wounds that only a zombie could have inflicted. Did that mean that Shigemoto's intelligent zombie and one of us were working together?

… If so, that would explain a lot of what had happened. The culprit drugged us and then, when night fell, theyd ragged Tatsunami out of his room and let the intelligent zombie in through the emergency exit. The intelligent zombie then bit and killed Tatsunami, and obediently left the lounge again. It was the same with Shindō's murder. The culprit let the intelligent zombie in through the emergency exit, and together they went to Shindō's room. The culprit made up some excuse to get Shindō to open his door. They forced their way inside, the intelligent zombie set its teeth in Shindō and, once the culprit left the notes, it was all done.

Surely that couldn't be the solution, could it!? The line between reality and fantasy was starting to fade in my mind. At that very moment, Nabari returned from the third floor.

'He really disappeared into his room. And the other two are fine.'

Upon hearing that news, Hiruko decided to tackle the matter from a different angle. She clapped her hands together loudly.

'Let's put the matter of what trick was used aside for the moment and concentrate on the objective facts before us. First, Tatsunami was moved out of his room. He was bitten and killed by zombies inside the elevator. Those events we know occurred. Forget about the note from the killer and the zombies in the corridor. Which brings a curious matter to light.'

Hiruko had simplified the problem by cutting away the factors that had confused us.

'What's curious?' I asked.

'Why was the elevator chosen as the scene of the crime? It doesn't matter whether the murderer was a human or a zombie. Why wasn't Tatsunami killed in his room, like Shindō?'

The other three in the lounge looked as if they had no idea, so I just said what came to mind.

'The murderer is determined to kill their targets by having a zombie attack them. That's easier done if Tatsunami is out of his room.'

Hiruko pointed at me.

172

'That's exactly what I mean. You're supposing that Tatsunami was moved out of his room so that a zombie could attack him. But there are simpler methods to have a zombie sink their teeth into him.

'For example, after tying Tatsunami up, the culprit could have just dropped him off in the south corridor, then opened the emergency exit, made a run for the lounge, and locked the south wing door. Only Tatsunami in the corridor would have been attacked. And the job would be done. See? That method would be easier. That's how I would have done it.'

She was right. Once again I had been focusing too much on the trickery, the howdunnit, and lost sight of why it had to be done like that, the whydunnit. Still, that was a very clever murder method she had come up with. Let's dub it the Hiruko Method.

'And yet the culprit showed they had a clear objective, by deliberately moving Tatsunami to the third-floor elevator,' Hiruko continued.

A certain intention, a certain aim, which presumably could not have been achieved through Hiruko's suggested murder method. Suddenly, Hiruko, who had been staring at the pool of blood in the elevator, noticed something.

'Darn. I must still be half asleep,' she said as she stepped closer to the body, but stopped just inches in front of it. She called out to me in a tense voice.

'Ye—yes?'

'Let's make a deal.'

It felt like ages since she had first used those words, the words that had brought us to the Villa Violet.

'What kind of deal?'

'Move Tatsunami's body. If you do that, I'll give you a kiss.'

'Uwwaa!' I let out a pathetic cry.

The body? In that squishy state? At the risk of being rude to Tatsunami, his body was not something anyone should touch. Parts that shouldn't be visible were visible, and didn't the news say we shouldn't even come in contact with the injured?

'I'm not asking you to move it far. Just outside the cage. Please.'

Needless to say, I wanted to help Hiruko, and there was an alluring reward waiting for me as well, but it was an even more difficult task than touching a Komodo dragon or a tarantula. Seeing me hesitate, the housemanager, beacon of responsibility that he was, spoke up timidly.

'Shall I move it, then?'

Nabari was the quickest to react.

'Mr.Kanno! For a kiss! For shame!'

'No—no, that's not it. I just thought I should do it as the oldest here....'

We eventually placed Tatsunami's body on a mattress we had taken out of his room and moved him out of the elevator. The deal was off, of course. But since when did Nabari start minding about Kanno's behaviour?

'So, what did you learn?'

Instead of approaching the displaced body, Hiruko went over to the blood-splashed elevator.

'Let's make a deal.'

'Forget about it. Just tell me what you want me to do,' I sighed, but the mission she offered was another gruelling one.

'I want you to get inside the elevator cage and close the doors.'

There was nowhere clean to stand because of the blood. I placed a bedsheet on the floor and stood, surrounded by the blood of someone I had liked, inside the terrifying cage, fighting back tears. I placed a stopper to prevent the doors from closing completely and pushed the "Door Close" button. Slowly the doors moved together, but when they reached the stopper, they opened again.That was when I understood what had been on Hiruko's mind.

'And?'

'There's barely any blood on the doors, even though the walls are covered in it. Which means....'

'...that Tatsunami was killed by the zombies whilst on the first floor,' whispered Hiruko. The others looked shocked.

'What did you find?'

'It's what he didn't find. There are no bloodstains on the inside of the doors. And take a look at that.'

Hiruko pointed to the carpet in front of the elevator opening. Save for the spot where Tatsunami had been lying, there was hardly any blood on it.

'You see, it's relatively clean. That's why my first thought was that the elevator doors were closed at the time Tatsunami was killed. But Hamura just checked and found there was no blood on the doors. Which means that the elevator was open at the time of the murder.'

Shigemoto seemed puzzled.

'But if the doors were open, blood would have sprayed on the carpet... Ah!'

It finally dawned on him.

'There were no traces of blood on the third or second floor, which means that Tatsunami was murdered on the first floor,' explained Hiruko.

Everyone looked pale. They couldn't believe it.

'But how? Did the murderer go down in the elevator with him?'

'No way. They would have been attacked by the zombies as well.'

I began to see what Hiruko was saying.

'The murderer didn't need to be in the elevator themselves in order to move it. After moving Tatsunami's body inside, the killer pushed the 1F button, got out and watched the elevator go down. They could call it up again later.'

That way, the culprit could offer up Tatsunami to the zombies without getting on the elevator themselves. But there was a problem with that hypothesis, which Nabari pointed out.

'Interesting idea, but too dangerous. If the elevator were to be called up whilst the zombies were munching on Mr. Tatsunami, they would have been brought up as well.'

She was right, of course. The zombies weren't like the tissue box we had used, and wouldn't necessarily stay in one place to block the elevator doors. If they entered the elevator cage completely, the doors would close as usual, and the zombies would arrive upstairs, which would endanger the culprit himself as he waited for the elevator. So why would they choose such a complicated approach and not just use the Hiruko Method?

'But if that's what happened, why let the zombies in through the emergency exit? Was the culprit trying to get Hiruko and Takagi killed?' I wondered out loud.

'I don't think so. We were only saved because the culprit called us. If we think about it in simple terms, it could just be bad luck that the zombies managed to break through the emergency exit, or perhaps there was something in the corridor the culprit didn't want us to see. But let's put that aside for the moment.'

For the moment, she said... So she was not planning to give up on the matter. The feeling in my heart became heavier and heavier.

7

Next, Hiruko asked Kanno permission to enter his room 203. We watched her pick up the phone.

'Mr. Kanno, do these phones have a redial function?'

175

'If you push the small button on the lower right, it will redial the last number called.'

Hiruko nodded and turned to me.

'Could you go upstairs, to the room right above Takagi's?'

She meant 302, which had been used by Kudamatsu.

'Ah, you want me to check if I can hear the phone in Takagi's room ringing?'

'Full marks. I'll call in a minute.'

We couldn't go to Takagi's room 202 because it was surrounded by zombies, but we might be able to hear what was happening there from the room right above. Upstairs, I found Takagi and Shizuhara hanging around in the elevator hall and they tagged along.

'What are you doing?' asked Takagi.

'Testing the redial.'

We entered room 302, which was the one next to Nanamiya's room, and the room we had used when we saved Takagi. I went out onto the balcony. The rain had stopped, and it was now light outside. It was just past six in the morning. I explained the nature of the experiment to the two of them.

'Earlier this morning, Hiruko and you, Takagi, each received an anonymous call, which we assume came from the culprit. If they only called you two, then the redial function of the phone the culprit used must still have either your or Hiruko's phone in its memory. Hiruko is going to try the redial function on all the phones, and find out which phone the culprit used.'

Almost a minute went by. I leant over the balcony railing to try and catch any sound from the room below. But no matter how long I waited, I couldn't hear any phone ringing. Which meant that Kanno's phone hadn't been used to make the calls.

As long as I was there anyway, I decided to try 302's phone, but there was no noise from below, nor anywhere else. The call might have gone to the reception or somewhere else. We were just leaving the room when Takagi spoke up.

'But it's also possible that it's an old call in the redial memory, isn't it? Even if the phone in my room had rung, there's no guarantee that the phone in question had called there recently.'

She had a point there. But in an age where everyone has their own mobile, you're not likely to use the extension to call someone you know who's staying in another room. You'd probably only use it to contact reception. If we checked all the phones and only one of them had called either Hiruko's or Takagi's room, there was a very high probability that that phone had indeed been used by the culprit.

With a bit of luck, or bad luck, depending on who you ask, that process could lead us straight to the murderer. I could feel beads of perspiration run down my back.

We returned downstairs and told Hiruko that it had come up empty. We repeated the experiment with different rooms. I stayed in 302 until I could hear a phone ringing. After about ten minutes, I could make out a faint ringing sound in Takagi's room. I ran downstairs and found Hiruko and the others in room 206, the empty room in the east wing which Nabari had originally used.

'It rang!'

Nabari turned pale as I spoke.

'But that's the room I first used. That's curious. On the first day, right after I arrived, I noticed the batteries of the wall clock were dead, so I called reception. Isn't that so, Mr. Kanno?'

'Yes, I received the call and put in new batteries.'

It was indeed strange, in that case, that the redial function hadn't called reception. Which meant that the phone had been used after that first day. And it was very likely that it had been used by the culprit, only a couple of hours earlier.

'But they could just have called reception or anywhere else to overwrite the memory. Did they forget about the redial function?'

Hiruko frowned at my suggestion.

'Hard to tell. Perhaps they didn't care because it wasn't their own room anyway, or perhaps they simply didn't have the time.'

'The time?'

'Perhaps the culprit themselves hadn't expected the zombies to break through the emergency exit. They didn't want me or Takagi to fall victim because we had been drugged. That's why they ran into the closest room, 206, and tried to wake us by phone. But the culprit had to realise that, once I knew what was happening, everyone here would come running to save us. Which meant that the culprit had to get back to their own room before anyone saw them. So they wouldn't have had any time to think of the redial function.'

That did sound like a plausible scenario.Nabari interrupted us again. She seemed sorry.

'Do things look bad for Mr. Kanno because he has the master keycard? Because he would be able to enter Mr. Tatsunami's room?'

She looked at us. She had returned the master keycard to Kanno because she hadn't wanted to be a suspect herself. She seemed worried that Kanno would now be a suspect because of her action.

'For the moment, I'd say it's very unlikely that Mr. Kanno's the murderer.'

'Why?'

It was Kanno himself who seemed most surprised by that. He had probably expected himself to be a suspect.

'It's just an estimate, but if we put everything on a timeline, you have an alibi. Takagi said that before she got my call, her phone had been ringing for over a minute. If that was from the killer, we can make the following timeline.

1. The killer called me.
2. I called Mr. Kanno. It took me at least two minutes to explain the situation and ask for help.
3. I immediately called Takagi afterwards. She answered the phone within ten seconds.
4. But Takagi said the killer had been calling her for over a minute before I called her.'

She was right. Whilst the killer had been in 206 and calling Takagi for over a minute, Kanno had been on the phone with Hiruko. It was impossible to pull the receiver of the phone in Kanno's room all the way to 206, and if Takagi had answered the call from the killer, he'd have to speak with the two of them simultaneously. It was only for a few seconds, but Kanno had an alibi for the phone.

'I'm glad to hear that.' Nabari looked relieved.

'And to add one more thing, since I was on the phone with Mr. Kanno, I myself have an alibi as well. Sorry for pointing that out myself,' said Hiruko.

I then realised one more person had an alibi.

'Then Takagi must be out as well! When the phone in 206 was being used, the south corridor had already been overrun by zombies. She would not have been able to return to her room.'

Hiruko shook her head sorrowfully.

'That's not exactly right. There's a possibility that her story that her phone had been ringing for over a minute is a lie, and that the redial function is actually a trap. For example, after killing Tatsunami, she could have gone to 206 and called her own room so it would be recorded in the redial function. She could then have let the zombies in through the emergency exit, escaped into her own room and then used her own phone to call me.'

I had to object to the theory that Takagi had lied to us.

'But if Takagi is lying, then Mr. Kanno's alibi would also fall apart.'

'In that were the case, he would not have prepared the redial function as he did, because he couldn't have foreseen that Takagi would lie about a non-existent phone call.'

There was nothing I could bring up to counter that. Their alibis only existed because Hiruko *happened* to call Takagi and Kanno. It was impossible to deliberately control their actions, which is why their alibis were trustworthy. Takagi scratched her head, not quite able to grasp what was being said.

'This is getting difficult. So am I still a suspect or not?'

'Yes. Because the key to the wing doors was left on the television stand. If only the south wing door had been locked, then that would mean the culprit had locked the door from the lounge side, in which case, you could proudly declare your innocence.'

So Takagi still remained a suspect, solely because that one door hadn't been locked. Perhaps the culprit had realised that and left the door unlocked on purpose.

'But I do think the chances that you're the culprit are low. That's because Mr. Kanno's and my alibi rely on your testimony that someone had been calling for over a minute before I called you. If you're the murderer, I can't imagine you stating something that would only benefit Mr. Kanno and me, and not you.'

When we were discussing everyone's movements in the elevator hall earlier, Takagi's turn had come after Hiruko and Kanno's. Given that she was last, she could have come up with a better lie to benefit herself.

Anyway, working on the assumption that the culprit used the phone in 206, we searched the room for possible clues. Shigemoto, who had gone out onto the balcony, suddenly cried out.

'Look! Aren't those *yukata* (casual kimono) from the Villa Violet?'

He was pointing straight down below the balcony. Despite the zombies roaming the area, I could make out a pile of white fabric lying on the ground. The zombies had trampled all over it, so it was hard to see, but it didn't look as though there was only one *yukata*.

'Why are they lying there?'

'It must have been the killer. I think they must have donned a *yukata* before they dragged Tatsunami's body half out of the elevator, so as to prevent blood from spraying on their body when they smashed his head. If they run DNA tests on the *yukata*, the police might be able to determine who wore it, but there's no way we can retrieve it now.'

No other discoveries were made, so we stopped the investigation at that point and returned to the lounge. The loud banging from the other side of the south wing door continued, but for the moment, the door still held. To be safe, we locked the east wing door as well, and left the lounge behind us.

8

Back on the third floor, Hiruko said she wanted to have another look at Shindō's room 305. Kanno's master keycard opened the door. It was still as cold as winter inside because of the air conditioning. Fortunately it had delayed the rotting of the body up to a degree, but his remains still looked as gruesome as ever.

'Oh.'

I knew right away why Hiruko had cried out softly. The desk light was on.

'Did we forget to switch it off yesterday?'

'Last night, I could see from my room that it was still on. It can't be switched off from the nightstand, so we must have forgotten.'

I went over to the desk, and used the switch beneath the mirror to turn the light off.

'You can see this room from yours?'

'If you look diagonally to the left, that's my room at the back. The one before mine is Shizuhara's room.'

I made my way around the bloodstains and the pieces of human flesh on the carpet and, standing near the window, I pointed to Shizuhara's room.

'I see,' muttered Hiruko.

She played with her hair for a while, then went back to searching the room. We didn't speak, but I ended up checking the balcony. I looked for marks on the railing, or spots from where you might climb up to the rooftop or one of the other rooms, but my search ended up fruitless. Hiruko checked the top of the door, just as she had done in Tatsunami's room, but there was no sign of a tool having been used there.

'Now I think about it, considering that the balcony doors were open and Shindō was lying facing the outside, doesn't that mean he was trying to escape that way?' I suggested.

'It would seem so. That would mean that the zombie came from the direction of the door, from the corridor. But I can't find any trace of a zombie here.'

'Another thing that bothers me is that his sword was placed against the wall by the entrance, which suggests that Shindō hadn't been on his guard for the killer at all.'

'So was it one of us who managed to enter this locked room....?'

Hiruko grunted for a moment whilst she twisted her hair around her fingers, but then beckoned to me.

'Head!'

'Huh?'

'I can't do it with my own hair. I want to ruffle through your hair to think.'

'Eh? No! That's embarrassing!'

'Let's make a deal. Get onto the bed. I'll allow you to sleep on my lap.'

'Eh? No way, no way, look at all the blood there!'

I didn't mean I would have lain down on the bed but for the blood, of course.Hiruko looked upset that her lap deal hadn't gone through. Glaring at the bloodstains on the comforter, she pulled it away. The bed was empty, just as when we had checked yesterday.

'Huh?' she exclaimed, suddenly puzzled.

Hiruko was looking at the inside of the comforter, the side which had been in contact with the bed all the time.

'There's blood here.'

It was true, there was a blood-coloured smear there. Unlike the blood spatters on the outer side, however, it was a faint stain, as if the comforter had brushed against a minor injury. Hiruko turned the comforter over. There was blood there, of course.

'That's odd. How can there be blood on both sides of the comforter?'

We compared the two sides, but the location of the stains did not match. It wasn't that the stains on the outside had seeped all the way through to the other side. Had Shindō thrown the comforter at the zombie, or used it as a shield? But it had been lying neatly on the bed and didn't look rumpled at all.

'How....?'

I looked at Hiruko for an answer, but she was just standing there with her eyes open wide. They were not focused on the comforter in front of her, but somewhere faraway.

'Hiruko?'

'So... That would explain why it didn't feel right. It was only natural that I thought it curious.'

She started talking excitedly.

'I should have looked at myself first, before dismissing other people's ideas. I had a feeling something was off, and I should have paid more attention to it. I should have been more open.'

'Did you work something out?'

'Something about Shindō's murder. So now it's just Tatsunami's death.'

She turned to me.

'But first, could you lend me your phone? My battery's dead.'

'Of course, but there's no signal,' I said, as I took out my smartphone, but she shook her head.

'I want to take pictures.'

Aha. I took a picture of the bloodstains on the comforter.

'There's one more I want you to take.'

'Sure. Of what?'

'Of the inside of this bag.'

9

A gentle rain had started again. We spent some time in the limited space we had on the third floor. We all had been careful with our water consumption, so the water storage tank wasn't empty yet, but the main problem was food. We had brought everything we could take from the lounge, but that was only enough for another two days, at three meals a day. On the first day, Hiruko had estimated the time for the bodies of the zombies to rot at over a week, so not even half of that had passed. Shigemoto had estimated the period even longer than that, so there was little hope that the zombies would just disappear on their own.

There was also the problem of living space. There were more people than available rooms, so every room, except those of Shindō and Nanamiya, was kept open via the door guard, so anyone could use it at any time. With each passing day, the zombies had taken a new floor. The thought that, next time, we'd only be able to escape onto the empty rooftop was a source of great stress. And within this extremely limited space was also someone who had murdered two people.

Nevertheless, the others seemed surprisingly calm. Apart from Nanamiya in his room, none of us had given in to despair, or become extremely suspicious of the others. Which was probably because of the presence of the ultimate enemy, the zombies. There was no way to protect oneself from those horrifying corpses unless you were part of the group.

Food shortages, zombies and a killer: three monstrous waves that collided together, cancelling each other out, and ultimately leaving us floating in a mysteriously peaceful sea. Of course, I was well aware that such a peace could not last for long.

The long morning finally turned into noon.

'The news is on!' cried Shigemoto, popping his head out of his room. The seven people besides Nanamiya all gathered inside in front of the television. There was a shot of Sabea, which had become the most famous spot in Japan in just a few days, accompanied by shocking descriptions we hadn't seen before. "Terrorist Attack with a Killer Virus," "Explosive Infection Rates Feared," and more. The screen showed a group of men seated behind long desks, illuminated by camera flashes. The man in the middle was the Chief Cabinet Secretary. The fact that he himself would explain the incident was a sign of how grave the situation had become.

Shigemoto spoke very rapidly.

'It suddenly came on at noon. It's on all the channels.'

The Chief Cabinet Secretary held his text in front of him and started explaining the outlines of the crisis and the current situation in that euphemistic manner so typical of politicians. Given that we were right in the middle of the calamity, the roundabout, vague approach of the press conference made us very irritated, but we nevertheless learnt some new facts.

The main suspect was an associate-professor, together with several colleagues, who had been monitored by Public Security for some time. They had infiltrated the Sabea Rock Festival and spread an unknown virus which was extremely infectious. Once infected, death was inevitable. Those infected (they avoided calling them zombies) fell into a state of confusion. In the Sabea region, over a thousand cases of infection had already been confirmed. As there were probably already over five hundred zombies around the Villa Violet alone, and given that there are around a hundred thousand rock festival attendees every year, the number quoted on the news was more than suspicious.

It was the first time that the government had acknowledged that an act of bioterrorism had been committed.The Chief Cabinet Secretary also stated that there were communication restrictions in place in the

Lake Sabea area, in order to prevent misinformation from spreading. He also dared to say with a straight face that they had succeeded in containing all those infected, and that the situation was under control. Lying bastard. If he was right, get rid of the zombies around here as well.

The killer virus was being examined by the Institute of Infectious Diseases, and the Institute of Physical and Chemical Research in particular.

"Rescue units are being sent to evacuate the people within the sealed-off zone. People inside the zone are asked to seek refuge inside a safe building and calmly await the rescue units. We warn people not to come in contact, especially not orally or through the eyes, with the blood or other bodily fluids of those infected, due to the risk of infection. In the event you do come into contact, we strongly advise you to wash yourself thoroughly immediately, and to contact the police or fire departments."

Takagi was beside herself. She just couldn't believe what she had just heard.

'Wait for rescue? The zombies out there do a quicker job than any of them!'

'And, unlike the government, they actually actively pursue their goals,' added Shizuhara angrily.

Next, the cameras were trained on a well-known research institute, to explain the current thinking about the virus. The speaker spouted a lot of difficult specialist terms, but there was one piece of information that struck me.

'When the virus is transmitted via an injury or a mucous membrane, the time it takes for the brain functions to be destroyed, and the infected to fall into the aforementioned state of confusion, is between three and five hours.'

'The destruction of the brain functions. It seems your theory was correct,' said Hiruko, praising Shigemoto. The zombie master seemed pleased and smiled.

'Well, it was just a hunch.'

The press conference lasted for about an hour. The only other useful piece of information was that insects living in the area, such as mosquitos,which have sucked blood from the infected, have all died due to the toxicity, so there was no fear of vector transmission.

Kanno got up as the newsreaders and reporters from each channel appeared on the screen again.

'It means that rescue is coming. We should draw an SOS on the rooftop so they will find us sooner. Would anyone care to help me?'

'I'll help,' I offered. 'Do you have paint?'

'There should still be some in the storage.'

Shigemoto, however, wanted to stay and keep an eye on the news. Kanno and I stepped out under the concrete-coloured sky, which was still spewing its misty rain.

10

'Hopefully, we'll be able to leave all of this behind us soon.'

We had begun by wiping the rooftop as dry as possible. Kanno was now crouching down to paint the letters.

'Almost half of my guests have died, and I feel some responsibility. The least I can do is to make sure that every single one of the survivors makes it out safely.'

'You mustn't feel responsible. Not even the authorities know how to handle it.'

I tried to cheer him up as I painted a crooked S. But I did wonder whether he hadn't remained a bit too calm whilst the murders were occurring. The members of our group had, to some degree, an idea why someone would want to kill Shindō or Tatsunami. The same held true for Nanamiya, of course. But this friendly man, who had been working here since last fall, could not possibly know about the past history. How could anyone remain so calm whilst his guests were being brutally murdered? As I was thinking about this, Kanno sighed out loud.

'It's such a shame Mr. Tatsunami died.'

'You got on well with him?'

'No, it was the first time we had met. Mr. Nanamiya visited a few times after I started working here, but apparently Mr. Tatsunami and Mr. Deme only come in the summer. I wonder if they got killed because of last year's trip?'

So he did know. I looked straight at him, and he seemed to sense what I was thinking. He explained himself.

'Mr. Nanamiya always came here with women. I suspect his friends did as well.'

'Did the previous manager quit because of what happened on last year's trip?'

185

Kanno shook his head.

'I believe it was simply because of Mr. Nanamiya's outrageous orders. Telling him to cancel the reservation of another guest and give him the room, or have a pizza delivered to him immediately, despite the inconvenient location. All I heard was that there was some trouble involving women last year.'

Kanno got up, took a long look at the O he had painted, and continued.

'I don't remember when it was exactly, but one day I overheard a drunken Mr. Nanamiya talking to the woman he had brought along. He said that Mr. Tatsunami was always messing around with women, but that it never lasted long, because of a mother complex.'

'A complex?'

'Apparently, Mr. Tatsunami's parents divorced when he was in elementary school. The cause was his mother's adultery. His father took him away and brought him up. His mother had been unfaithful to his father on several previous occasions.'

I thought that was enough to explain why Tatsunami had such a twisted idea of women, but Kanno wasn't finished yet.

'A few years later, his father died in a strange accident, and his mother took him back. But then, soon after that, she was arrested.'

'Why?'

'His father's accident had been engineered by his mother and her lover. With his father gone, Mr. Tatsunami would receive both the insurance money and the inheritance. The plan was for her to take him back and get hold of all the money. His mother and her lover were deep in debt, it seems.'

What an awful, awful experience.I thought back to my conversation with Tatsunami on the roof yesterday.

"At the beginning, when you start dating, there's nothing more fun than that. But the more you learn about the other, the less clear it becomes that you're truly in love. Then you start doubting the other. And when it's all over, it's as though everything had been nothing but a deception," he had said.

Tatsunami might have cursed half of the blood flowing in his veins, the half from his mother. He would find a woman in order to prove his own mother was wrong, but eventually he would recognise his own mother in the woman and push her away. A Möbius strip with no front or back. An SOS. Perhaps he also had been calling for help, from beneath his handsome mask.

'His actions might have caused a lot of trouble... but I wish he were still alive.'

I hadn't disliked him either.

The last time I had painted anything as big as our SOS was back in elementary school, when after classes, I and my classmates decided to doodle on the schoolyard and our heads were treated to our teacher's knuckles. I couldn't have imagined then that I'd be doing it again.

Although it was summer, by the time we were done we were drenched and feeling cold. I would have loved a shower in order to warm up, but we had to be careful with our water. We went back down again.

When we left the storage room and entered the elevator hall, the women there expressed their appreciation for our work. There was no sign of Hiruko, however. Takagi and Hiruko couldn't return to their own rooms, so she should have been there. I assumed she must have gone to check the crime scene again, but when I returned to my own room, which I had kept open with the door guard, I found her inside.

'Thank you for your work. Bet you're wet all over,' she said, handing me a towel.

As I took it, I noticed that it was warm. Had she warmed it for me with the hairdryer? I also wanted to change my t-shirt. Originally we had planned to stay here for three days and engage in outdoor activities, so I still had a few clean shirts left.

'Should I leave the room?'

'No, it's okay.'

I didn't give the ever-discreet Hiruko time to think it over, and changed shirts in a second.

'Take a seat,' she said, pointing to the chair in front of the desk. Once I sat down, she came to stand behind me, using the hairdryer. What service! What a reward for services rendered!

The sound of the hairdryer and the touch of her soft fingers on my head felt good, and my hair was dry in no time. After she switched it off, her fingers remained in my hair and she said softly: 'We don't have any time left.'

Were the zombies going to invade the third floor as well? No, no, I had to learn to keep up. Hiruko was trying to solve the mystery so as to survive herself, and not allow more people to die. The note left on Tatsunami's body had said, "One more to go. I'll be sure to devour you." The chances of us being rescued soon had become more realistic, thanks to the news. The murderer would probably try to kill their last target before the authorities arrived. That was what was worrying Hiruko.

'The zombies have us almost cornered. Would the killer really keep to their plan despite that?'

'… I don't know. But the likely last target, Nanamiya, is holed up in his room, and we are nearby as well. It's obvious that the killer can't act recklessly. It's even possible that rescue could arrive before evening. But the killer has executed their plans before, despite difficult circumstances, so I doubt they will give up now.'

By now Hiruko's fingers weren't simply combing my hair, but almost seductively enjoying the touch of it. Her fingers crawled over my head and I even imagined they would dig into my skull next. I did my best to not shudder.

'But I don't get it. On the one hand, I can sense a strong hatred towards the killer's targets, yet on the other hand I can feel mercy, such as when they called us to warn us of danger. Even though, to the culprit, someone like me should be nothing more than a mere obstacle. Is it hesitation? No, the culprit still listens to reason. They know the difference between the people they want to kill, and the people they should not kill, even if it would advance their goal. And despite all that, they can become merciless when it concerns their targets. It's almost as if….'

That was when she finally realised she had been playing with my hair. She gasped and hurried to make it neat again.

'Oh, I'm so sorry. I just think better when I run my hands through other people's hair.'

'It's okay. By the way, I was thinking about the motive.'

I told Hiruko what Takagi had told me, about what had happened on last year's trip. How the three alumni had messed around with the female members of the Film Club. How Deme had failed in his attempt to slip into one of the women's rooms, but that the other two had successfully dated those same girls and eventually dumped them. And how one of them had quit university and the other had committed suicide.

'Shindō had known all about what had happened and still went on to organise the exact same event this year. Which could explain why someone wanted him dead.'

'Yes. The manner in which the notes talk about sacrifices and eating could be an expression of the killer's rage about how those men treated those women. And the last note mentioned one last victim, which would be Nanamiya, of course.'

Wait, Hiruko, your fingers are going wild again!

'But that line of thought leads us to new questions. Nanamiya has been on his guard from the start, hiding in his room. The murderer must have known that, if they announced there was "one more to go," he would never leave his room. What would happen if this were a detective story?'

'Nanamiya would appear to commit suicide, leaving a note confessing that he had been the murderer. But actually, it would be the handiwork of the real culprit.'

'Aha, how thought-provoking. But I don't see that happening here. He hadn't shown his face in the lounge even once since yesterday noon, until this morning when he joined the rest of us. He couldn't have drugged us, so we know he can't be the murderer. But, setting that aside, I'm not sure what we should do with Nanamiya. I have a feeling it would be dangerous to leave him alone, but I also have a feeling it might be safer for him to stay in his room, because we can keep an eye on everyone else concurrently.'

It was not the appropriate time, but at that moment, I realised this turn of events was one you rarely saw in mystery stories.Usually, in a closed circle murder case, the characters all become suspicious of one another, because they don't know who will be killed next. In our case, however, we all had a common understanding that—although we couldn't be absolutely sure—Nanamiya seemed the likeliest to be killed next. He himself was aware of that, too. It was that realisation which had caused him to hide in his room with a weapon, knowing that the murderer had to finish the job before rescue came. Both sides were probably on edge. Then I recalled Hiruko's unique tendency to attract danger.

'If we aren't viewed as enemies by the murderer, couldn't we just leave Nanamiya alone in his room?'

Hiruko, however, protested that it was something we couldn't do. For a moment I was impressed by her strong views about justice.

'Our biggest threat now is the zombies. The situation will only worsen from now on, so in order to survive, we'll need the help of everyone, including him. His death would definitely be inconvenient.'

Her unemotional but correct observation made sense to me. That was her trademark. Hiruko-ism.

'By the way, this room of yours, 308, is located rather unfortunately, isn't it? It's hard to get away from here.'

My head was finally released from her grip. She sat down on the bed and continued.

'It's closest to the stairs and furthest from the rooftop. I really don't want to climb that rope ladder again. They really should design that thing better, so it's easier to climb. It's so unstable it's easy to miss a rung, and it forces you to use muscles you never knew you had. I never want to do that again.'

'There are no railings on the rooftop, so I don't think we can use the rope ladder anyway.'

'What should we do if we get trapped here?'

'Pfft. There aren't any ropes lying around here, so I guess they'd have to tie some bed sheets together and use that as a rope?'

'That's even harder than a rope ladder. Okay, you'll have to carry me up then.'

'That would exceed the maximum capacity,' I joked. But there was no reaction from Hiruko. A bead of perspiration ran down my back. Was her weight a taboo topic?

She shouted suddenly and jumped off the bed.

'Aha, so that's it.'

'Where are you going?'

'To the lounge! You really are the best!'

11

We borrowed the key to open the wing doors from Kanno and entered the second-floor lounge. I had the feeling that the smell of blood had become stronger since this morning and had to cover my nose and mouth. Where was my mask?

'Hiruko, the door.'

I pointed to the south wing door, which was keeping the zombies on the other side. It had been a victim of zombie attacks all morning and was already creaking loudly. It could break at any moment.

'We don't have time, let's hurry.'

Hiruko switched the lights on. I thought she would head for the elevator, but went over to the bronze statues of the Nine Worthies, each of them about one metre high, standing around the television. I took up a position between her and the door, standing ready with my sword in case the zombies broke through.

Was I imagining things, or was the door creaking even louder now? I looked around the room, but there was no furniture left here which could function as a barricade. It was all very risky. We had to leave as soon as possible. But I couldn't interrupt Hiruko's thoughts, either. She had come here because she was looking for something. I had to buy her enough time.After a few minutes, which seemed to last an eternity, she called out to me.

'Could you take a picture of this?'

'Of the statues?'

'Just their feet.'

When I took a better look, I noticed that just above the spot where they touch the ground, there was a dark-red stain. I made sure not to wipe it away as I took pictures from several angles.

'Is that blood? Why is there blood there?'

'It's the key to the trick behind the murder of Tatsunami.'

She had spoken the sentence so suddenly and without any hesitation, that I could hardly keep up.

'Err, do you mean you know how he was killed?'

'Yes. Using these, it's absolutely possible to create the situation. However, I don't know why this method was chosen.'

Hiruko was still focused on the matter of whydunnit. Just then it happened.

CRACK!

The sound of splitting wood. The door which had been holding the zombies away suddenly gave way. In the opening stood a blood-covered zombie.

Oh no! We were standing deep in the lounge, furthest away from the east wing door. We wouldn't be able to make it.The moment I realised that, I started swinging my sword at the mob of zombies.

'Hiruko, run!'

I smashed the head of the zombie which was already halfway through the doorway. But my attack was too weak. There was a dent in its skull, but its nailless hands still reached out to me.

'Damn!'

It took me another swing to take the first zombie down. But the second and third zombies were now inside the lounge. I began to realise the overwhelming, primitive power of a whole group. It took me more time to take down one of them than for one of them to get to me.

Hiruko called out to me as she backed away. I shook the zombies off and got out of the lounge. But before I could lock the east wing door, one of the zombies managed to get its fingers in between the door and the frame. An enormous force was pressing against the door from the other side, and the small Hiruko was nearly thrown back. I quickly body-slammed the door, but althoughI succeeded in pushing them back a bit, the zombie's fingers were still in the way. The two of us were barely managing to hold the door.

'Help! Someone, help!'

Takagi, Shizuhara and Nabari came running down with their weapons, having heard our cries.

'No…' said Nabari tensely when she saw the deadly struggle for the door. For a moment the enemies gained the advantage, pushing the door open wide enough for two fists. A zombie was forcing its head through. Takagi screamed when she saw it.

'Deme!'

Every hair on my body stood straight up as I looked at the zombie's face.It was indeed Deme, who had gone missing during the Trial of Courage. The left half of his face had been gnawed horribly, but we couldn't mistake his fish-like face and his hair. Deme's unfocused eyes were looking at us, as white foam escaped from the corner of his mouth.

'Yaaaaaah!'

We had been frozen in shock, but from behind us came Shizuhara, who shouted bravely as she thrust her spear through Deme's right eye, pushing him back into the lounge. Takagi and the others all snapped out of it and helped close the door and lock it.

'Tha—thanks… you saved us.'

Shizuhara looked at her bloody spear and sank down on the floor. Hiruko and I were leaning against the wall, catching our breath.

'He, he really became a zombie. He didn't recognise us anymore….'

Nabari's voice trembled. She didn't have fond memories of Deme, but seeing him in that inhuman state, she couldn't help but feel sorry for him.

Had Akechi, too, become like that? He could have lost his self, roaming around the boarding house, not able to recognise me anymore.

If he appeared in front of me, would I be able to kill him?

12

We had somehow managed to survive the latest zombie attack, but mentally, we were in a tight corner. Which was only natural. The lounge had been our place of rest, but it had now fallen, and we had for the first time seen a person we personally knew turned into a zombie. Which was more than enough to drive us to despair.

Kanno and Shigemoto had been watching television in Shigemoto's room and had not noticed what had gone on below, but when they were told about what had happened, they both let out a deep sigh.

As I scanned our exhausted faces, I wondered about something. Deme had been bitten all over, but his face was recognisable. And that was the same for the other zombies. They had all sustained wounds to different degrees, but there was not one of them whose face you couldn't make out. So then why had Shindō's face been gnawed all over? Did that mean that it had been a human with a clear objective, and not a zombie, who had attacked him?

It was two o' clock in the afternoon. The seven of us had gathered in the elevator hall, silently eating the emergency rations we had grown tired of. We hardly spoke.

'Is Nanamiya still in his room?' asked Hiruko, as if she had suddenly remembered him. She looked at everyone, but it was Kanno who nodded.

'Mr. Shigemoto and I called out to him this morning, but he didn't want to listen at all.'

'He actually threatened us, saying he'd shoot if we tried to open his door. He's probably sitting there ready with his crossbow. The phone won't connect, so I suppose he must have pulled the line out. He really does intend to wait until rescue arrives,' said Shigemoto, shrugging.

'Forget about him. We'll just get shot at if we bother him. Let him stay where he is,' said Takagi bluntly.

There was another awkward silence. Shigemoto had apparently gone through his stash of cola, because he was now drinking instant café au lait and not enjoying it. Takagi was leaning back on her chair with her eyes closed and arms crossed. Shizuhara was motionless, her eyes staring at the bottom of her paper cup. Nabari was sitting silently and looked the most exhausted of us all.

I glanced at Hiruko. How close was she to the truth? What was going through her head as she watched the others?

'I'm almost starting to miss the music,' said Kanno. He was talking about the rock music Tatsunami used to play.

'It was so loud, but at times like these, when it has suddenly become silent, I....'

A few others nodded hesitantly. Shigemoto mumbled to himself: 'Bruce Springsteen, huh.'

I looked up. I hadn't expected him to know the name.

'You know him?'

'Just a little. *Hungry Heart* had been playing on the music player. That song was used in a zombie film.'

I could read Takagi and Shizuhara's minds as they glared at me. "Don't ever mention zombies to him." But there was no way I could have guessed that my question would bring the topic up!The zombie master remained oblivious and continued.

'It's called *Warm Bodies*. Wanna watch it?' he asked, taking his laptop and a DVD out of his bag.

'A zombie film? Now? Please, no!' protested Nabari.

'Don't worry, it's not a panic horror film. It has a lot of rom-com elements.'

Urged on by Shigemoto, we all sat around the small screen.In the film, a boy who has been changed into a zombie falls in love with a human girl. He takes her to his secret hide-out, but because he's dead, he's not able to communicate with her. But, after saving her from other zombies when she tries to escape, the two grow closer, and listen to the boy's record collection together. A familiar song plays during the scene. I had heard it often, but this was the first time I actually understood the meaning of the lyrics, thanks to the subtitles.The lyrics about a hungry heart had parallels with Tatsunami's own life. The two on the screen would probably end up together. But Tatsunami was...No, I shouldn't think about him now.

As the story entered its second half, Shigemoto suddenly spoke up.

'Oh, speaking of the CD player, didn't the music suddenly stop late yesterday afternoon?'

'It stopped?' I had no recollection of that happening.

'Just for a few seconds. And then it started from the first track again. Mr. Kanno had been in my room to collect the garbage, and we had been talking about films.'

Kanno nodded his agreement.

'Yes, the music did stop. He probably wanted to change the music, but then decided not to.'

Hiruko interrupted us.

'What time did it happen?'

'I don't remember the exact time. I didn't check my watch.'

'I know. It was right after I had finished a 90-minute film. I started watching at three, so it must have been half past four. I didn't fast-forward at any time, and I've seen the DVD many times, so I'm sure.'

I searched my memory. It was when I had returned to my room after talking with Tatsunami on the rooftop. That was exactly half past four.

'But wait. At that time, Tatsunami should still have been smoking on the rooftop. Nabari was there with him as well.'

Nabari frowned at me. 'I wasn't there *with* him. But yes, he was smoking on the rooftop. I left my room and went up there around twenty-five past, so that's correct. Perhaps you're wrong about the time?' She looked at Shigemoto. He seemed annoyed.

'Absolutely not. I checked the clock before I started watching. And if you want, we can check the length of the DVD right now.'

He seemed absolutely convinced about the time and had no intention of backing down. I was puzzled. The clocks hanging in the Villa Violet were all digital radio-controlled clocks. Dying batteries could make the display fade, but wouldn't make the timepiece run slow.

'So what does it mean? Did someone have enough of the loud music and stop it whilst Tatsunami was out of his room?' asked Takagi, puzzled, and Shizuhara added timidly: 'But they say the music went back on again....'

'Perhaps you just imagined it?'

'No, it did happen. Two of us heard it,' retorted Shigemoto.

Hiruko changed the topic abruptly.

'Mr. Kanno, I assume you did your rounds last night before you went to bed? Did you take a look inside Shindō's room 305?'

Kanno was surprised by the sudden question, but nodded.

'Yes. We still don't know how he died, so I thought it would be wise to check the room, just to be on the safe side.'

The master keycard had been returned to him last night by Nabari, so he would have had no trouble entering Shindō's room.

'Did you turn the lights on at that time?'

She was asking about the desk light I had seen last night. Kanno, of course, confirmed my story.

'The small desk light was on. It had not been switched off, and doing so would have made the room feel creepy, so I left it on.'

'...Oh,' muttered Hiruko, her mind elsewhere.

I wanted to ask her what was wrong, when she suddenly stood up, said she needed me for a second, and pulled me away. Everyone watched us as we left the elevator hall. She took me to my room.

'What's the matter?'

As soon as we were inside, she declared confidently: 'I've solved everything except for the whydunnit.'

It took me a few seconds to digest her words. She meant she had solved the howdunnit and the whodunnit. She knew who the murderer

195

was, and how it had been done, but there were still a few mysteries remaining to be solved.

'But we still don't know how the murderer gained entry to Tatsunami's room to kill him.'

To my surprise, Hiruko nodded nonchalantly.

'Oh, that. I have a pretty good idea how it was done. I could try it out right now.'

'Now?'

'Yes, it's actually a very simple trick,' she said, going to the door.

'So, you can play Tatsunami. Actually, the door guard was on as well, but you know how that was opened, so we can skip that part.'

Leaving me alone inside the room, she stepped out into the corridor and closed the door tightly. I made sure the door was really closed and locked. The keycard was in the holder on the wall.

I watched the door in anticipation. Immediately, there was the sound of the door unlocking, and Hiruko stepped back inside. I stared at her wide-eyed. It had barely taken a second.She was holding a keycard in her hand.

'Oh, you have the master keycard,' I said disappointedly, but Hiruko smiled mischievously back at me.

'No. It's the keycard to this room.'

She showed the keycard to me. 308 was printed on it. It was only then that I understood what she had done. She had swapped my keycard, which I kept inside the holder in the wall, with another keycard at some point. No, wait, I knew exactly when she had done it. My door had been left open, so she must have swapped our keycards whilst I was painting SOS on the rooftop. On my return, I had simply assumed that the keycard in the holder was still my own. I gasped and kicked myself as I realised the trick.

'I see you understand how it was done. You did the exact same thing as Tatsunami. During the day you kept your door open, using the door guard as a stopper in case of emergencies, and assumed you'd be safe as long as you closed the door once you were inside. You never noticed your keycard had been switched, because the power was still working.'

As the user of the room, you would naturally assume there was nothing wrong if a keycard was still in the holder. Last night, Tatsunami had remarked that locking your room when you weren't inside was nuts. And he himself had indeed left his door ajar whenever he was out of his room, which is why we could hear his music from the lounge.

196

'So, someone switched the keycard of Tatsunami's room sometime before the evening?'

'Yes. He was almost never there. He would often leave the lounge to go up the rooftop to smoke, or to try to talk to Nanamiya. The culprit only needed a few seconds to swap the keycards. The correct keycard could be returned to its place after the culprit got into the room to commit the murder.'

So that meant that anyone could have swapped the keycards.But didn't that also mean that it would be impossible to identify the murderer?

Just then, we all heard the noise of something falling down, coming from the direction of Nanamiya's room. It was followed by the loud ringing of the personal alarm.

CHAPTER SIX
A COLD SPEAR

1

We all knew what had happened. The third-floor emergency exit had been broken open. Compared to the one on the second floor, which had only lasted until the early morning, the third-floor door had managed to last for some time.

Kanno and I immediately picked up our swords and ran to the south wing. We had to hurry, or Nanamiya would be trapped inside his room. If that happened, it would be very difficult to save him, as it wasn't possible to lower the rope ladder down from the rooftop. I put my mask on as I sprinted. But as I turned the corner to reach Nanamiya's room, a figure appeared from the other direction. A zombie!

'Uuuhaaa!'

I screamed to work myself into a state and swung at the head of the zombie in front of me with all my might. A dull shock ran through my body as the impact of my sword cracked its temple, causing bits of flesh to fly around. The male zombie was thrown against the wall and collapsed on the spot.

I hesitated between finishing him off or getting to Nanamiya's room, but neither option was in fact available. More and more zombies had appeared, which meant that Nanamiya's room was already surrounded. I remembered the hopeless fight in the lounge earlier, and quickly decided to retreat.

'It's too late. We have to retreat!'

'Mr. Nanamiya! Don't leave your room!'

Kanno and I called out to him, then quickly withdrew. Kanno locked the door behind him after we left the south wing. The others had all gathered in the elevator hall. Hiruko looked anxiously at us and enquired about Nanamiya. I shook my head.

'It's too late, the zombies have taken the corridor.'

'Perhaps he doesn't know what's going on?' Takagi wondered.

'With that noise? Impossible.'

It wasn't just the groaning of the zombies or the noise of them banging on the door. It was that intensely loud alarm. We could hear it even here in the elevator hall, with a corner and a door between. Nanamiya's room was closest to the emergency exit, so there was no possibility that he hadn't heard the noise.

'Can we get him out through another room?' asked Hiruko, but Kanno frowned.

'The way the building is constructed, the balconies of the south wing rooms can't be reached from here. We can't get there anymore.'

But Hiruko refused to concede defeat.

'So, we'll have to go the rooftop and see if we can work something out.'

We split up in groups. Fortunately, we still had the storage room door to act as a last line of defence if the south wing door failed and we had to escape to the rooftop. Takagi, Nabari and Shizuhara carried the necessary supplies to the storage room. Hiruko and Kanno tried to call out to Nanamiya from the rooftop. Shigemoto and I were standing guard just in case the zombies managed to break through the door.

'I can't believe our barricade managed to hold longer than the two emergency exits,' said Shigemoto as he held his spear awkwardly.

'In terms of sturdiness, those doors were much better.'

'What's important is whether they have something firm to stand on or not. Zombies have infinite stamina. And they feel no pain, so when it's a matter of breaking something down quickly, they are far superior to us humans.'

The south wing door on the second floor hadn't even lasted half a day. How long would we have until we were cornered on the rooftop? And what steps would the murderer take to kill Nanamiya in the meantime?

After a while the duo on the rooftop came down. They looked very worried.

'There's something wrong. He won't come out onto the balcony, even though we keep calling out to him.'

Hiruko's anxious tone told me she was already assuming the worst. The worst being that the murderer had already succeeded. We all tried to think of a way to get to Nanamiya's room. There was no railing on the rooftop to which to attach the rope ladder. The idea I had thought of earlier, to tie some bed sheets together to pull him up, was too dangerous.We gave up on the idea of lifting a person up and decided to tie Shigemoto's camcorder to the end of a bed sheet instead. We could lower it from the rooftop and take a look inside his room.

'Hmmm, the camcorder keeps spinning around.'

'Doesn't matter, it doesn't take long to get an idea of what's going on inside.'

After a few minutes we pulled the camcorder up. We viewed the footage in the storage room.For about three seconds, the camera had been aimed inside the room, but the view kept spinning around.

'Pause it there.'

Nanamiya was indeed visible in the still.

'He's....' Hiruko gasped.

'He's collapsed,' announced Kanno. A feeling of despair took over the room. The door had not yet been broken down, and the inside of the room looked the same as in the morning. But Nanamiya was lying in front of the door on his side. His body was bent backwards and his hands were clutching his head, as if in pain. We checked the footage multiple times, but he didn't appear to be moving.

'We're too late,' sighed Hiruko in frustration. It was clear what she meant. The murderer had managed to take the life of their last target, Nanamiya.

'Aah... why him?' exclaimed Kanno, his shoulders drooping. Was he lamenting the loss of another one of us? Or was it out of regret, because he was the manager? Or was he blaming himself for allowing the son of his employer to die?

Takagi and Shizuhara looked away from the screen uncomfortably, but neither of them let out any words of sorrow. Nabari, who had been fighting with Nanamiya just that morning, sat down on the floor. Shigemoto silently switched the camcorder off.

I stared at Hiruko. We had thought that Nanamiya would be absolutely safe, but the murderer had somehow managed to take his life, and now there was a new locked room mystery to add to the list. Nanamiya had been killed inside a room where he had been hiding by himself since the morning, allowing nobody inside. Everyone present had been within sight of someone else. His murder was absolutely unthinkable.

Would she give up? Or did she have a trump card up her sleeve to turn everything around? To my surprise, Hiruko spoke calmly.

'Listen, everyone. Let's focus on staying alive until rescue comes. Our biggest threat is the zombies. It's only a matter of time before they take the third floor. We need to move to the storage area and strengthen our defences.'

Kanno made a suggestion.

'We should make a distress flare by gathering the available bed sheets. Does anyone have a lighter?'

'I do. I stopped smoking, but I still have my lighter,' said Takagi.

Everyone had moved on from the murder.

'No, wait.'

It was Shizuhara who had called out. She seldom spoke on her own in front of others, so everyone looked at her in surprise.

'What's the matter, Mifuyu?' asked Takagi. Shizuhara, however, kept looking at Hiruko.

'Could it be that... that you already know who the murderer is?'

I was startled by the question. Hiruko turned to Shizuhara and sighed gently. So she did know. She knew everything, but had chosen to keep silent for our sakes.

'I thought so. You were acting so strangely just now. Can't you tell us? Can't you say who's been haunting us for the last three days?' Shizuhara stared intensely at Hiruko, who slowly shook her head.

'The culprit has already accomplished their goals. What good would it do if I revealed their crimes and identified them as the killer? We have to work together to survive. Apprehending the murderer can come after we're rescued and the police have arrived.'

'No, we have a right to know. We have a right to be angry. No matter the reason, the murderer took the lives of three people.'

Shizuhara wouldn't back down. Takagi and the others looked hesitantly between the two as the discussion continued, which was only natural. The surviving members had overcome unbelievable hardships together as comrades these last three days. Was it really necessary to accuse one of us of the crimes, here and now, and throw them out of our circle, with perhaps only a few days to go where we needed to work together? But I realised that I was probably the only one absolutely against solving the mystery at this point in time.

'I understand. If you truly wish to listen to my meaningless reasoning, I will explain.'

Hiruko closed her eyes tightly once and began.

2

'Before I explain each mystery, I want to focus on the profile of the culprit behind this series of crimes. I'm assuming that the motive behind the murders is tied to the twisted outcomes of the sexual relations initiated by Nanamiya, Tatsunami and Deme during the trip last summer. The precise details are unclear to me, but the fact that the culprit brought strong sleeping drugs with them indicates that they became a participant on this trip with the clear intention of killing the three alumni, as well as Shindō, the organiser. But then we were all confronted with an unforeseen crisis: the attack of the zombies. Despite the situation, the culprit decided to make use of what fate had wrought, and thanks to a devilishly inspired plan, they succeeded in accomplishing their goals.

'The whole series of murders was completely incomprehensible to me. Why take such risks and commit such diabolical crimes, putting the lives of innocent parties at stake? It suggested an unimaginably deep hatred towards those four victims. But the culprit also showed a very humane side at times, such as when they called me to warn me of danger. Intense hate, and human compassion. I couldn't picture the psychology of the culprit, having those two contradictory sides, and that's what kept confusing me until the very end.

'I'm sorry for the long preamble. From now on, I'll only talk about solving the mysteries, beginning with the first, the murder of Shindō.

'Shindō died with bite marks all over his body, inside his locked room. Based on the state of his body and the room, there's no doubt that Shindō had been attacked by someone inside the room and was bitten to death. It was, however, a highly peculiar situation. That evening, we had erected a barricade to prevent the zombies from coming in, and the elevator had been stopped as well. The emergency exits can't be opened from outside, the walls don't allow for anyone to scale them, there are no indications that a rope ladder had been used. So, in theory, there was not a single route available for someone outside to come in.

'It was possible, in principle, that one of us could have made up some excuse so Shindō would let them into his room, but none of us had signs that our mouths had been used to commit the murder. Likewise, a zombie could have killed Shindō, but could not, in theory, have got into his room. In addition, a note was found, wedged between the door and the frame, clearly from the elevator hall side. Which implied that the culprit had left the room and was inside the building. All those contradictions troubled me.'

Having said all that, Hiruko took a deep breath.

'In addition, I felt it was odd that the first murder was so different from the second. Shindō had been killed inside his room, but Tatsunami had been moved out of his to be killed. Shindō had been bitten all over, but his body had been left as it was, whereas Tatsunami's head had been cruelly and deliberately crushed. But in fact, it was totally understandable. For the two murders were committed by two different beings.'

'What! You mean there are two murderers amongst us!?' cried Kanno in surprise. Hiruko shook her head.

'No. There is only one culprit amongst us. For the other culprit isn't human anymore.'

'Not human?'

Hiruko looked at me.

'Photograph.'

I took out my smartphone and showed the pictures I had taken of the bloodstains on the comforter in Shindō's room.

'Don't you think this is odd? The blood that was splashed during the murder stained the front of the comforter. But, even though the blood didn't seep all the way through, there's also blood on the back,' observed Hiruko.

'I see, it's impossible for the blood to have splashed both sides of the comforter.'

'But what does it mean?' asked Takagi.

'It means that someone wounded was already lying on the bed before Shindō was attacked. Shindō had brought someone into his room and was taking care of her, but during the night, her situation worsened. She turned into a zombie and killed him.'

'You don't mean....'

'Shindō desperately wanted to save this person and brought her into his room, but kept her presence a secret from us. That person could only have been his girlfriend, Reika Hoshikawa. Shindō was killed by Hoshikawa after she turned into a zombie.'

Everyone shouted at once.

'It can't be!'

'Remember, that evening Shindō returned from the Trial alone. We all saw him arrive at the front entrance. But none of us saw her.' Shigemoto was thinking back to what had happened after the game had to be cancelled.

'Just think back more carefully. Shindō appeared from the rear of the building. I suspect that Hoshikawa was hiding outside in the rear at that time, and Shindō went inside in order to open the emergency exit for her. She could thus slip inside without anyone knowing, using the emergency stairs. That's how he let her in from the rear without any of us knowing.'

Takagi raised an objection.

'Wait. Why didn't he just ask for our help? None of us knew anything about zombies at that time.'

For the first time, Hiruko hesitated. After a short pause, she replied.

'Remember what happened just before Shindō arrived. We had been chased by the zombies and had fled from the plaza up to the house. Tatsunami had barely managed to kill off a zombie who had followed us up the stairs. Shigemoto was watching and said: "It's all over if a zombie manages to bite you. They're not human. We have to kill them!"'

'Ah...' Shigemoto let out a bewildered gasp.

'Shindō had probably been watching the scene from behind us. At that moment, he couldn't have known whether Shigemoto was right or not, but he must have feared that if he brought Hoshikawa, who had already been bitten, along, we would have killed her.'

In the end, it turned out that Shigemoto had been right and that Hoshikawa's transformation into a zombie had been inevitable. But because of what Shigemoto had said, Shindō decided to hide his girlfriend, which led to his horrible death.

Hiruko continued.

'Shindō played his role perfectly, pretending to look desperately for Hoshikawa, so that none of us suspected that she was already inside the house. That was why he hadn't wanted to spend the night together in the group. His attempt at nursing her was doomed from the start, however, and she turned into a zombie. On the news they said it takes three to five hours for the symptoms to show, after infection. There wasn't much blood on the comforter, so Hoshikawa had probably only a small wound, meaning it could have taken as much as five hours after she was attacked for her to turn into zombie. The Trial of Courage had started at nine, so if she had become infected at half past nine, she probably changed and attacked Shindō at half past two, the time Nabari heard noises from the room above. I can't say for sure, but going by the traces of blood on the balcony, I think Hoshikawa and Shindō struggled and she fell over the railing to the ground below. Zombies can survive as long as the brain is intact, so she's probably roaming around there now.'

Nabariinterrupted Hirukohesitantly.

'But that's just a guess, isn't it? You don't have any proof....'

'Actually, I do.'

I had to show my phone again.

'I took the liberty of checking Hoshikawa's bag as it was lying in Shindō's room.'

Everyone gasped when they saw what was in the picture.

'Her shoes!'

'Those are her shoes!'

205

They were the white pumps that Hoshikawa had been wearing that day.

'Yes. On the first day, before we left for the ruins, she said she hadn't brought any spare shoes with her. So why are her shoes in her bag, even though she went missing? There's only one answer. She *did* return after the Trial. She had taken her shoes off and was lying on the bed. Shindō hid her shoes in her bag. That is the only possible explanation.'

To think that Hoshikawa had been in Shindō's room that night, with him knowing that she had been infected... Nabari looked at the floor, as if she was unable to face the horrible truth about her friend.

'Somehow the culprit learnt what had happened in Shindō's room. Shindō had been killed by a zombie, and his was the only body left inside the room. The culprit realised they could use the situation to their own advantage. They made it appear to us that his death had been a murder. Then later, if they became a suspect in the planned murders of Tatsunami and Nanamiya, they could counter any such suspicion by claiming they couldn't have killed Shindō. All the time, we were trying to work out how a human could shift the blame to a zombie. But, in fact, it was the other way around.

'In order for the scheme to succeed, however, the culprit needed to leave clues to indicate that a human had done it. That's why they wrote two notes and wedged one of them in between the door and frame. The other note was thrown into a corner near the door on the inside of the room the following morning, when all our eyes were fixed on Shindō's body. And, just as the culprit had planned, we became confused about whether the murder had been committed by a human or a zombie, simply because of those notes. We were completely ensnared in their trap.'

I interrupted with a question of my own.

'But why two notes? Wouldn't one have been enough?'

'If there had just been the one note wedged in the door from the outside, it wouldn't have left a strong enough impression that the killer had actually been inside. The second note made us believe that the murderer had been inside, and then gone out into the elevator hall.'

'But then surely the note left inside would have been enough.'

Hiruko shook her head.

'No, the note placed from the outside had another important function. Think about it, the culprit knew Hoshikawa had turned into a zombie. If Shindō in turn had become a zombie three to five hours later, it would be proof that he had been killed by one. Which would make it immediately clear that the notes had been left by a human. And that wouldn't be any good. There was no point to the notes unless they made us think a human killed Shindō. So the culprit needed us to discover Shindō's body before he turned into a zombie. That was why there was a note wedged in his door. The culprit hoped Kanno would find it on his hourly rounds.'

Kanno went pale at the sound of his name.

'But I didn't notice it, unfortunately....'

'Exactly. Which must have put the culprit in a panic. At that rate, Shindō would become a zombie. Luckily, Shigemoto found the note and informed everyone.'

Everyone's eyes were focused on Shigemoto. Had the culprit become tired of waiting and pretended to have found the note themselves....?

'No, I'm not the murderer, I....!'

'He's right. There's nothing suspicious about him being the first to find the note, because he occupied the room next door. Anyway, as soon as we read it, we went into Shindō's room, where we discovered his body. I believe the time was some time after six.'

Nabarihad said she had heard noises from above at around half past two. If that was the time that Hoshikawa had attacked Shindō, it meant that we found Shindō's body about four hours afterwards.

'...That was close.' I shuddered at the thought.

'Yes indeed, whilst we were in his room, he could have risen as a zombie at any time. He had been bitten all over his body, unlike Hoshikawa, so his symptoms might have shown earlier than hers.

And when we were in the room, Nanamiya had claimed to have seen Shindō's fingers move. Perhaps he hadn't imagined it, and Shindō had been just about to stand up as a zombie.

'That's the whole truth surrounding Shindō's murder. Now we can move on to Tatsunami's.'

3

Everyone was rendered speechless by the surprising truth behind Shindō's murder, but evidence necessary to pinpoint the human murderer had not been addressed yet. What would come next? I could feel my heart beat faster as I waited to hear what Hiruko had to say.

'There are two main mysteries surrounding the murder of Tatsunami. The first is the question of how the murderer got into his room. The second is the question of how the murderer arranged for zombies to attack him. I'll start with the second mystery first. As Hamura explained this morning, the murderer had tied Tatsunami up in the elevator and sent him below so the zombies could attack him. Once that was done, the murderer could theoretically call the elevator up again. The problem being, obviously,that with the elevator doors open, a zombie could also have been brought upwith Tatsunami's body.'

'That is indeed a major problem.' Nabari, who had brought the point up that morning, nodded.

'So, the culprit had to come up with a trick.'

Hiruko asked me to display a different picture, the one of the bronze statues surrounding the television.

'What about them?' asked Kanno, puzzled.

'It's hard to make out because of the crimson carpet, but look at the feet of the statues, where they touch the floor. There's a little bit of blood there.'

I zoomed in on the picture. As Hiruko had said, there was something red on their feet, which was clearly not the crimson carpet.

'I see. But how did the blood get there? The statues are standing quite far away from the body.'

'The statues were moved into the elevator along with Tatsunami.'

'But why?' Kanno looked flabbergasted.

'So no zombie could ride the elevator.'

Deep down, I was impressed by Hiruko's analytic abilities.

'The elevator has a weight capacity. The culprit added extra weight so it would go over the limit if a zombie got inside. Let's make some estimates. The elevator is very small, with a maximum capacity of four passengers. If we assume that an average person weighs 65 kilograms, then the maximum capacity is about 260 kilograms. Normally a buzzer would sound at 110% of capacity, which is around 290 kilograms. I estimate Tatsunami's body at 70 kilograms. The statues are about a metre high, so even at a low estimate, they would weigh at least 40 kilograms each. They're a bit heavy to carry around, but remember there were *yukata* (casual kimono) thrown down from the balcony of room 206. Anyone could spread a *yukata* on the floor, push statues onto it, tie them up and pull them across the floor. Suppose five of them were moved into the elevator. Together with Tatsunami's body, the total would be around 270 kilograms. If a zombie heavier than 20 kilograms stepped inside the elevator, the alarm would go off and the elevator doors wouldn't shut. Of course, my calculations aren't accurate to the last kilo. Perhaps the actual weight capacity is slightly more, and perhaps there was one statue less. And, considering bits of flesh had been ripped from the body, it might have been lighter. But it would have been possible to make minor adjustments using the weapons hanging on the lounge wall. The culprit could add just enough weapons to cause the buzzer to sound, and then remove the last one.

'If you sent the elevator down to the first floor like that, it would never come back up as long as there was a zombie inside. Zombies don't bite people in order to feed, but to spread the virus, so after some time with Tatsunami, they would have achieved their goal and left the elevator cage on their own. Then the elevator doors would have closed, and only Tatsunami's remains brought up.'

'But, using that method, you cannot know when the elevator will return. It's impossible to predict when the zombies would leave Mr. Tatsunami's remains.'

'Quite so. That's why the killer didn't just drug him with a strong sleeping medicine, they drugged all of us. Let's lay out everything in order. The killer waited for the drugs to start working and left for the lounge. Just to be sure no witnesses would appear, they used the key kept on the television stand to lock the two wing doors. After moving a number of statues into the elevator, they tied Tatsunami up and moved him out of his room. If by any chance he had woken up then, the culprit could have simply knocked him out again. Once Tatsunami was in the elevator, the killer could use the swords and spears and other small objects to add enough weight so the buzzer would almost go off. Then the elevator was sent down. Perhaps the zombies didn't attack Tatsunami the first time, and the culprit had to repeat the process several times. When Tatsunami's body finally returned, the culprit moved the extra weight out again and cleaned the blood off the statues. They then cracked the skull and left the note inside. That's how the culprit succeeded in carrying out their plan.

'But, by sheer coincidence, the zombies had managed to break through the second-floor emergency exit during the last phase of their plan. The murderer must have heard the zombies banging on the south wing door.

'The murderer probably didn't know what to do at that point. With their task done, they could theoretically just have returned to their room and pretended to know nothing. But if they didn't do anything, Takagi and I, who had been drugged, wouldn't be able to get away safely. That's why the culprit went into the empty 206 and called us. Perhaps they were in 206 anyway, to wash the blood off their body and clothes. The culprit then waited for Kanno and everyone else to start moving before they joined the rest.'

'But why did the murderer unlock the south wing door if they had previously locked it?' asked Kanno.

'I think it was to keep the possibility alive that it all had been an act by Takagi or myself. By simply unlocking one door, the two of us remained viable suspects.'

After considering Hiruko's reconstruction of the events, I commented: 'If you're right, the murder must have taken quite some time.'

The phone calls to warn them must have been made immediately after the murderer was done.

'Yes. Perhaps it was difficult to get the zombies to attack Tatsunami in the elevator, or perhaps cleaning up after the murder took longer than expected.'

That would explain why there were traces in the elevator cage that looked as though Tatsunami's body had been moved around. Although they were small, five statues inside the elevator would definitely have interrupted the natural flow of the blood on the floor. The body had been dragged around to erase the traces.

'I can see how the murder could have been committed like that,'said Shizuhara, 'but I don't see how that leads to the killer.' Hiruko nodded.

'You're right. We already knew a murder had been committed, so proving it was possible doesn't advance us much. From this point on, I shall start narrowing down the list of suspects. But in order to do so, I need to explain the first mystery, the question of how the murderer entered Tatsunami's room.'

Hiruko explained how the door of Tatsunami's room had been rigged so that my wire trick wouldn't work, and there were traces to show that a string had been used to unlock the door guard. She also explained the keycard swapping trick she had pulled on me.

'Swapping keycards. It's a very simple trick, but several circumstances turned out favourably for the murderer. First of all, Tatsunami always left his door ajar when not in his room, so he would seldom use his keycard. And he was often away from his room. That was why the murderer had no problems swapping keycards.'

That I understood. But could Hiruko really identify the murderer based on the fact the keycards had been swapped? People had been constantly going in and out of the lounge during the day, and it was impossible to say who had been alone in the lounge and when. Save for Nanamiya, who had been in his own room all the time, any of us would have had the opportunity.

'So the culprit swapped keycards with Tatsunami. Do you understand what that means? The culprit had to let go of the keycard to their own room. The keycards of the Villa Violet are quite sophisticated, and you can't switch on the power in the rooms by placing other kinds of card, such as a business card or a driver's license, in the holder. The only way to swap Tatsunami's keycard without him noticing, is by using your own keycard.'

Shigemoto interrupted her.

'Wait. Couldn't the murderer have got hold of the keycard of a different room? I'm sorry to have to say this, but although Mr. Kanno claimed that the only keycard he got from reception was the master keycard, he might be lying and carrying multiple keycards.'

'But why would I do such a thing?' retorted Kanno in response to the unexpected accusation.

'I'm just talking possibilities. If she's trying to narrow down the culprit, we can't just ignore some of the possibilities,' Shigemoto insisted.

Nabari jumped in as well.

'It's not fair to be suspicious only of Mr. Kanno. Setting aside keycards that have gone missing, such as those of Kudamatsu or Akechi, there's still the keycard to Shindō's room. We kept the air-conditioning running in there. The killer could have used the wire trick to open the door and taken the keycard.'

Hiruko had been nodding at all the theories presented, but returned to her own calm explanation.

'I can't deny the possibility that Mr. Kanno has been carrying multiple keycards on him from the start. However, there is a reason why he can be eliminated from the list of suspects. After Tatsunami's murder, Mr. Kanno and I were talking on the phone at the same time Takagi was being called by the person who is probably the murderer. He is therefore not the murderer.'

It was the alibi she had talked about on the second floor.

'Exactly,' agreed Nabari. Kanno looked relieved.

'And, as for the possibility that Shindō's keycard was taken: that's impossible. Last night, from supper onwards, everyone was in the lounge and Tatsunami was the first to retreat to his room. That means the culprit had to have swapped the keycards before supper. But, after we all said good night, Hamura saw from his own room that a light in Shindō's room had been left on. Mr. Kanno also noticed during his

211

rounds that the light had been left on. As I said before, a keycard is needed to switch on the power in a room, so that proves that the keycard was still in the holder in Shindō's room.'

Several people looked at me, and I nodded to confirm Hiruko's explanation.

'And so we all had one keycard on us. And, during supper, the culprit was already in possession of Tatsunami's keycard as well. Most of us drank the drugged coffee and went our separate ways after Tatsunami, who left first. But after that, there was a conversation we knew nothing about.'

Hiruko looked at Nabari.

'Before you went to bed, you went to Mr. Kanno, who had been cleaning up the lounge. You asked if you could swap keycards.'

'I didn't want the master keycard anymore. If someone was killed again, I'd be the first to be suspected, because of it.'

Hiruko nodded at her reply, then looked at Kanno.

'And are you sure you were given the master keycard?'

'Of course. I opened the door to her room for her with the master keycard and made sure she got safely inside.'

'So after Tatsunami's keycard had been swapped, Nabari had still been in possession of the master keycard. Which means she isn't the killer.'

With that, Kanno and Nabari's names were crossed off the list as well. There were five names remaining.

'The other point I want to focus on, is what Shigemoto and Mr. Kanno were talking about earlier.'

'That the music from Mr. Tatsunami's room had been interrupted once yesterday, during the day?'

Hiruko nodded.

'Yes. Now let me ask a question. Is there anyone here who's prepared to say it was they who touched Tatsunami's music player just then?'

Nobody raised their hands, so she continued.

'Thanks to Shigemoto's calculations, we can assume the music was interrupted at half past four. But Nabari's testimony puts Tatsunami on the rooftop at that time. So why did the music stop for a moment? The answer is simple. That was the exact moment the murderer pulled Tatsunami's keycard out of the holder, thus switching off the power in the room and turning off the radio cassette CD player. When I looked in Tatsunami's room this morning, I saw that the music player was connected to an outlet behind the bed in a blind spot from the entrance, on the left side of the room. That's why the culprit made such a mistake. They probably assumed it was running on batteries, as it had been during the barbecue. Or perhaps it was just a true slip-up.

'At any rate, the moment they pulled the keycard out of the holder, the loud music suddenly stopped. The shock must have stopped the culprit's heart for a moment. In their panic, the only thought would be to get the music going again. If anyone noticed it had stopped, it would be discovered that the culprit had gone into the room, or that they had swapped keycards. So they quickly inserted their own keycard in the holder and pushed the play button on the music player. Which means that anyone who can provide an alibi for the moment the music stopped can be eliminated from the list of suspects. Mr. Kanno has already been ruled out, therefore the alibi of Mr. Shigemoto, who had been with him, also holds. He's out as well.'

Three names had now been eliminated. Four names remained: Hiruko, Takagi, Shizuhara and myself.

'And now we make our final dash to the finishing line.'

Hiruko's voice had turned cold and sharp.

'I just said that swapping keycards meant the culprit had to let go of the keycard to their own room. Which meant that,after we retreated for the night, the culprit wouldn't be able to unlock the door to their own room.'

Nabari interrupted again.

'But you could use the wire trick. Or the culprit could simply return to their own room, if they had used the door guard as a stopper, as Mr. Tatsunami did.'

'True enough, but that's not the point. What I'm saying is that anyone who can prove that they re-entered their room after supper by using their own keycard to unlock the door, can be eliminated as a suspect.'

Ooooh, so that was it. She had made it to the finishing line.

'In my case, Hamura walked me to my room.'

I nodded.

'Yes, I watched her unlock the door with her keycard. I'm sure of it.'

Hiruko was off the hook. Three remaining.

'And then you said you chatted with Takagi, correct?'

'Yes. I had trouble unlocking my door, so he helped me,' replied Takagi.

I nodded again.Takagi was safe as well. The ten eyes of the innocent five were now levelled at the remaining two.

Shizuhara and myself.

I had already given up in my mind. Hiruko knew. She knew I had been deceiving her. How she had worked it out, I don't know, but did she also know why? Hiruko's large eyes were looking at me.

'And finally, Hamura, you went up to the third floor together with Shizuhara. Answer me. Which of you went inside their room first?'

It was her final warning to us. We were the only ones to know the truth. And that's why I....

'He went first.'

Shizuhara had spoken up before I could say anything.

'He unlocked his door right in front of me and stepped inside his room. I am his witness,' she declared defiantly.

Shizuhara was the murderer.

4

It wasn't as if there was another suspicious figure amongst us. Nevertheless, we all could scarcely believe it.

'Mifuyu... no...'

Takagi, who was closest to Shizuhara, was visibly devastated. She hadn't looked nearly as shocked when she had been confronted by dead bodies. Shizuhara, however, remained calm and spoke in an unperturbed manner.

'I suppose I should congratulate you,' she said, looking at Hiruko.

It had been Shizuhara herself who had pushed Hiruko to solve the mystery, so she must have prepared herself for the outcome. Nobody knew how to react. She appeared so tranquil, yet a seething hatred could be inferred from her horrible crimes.

'I don't wish to be a sore loser, but I would like to know. If I hadn't confessed, or if I had lied to you, would you still have been able to identify me as the murderer?'

Hiruko considered the question for a moment, then nodded her head slowly.

'Yes, there was actually another clue which indicated you as the murderer. There was a clear contradiction when we discussed what everyone did after waking up this morning.'

'There was? I was sure to be careful....'

'It wasn't your mistake.'

Hiruko turned to look at me.

'It was you. There was an unquestionable contradiction in your account.'

I didn't say anything, but merely let her continue. How much had she discerned?

'You woke up early because you hadn't taken any of the drugged coffee, and heard Mr. Kanno shouting. "It was just before half past four," you said, speaking about the time.'

Nabari looked at Hiruko in bewilderment.

'Wait. I don't see what's wrong with that. You called Mr. Kanno at twenty-five past and talked for two or three minutes. Mr. Kanno then stumbled upon the body and had to check the door, so that would indeed have been about the time that he reached the third floor.'

'It wasn't the time that bothered me. It was his choice of words. There were several amongst us who mentioned times, but those who checked the clocks mentioned precise times, like twenty-five or twenty-eight past. None of us talked about the time as "just before half past four" as Hamura did. And why was that? It was because he was looking at an analogue timepiece.'

None of the others, including Shizuhara, understood the implications of what Hiruko had said. I, on the other hand, knew she had seen through everything.

'So he checked his own wristwatch instead of the clock on the wall. What's odd about that?'

Kanno's question was immediately followed by puzzled remarks from Takagi and Nabari, however.

'Wait. Didn't you say you lost your watch after the barbecue?'

'So, did you find your watch?'

I couldn't answer them. Hiruko continued.

'Another contradiction will explain what happened. After Mr. Kanno ran past the room, you put the door guard on, pushed the door ajar and peered outside. Shizuhara did the same thing at the very same moment, and you looked each other in the eye.'

Nabari interrupted Hiruko yet again.

'There's nothing strange about Shizuhara being in her room by then, surely? The killer's call to Takagi was before twenty-eight past four. Mr. Kanno would have been running past the rooms and warning us around half past. There would have been enough time to return to her room after the phone call.'

'That's not the contradiction.The problem is what they did.'

I myself had no idea what the contradiction was. I had simply recounted exactly what I had experienced at the time to Hiruko.

'It's better for you to see for yourself. Take a look at how those two could have looked at each other from their respective door openings.'

Hiruko left the storage room and headed for the east wing. Everyone followed. She pointed at our two doors.

'Aah!'

We all gasped.The doors of our two rooms wung open towards each other. Shizuhara and I finally realised the fatal mistake we had made.

'The only way two people in these specific two rooms can look at each other from the doorway, is by stepping out into the corridor and looking *around* the doors. But that's impossible todo with the door guard in place, which only allows you open the door partially. So why did Hamura lie in his testimony? At first, I couldn't think of any reason. But the answer came to me when I combined this question with the problem of his watch. The two of them did actually look at each other through the door opening with the door guard in place.'

Shigemoto looked puzzled.

'But that's impossible, the way the doors are oriented....'

'They weren't on the third floor, they were on the second. Shizuhara was in room 206, from where the calls had been made. Meanwhile Hamura was in 207, the room which had belonged to Deme. They heard Mr. Kanno as he ran past to take the stairs up to the third floor.'

Everyone looked at the adjoining rooms. The orientation of the doors of rooms 306 and 307, which followed the same arrangement as 206 and 207 below, did allow the people inside to look at each other from their own doorway, unlike rooms 307 and 308.

Takagi put her hand to her mouth, as she finally realised what I had done.

'You were in Deme's room... oh!'

Hiruko looked questioningly at me. She was asking me if she could tell the others. I nodded back. I had lost the right to say anything the moment I had decided to deceive her.

'Yes, Hamura had gone to Deme's room to search his belongings for the wristwatch. He probably intended to be finished before any of the others woke up. And he did indeed find it. But, just as he was about to return to his own room, Mr. Kanno came running past. And he reflexively checked the time on his watch.'

Yes, the hand on my watch was just about to point at the 6. If I'dbeen looking at a digital display, I would have stated the time at exactly twenty-nine past, but instead I testified using the less precise time.

'Meanwhile, Shizuhara had intended to slip back into her room after Mr. Kanno had gone by. But then Hamura appeared from a room he shouldn't have been in, and they looked straight at each other.They were each in a place where they didn't want to be seen, so they agreed to keep it secret and pretend that they had been in their own rooms all the time.'

Nabari spoke out again: 'But that doesn't make any sense! He only went there to retrieve what was stolen from him. That's nothing compared to murder.'

Perhaps she was right. Most people would consider my act justified.

'To us, his act might seem excusable, but to himself, it was an act of evil. An act equivalent to murder.'

I looked in surprise at Hiruko. How did she know? She looked apologetically back at me.

'After the trouble with the notebook in the abandoned hotel, Akechi told me what had happened to you as a boy. You didn't get that scar on your temple from an earthquake or a tsunami. One day, whilst you were still an evacuee, you returned home to find looters, who attacked you.'

So it was Akechi who had told her. There had been a disastrous earthquake, but my family had managed to escape the ensuing tsunami, and we had evacuated to elevated ground nearby. Many buildings had been swept away by the waves, but our home was somehow one of those still standing. But it could have collapsed at any time, so we had to live in an evacuation shelter for some time.

One day I went home to pick up some things we could use, and ran into two people who had broken into our house. Furious, I got into a fight with them and was struck on the head with a brick.

A dark rage smouldered within me after that. Earthquakes and tsunamis are calamities. There's nothing you can do about them. But those two looters were different. They were stealing things from refugees. I could never forgive scum like them. Trash nobody would care about, even if they did get murdered.

The years went by, and no matter how often I looked back, the hatred within me never faded. On this trip, I felt uncontrollable rage towards Shigemoto, who took someone else's notebook from the hotel, and Deme, who stole my watch. They reignited my dark hatred of looters. And so the act of going through the belongings of someone deceased was an unbearable shame to me. Even if it was to retrieve the watch given to me by my younger sister. Even if it was Deme. But it was the only way to get my watch back. If I had waited any longer, the zombies might have taken over the second floor and I would never have got it back.

So, the moment my eyes met those of Shizuhara, I wasn't thinking about the murders. The one thing that occupied my mind was wanting her to keep quiet about what I had done. I couldn't bear anyone knowing about my sin. It meant little to me to keep her crimes a secret, as long as she kept mine a secret as well.

Let's make a deal.

I was about to confess all of this, when Shizuhara suddenly interrupted my story.

'No, we didn't agree on a story together. I threatened to kill him if he told anyone. He was only following my orders.'

Why? Why would you do that for me?

'Wait a second, Hiruko.' Takagi didn't want Shizuhara to say any more.'You still haven't explained Nanamiya's death. Mifuyu has been with me ever since this morning. She never had time to kill him.'

Kanno nodded.

'It's not just Ms. Shizuhara, none of us could have done it. Mr. Nanamiya barely went out his room the last three days. Nobody could have swapped his keycard, nor did anyone have an opportunity to kill him.'

'There was, though,' said Hiruko clearly. 'Because Nanamiya was poisoned.'

'Poisoned!' Everyone was surprised.

'Yes. From the video we saw, he didn't appear to have sustained any injuries, and since he had been in his room all the time, that's the only possible way.'

Questions followed immediately.

'But how could anyone have poisoned him?' asked Kanno.

'Perhaps the water and food he brought to his room had been tampered with in advance?' suggested Takagi.

'Impossible,' said Nabari. 'He picked randomly from the supplies in the lounge. What if somebody else had taken something that had been poisoned?'

Hiruko shook her head.

'There was one occasion when it was possible to enter his room. This morning, when the rope ladder was lowered to my room.'

Somebody cried out. That was the only moment we ever set foot inside Nanamiya's room.

'But how could you make him take the poison? The bottles of water on his table were still sealed,' I asked, to which Nabari replied with a guess.

'Perhaps the poison was put on his toothbrush, or the cup in the bathroom, whilst nobody was watching.'

Shigemoto, however, refuted this theory.

'No, Mr. Nanamiya, Mr. Kanno and Hamura went out on the balcony, but I was still in the room with Shizuhara. I wasn't watching her all the time, but she certainly didn't go into the bathroom.'

I, too, thought back to what had happened then.

'The emergency rations on the table hadn't been opened yet, and his face masks were also still sealed. And he was obsessed with staying clean, so he'd never leave something already opened out on the table. And as for his painkillers, you need to pop them out of the blister strip one by one, so you can't insert a poisoned pill in advance.'

'What if you had a poisoned bottle of water and switched them?' Kanno suggested.

'No, I ran up to the third floor together with Shizuhara, and I'm sure she was not carrying anything as big as a bottle of water.'

Considering she was wearing light summer wear, I would have noticed it immediately if she had been hiding a bottle of water beneath her clothes.

'I said "poison," but it doesn't necessarily have to be taken orally,' said Hiruko.

'Not orally? But how then?'

'Through the eyes.'

She her index finger and thumb to stretch her right eyelid.

'The poison only needed to be taken in via the mucous membrane of the eye. He was using eye drops all the time, probably because he was wearing overcorrected contact lenses. His eye drop case is coloured, so you can't see if anything is introduced inside, and it's small enough to be able to carry around without it being noticed. I believe Shizuhara uses the same eye drops.'

I recalled Takagi had mentioned that earlier.

'But, even supposing a poison was introduced into his eyes somehow, I can imagine him becoming blind in the worst case, but dying? Did she come here having prepared such a strong poison?'

'No. She procured the poison here on-site.'

Kanno looked pale as he quickly objected: 'We don't keep such a poison here at the boarding house!'

'But we do. In fact, they've been talking about it all the time on the television, warning us to not allow it to come in contact with our eyes or in our mouths as it is horribly deadly and infectious.'

We were at a loss for words. It was as if we had been struck by lightning. So that was it. The zombie blood of Shindō and Tatsunami. I could imagine what could happen if you introduced that blood into the body via the mucous membrane of the eye, so close to the brain. The virus would reach the brain immediately. Nanamiya was probably in the process of turning into a non-human at this very moment.

'You impress me. So when you worked that out, you became convinced I had to be the killer.'

'I couldn't be sure nobody else was carrying eye drops, so my suspicions of you merely strengthened.'

'It doesn't matter either way. Rescue will arrive here soon. Once the official investigation starts, all of my little tricks will be exposed and it will become clear that I am the murderer.'

I recalled an earlier conversation with Hiruko, when she talked about the aim of the murderer. If we were to believe Shizuhara, she did not put any effort into erasing physical evidence, such as fingerprints. Her intricate plan had been executed solely so she could kill her three targets before the rescue units arrived.

'But Mifuyu, why, why would you do all this?'

Takagi's voice was trembling. For the first time, Shizuhara showed an expression of agony.

'I'm sorry. But I had to take revenge for Sachi. She is the reason I went to Shinkō University.'

Hiruko looked around at the others at the mention of the unfamiliar name.

'Sachi Endō. She was a senior member of the club. Last year, she broke up with Tatsunami, quit university and returned to her parental home,' explained Shigemoto.

'Revenge? For what?'

'Sachi committed suicide in December.'

The expressions on Takagi and Shigemoto's faces tensed. Takagi had told me that only Nanamiya's ex, Megumi, had committed suicide. Which meant that Sachi Endō's suicide occurred some time after she had returned home. None of the current club members had known about it. Shizuhara started to speak calmly.

'Sachi lived nearby, and she had always looked after me since we were children, treating me like her little sister. She was so pretty and nice. But last October, I heard she had suddenly quit university and returned home. I had a nasty feeling, so I went to see her.'

At first Sachi wouldn't see Shizuhara, but after a few visits Shizuhara was finally invited up to Sachi's room. She had grown unbelievably thin, almost unrecognisable. Sachi Endō had not explained anything to her family, but confessed to Shizuhara what had happened. A man she had met at her university club's summer trip had deceived her. She had been used and dumped.

'Sachi had always been so pure-minded. She had never been in a relationship before she left for university and never learned to doubt men. I tried to get her out of it, but to no avail. Two months later, she took her own life. I don't know whether she was still trying to protect the man, but she didn't even mention the trip in her suicide note. I was the only person who knew the truth.

'An inferno had taken over Sachi's body and my mind. All that was left was revenge. Not just Tatsunami. I vowed to send him and all the other tormentors to hell. That's why I decided to take the entrance exams for Shinkō University. I had to change my plans suddenly and prepare all over again for the examination subjects, so I was only able to get into Nursing Studies.'

'Was Shindō's murder also part of the plan from the start?' asked Hiruko. Anger crept into Shizuhara's voice.

'Of course. That piece of scum, he knew that the women were going to be sacrificed to those three, to be eaten alive by them, and he still tried to keep everything a secret. He even invited me on this trip. I would have joined anyway, even if he hadn't contacted me. But I couldn't believe he also dragged in you and Nabari from the Drama Club, just because there were too few people. He only saw women as sacrifices in exchange for a job.'

It was then that I noticed something important was missing from her confession, so I interrupted her.

'Wait. So you didn't write that first threatening note?'

If Shizuhara had planned to come along on the trip to exact her revenge, she wouldn't have written a threatening note which could have led to a cancellation of the trip. As I had expected, she shook her head.

'That wasn't me. I think a senior who went last year wrote the note to warn us. If Shindō had cancelled the trip then, I might have let him go.'

Nabari couldn't contain herself.

'How can you be so stupid! I understand your pain, I really do. I won't ever shed a tear for that trash. But why, why do you have to commit a sin yourself? It's so foolish... why....'

Nabari covered her face. Shizuhara silently bowed to her.

'Thank you, but I'm really not the person you believe I am. These last few months, the only thing I have been thinking of has been how I would kill them. I joined this trip in order to do so. Originally, I only had a rough idea that I'd lure them out one by one, or use sleeping drugs so I could kill them. Allowing the law to judge them had never been on my mind. The attack of the zombies was a sign to me, guidance for my revenge. The police couldn't come, no matter what I did, and my victims wouldn't be able to escape. The existence of the zombies themselves also gave my plan a boost. The zombies were a sign. The devoured turned into the devouring.'

'Still, your plans made surprisingly good use of the circumstances. Do you have any connection to the people behind the terrorist attack?' asked Hiruko, but Shizuhara shook her head.

'No. All of this was just divine—no, devilish—intervention and coincidence. The first night, I just happened to see Shindō being attacked on the balcony by Hoshikawa, who had turned into a zombie. He was struggling to keep her pinned to the window whilst she was trying to bite him, but he never cried out for help. He knew that she'd be killed if the others found out about her. I only watched as he desperately tried to hold her. No, I was cheering for Hoshikawa. Go for it! Do it! Kill him!'

She was speaking in a monotonous manner, but her eyes sparkled.

'After about thirty minutes of struggling with the never-tiring Hoshikawa, Shindō finally ran out of steam. And finally... haha, do you want to know why his face was gnawed all over? In his last moments, he kissed her. She had been a zombie for a long time by then. That changed my opinion of him slightly. Not that I had forgiven him. She bit him in the face and all over his body and then finally got up. She happened to notice me then, standing on my balcony watching them. She tried to reach my balcony. But zombies are rather stupid. She climbed over the railing and fell down.'

I remembered what had happened on the rooftop. The zombies which had taken over the emergency stairs had noticed my presence and started climbing one after another over the railing, plummeting to the ground. Hoshikawa had done the same, trying to reach Shizuhara's balcony, and had fallen down.

'I took a look at the room where Shindōwas still lying. It was at that moment I came up with my plan. If I could make it appear as if Shindō had been killed by a human, I could avert suspicion away from myself in the ensuing murders. Thinking back to the Trial of Courage, I estimated the time to turn into a zombie was five hours or less. It was then I knew it had been a sign from heaven. I made new plans to use the zombies to kill Tatsunami and Nanamiya. Nanamiya had been hiding in his room from the start, so I decided to kill Tatsunami first. Whilst I was observing him, I came up with the idea of swapping our keycards and using the elevator.'

Here Shizuhara's look wavered.

'But when it became time for me to commit the murder, there was one reason that caused me to hesitate. That reason was Akechi. I had started to despise all men after Sachi's death, but a tremendous doubt had started to creep inside me after Akechi saved my life. I had effectively sacrificed him to save my own life. Did I then have the right to take the lives of others? That is why I asked someone for the answer to my question.'

I could still recall what Shizuhara had said to me last night. "If there's any way I can make up for what I have done, please tell me. Money, my body, anything."

That moment had been the last chance to stop Shizuhara. I should have asked for something. Money. Her body. She would have thought the worse of me, but I could have kept her with me, so she wouldn't have needed to stain her hands with blood.

But my answer had been "Live your life the way you want. That's all I want." She had taken my reply as a green light. My petty sense of doing the right thing had given her the final push onto the path of the wicked.

What a hopeless, useless fool I am.

'I was told it was all right for me to proceed.'

An insane smile appeared on her face. There was no sadness anymore, no rage.

'And the sleeping drugs?'

'I had brought some with me, thinking I'd probably need them at some point to kill those three and Shindō. But then suspicion fell on Nabari because of the drugs. It had been my intention to have nobody specific be suspected of the murders until I was done. I'm sorry.'

Nabari shook her head. It wouldn't change anything anymore.

'The zombies had managed to break into the south wing just after I was done killing Tatsunami and had moved the statues back to their original place. I was in a panic, because I knew Rin and Kenzaki were trapped in their rooms. But it was once again the devil who whispered in my ears. I could use this chance to get inside Nanamiya's room, pretending to save Kenzaki. I added some of Tatsunami's blood to the eye drops I always carry around. I had been more concerned with accomplishing my task than the zombies, but once again everything happened in such a way as to aid me.

'Feel free to despise me. I called the two of you, partially because I was worried for you, but also because I wanted to kill Nanamiya. I even unlocked the south wing door to keep the possibility alive that one of you two had faked the call yourself. I ran inside 206, with two things to do. I had to call Kenzaki and Rin and wake either one or both of them. And then I had to get out and return to my own room 307 without being seen.

'After calling Kenzaki, I got rid of the bloody *yukata* by throwing them out from the balcony and then waited for someone to save the two of them. That would be the two or three minutes during which you were speaking with Mr. Kanno. It took so long that I also made a call to Rin, but by that time Mr. Kanno had stepped out into the lounge, and I had to grab my chance to leave the room.

'The rest happened just as you guessed. Mr. Kanno ran down the corridor shouting about the zombies and, after making sure he had gone upstairs, I opened the door of 206 and looked outside. It was then that I looked Hamura in the eye.'

And with that, Shizuhara ended her confession of the matter of howdunnit. But there was still one other mystery. Hiruko placed her right hand over her face and dug her nails in. She was trying to hide her distress with physical pain.

'There is one thing I just don't understand, no matter how much thought I give it.'

'What is it? I will answer you if I can.'

'Why were you so determined to use that trick with the elevator to kill Tatsunami? If you simply wanted the zombies to get him, there would have been other, less convoluted options. You had to move more than 200 kilograms in and out of the elevator and wipe blood away from those weights. I don't understand why you used a trick that required so much labour.'

It was the question of whydunnit which had troubled Hiruko all this time.Shizuhara nodded as if the question had been nothing special.

'Oh, that's easy to answer. It was the only way I could get Tatsunami's body back after he had been attacked by the zombies.'

'You had to retrieve his body?' repeated Hiruko, aghast.

The Hiruko Method would have left Tatsunami's body with the zombies. So why didn't Shizuhara want that to happen?

'I told you that the zombies were a sign to me. Do you know why? Because you can kill a zombie twice. Once as a human, and once as a zombie. Tatsunami was the direct cause of Sachi's death and I needed to kill him twice. Because he... he took two lives. Sachi, and the baby inside her.'

'She was... pregnant?' gasped Takagi.

'Yes. And Sachi told him she was pregnant. But do you know what he did? He sent her an envelope with money to pay for the abortion. She took her life two days after she received it.'

I couldn't believe it. Shizuhara had gone through all that trouble because, in that way, she could kill Tatsunami, have him rise as a zombie,and kill him a second time. This was the answer to the question of whydunnit which had haunted Hiruko.

Shigemoto's earlier analysis had been on the spot. Zombies were reflections of the mind-sets and egos of man. To Shigemoto, they were mysterious beings that provided endless amusement. To me, they symbolised the powerlessness of man. To Hiruko, they were the worst threat she ever faced, due to her unusual fate. To Tatsunami, they were patients dancing to the tune of the mysterious disease that is love. And to Shizuhara, they were a tool which allowed her to take her unprecedented revenge, by killing the same person twice.

Shizuhara was looking at her own two hands, as if she were reliving the physical sensation of the murder. She reminded me of the Virgin Mary cradling the Son of God.

'I can still remember the moment. I put Tatsunami in the elevator and sent it down. The moment I heard a muffled cry coming from below via the lift well, I put my ear to the ground so that I would not miss a single moment. With his hands and legs tied, there was nothing he could do to fight back. He was writhing in agony as the zombies surrounded him and started ravishing his body. I guess the gag came off, because he started to shriek like a little girl. It was like a melody from heaven, a melody that cleansed the hate that had been blazing in my mind for these last few months.

'Do you understand? I'm not a sane person anymore. By calling the elevator back up, I got Tatsunami's body back. Whilst I was doing the remaining tasks, such as returning the statues to their original positions I waited, I yearned for Tatsunami to become a zombie. The murder didn't occur until the morning because I was having problems.

It was because I was waiting for him to turn into a zombie. He turned slightly faster than Shindō. Exactly four hours later, his body started to change. I had been waiting for the moment. Holding the mace tightly, I smashed his head again and again. What a perfect summer game, like the classic watermelon splitting game at the beach.'

Her red tongue showed bewitchingly from between her lips. She had finally removed her silent mask, revealing a stunning, beautiful woman.

'And what's more, I couldn't have been luckier when I was given the opportunity to finish off the zombiefied Deme. It had been my only regret until then, that I had not been able to do the job myself.

'These have been three long days. I've had to pull off all kinds of tricks to accomplish the murders the way I wanted within the limited circumstances. But I have accomplished all I wanted to do. As for what happens next, I don't care anymore.'

All I could do was bite down on my lip. I know. I had no right to say anything to Shizuhara. I had kept silent about her crimes, so I was her accomplice.I was the only person Shizuhara wouldn't want to hear anything from. I know all of that. I know, but couldn't things have worked out differently?

Shizuhara, I understand the hatred you feel. The person you admired had been toyed with and dumped. She died with a baby inside her. It was an unforgivable act. You had to kill them.

If I had been you, my wish would have been exactly the same. They had committed what you deemed to be the most unforgivable act in this world. If they had done anything else, you could have forgiven them.That is why you don't feel any regret now.

But Shizuhara, you saw it for yourself. Shindō tried to protect his girlfriend who had turned into a zombie, all by himself. He kept trying until the very end, and ended his life with a kiss.He may have been a cowardly, egoistic scumbag who betrayed women, but he gave his own life to protect the person whom he deemed most important.

Tatsunami too. You wouldn't know it, but he had been living with a trauma after an experience none of us could begin to imagine, and he couldn't believe in love anymore. He threw himself on women in the hopes of understanding love. I can sympathise with him, up to a point.

Perhaps they just displayed the worst side of man too clearly, just like those looters. Apart from that, they might not be all that bad. If you or I or anyone else would show us at our worst, we too would be called inhuman.

So was your anger justified? Can you be sure you will never regret what you have done? You and I have shown ourselves at our worst. Can we still continue as living humans?

I don't know anymore. That's why I don't want to learn anything more about Deme and Nanamiya. I want to keep thinking of them as hopeless trash.

Or else I won't know what I can hate anymore.

It was at that moment the alarm we had placed on the eastern stairway barricade went off.

5

We all knew what that noise meant. Some started to cry out.

'They're through the barricade!'

'They're coming!'

Zombies, fortunately, move awkwardly. There was still time to escape. I picked up a spear that was lying around. Whilst the rest hurried to carry the supplies from the storage room up to the rooftop, Kanno and I took up position on the eastern staircase. We had to buy everyone time. The zombies slowly made their way up.

'They're here.'

'We don't need to kill them. We only need to push them down the stairs,' I told Kanno. We both swallowed hard as we held our weapons ready.

But then the unexpected happened. From the opposite direction came the noise of wood breaking and the screams of women. The zombies had broken in from the other side of the elevator hall, through the south wing door.

'No!'

That door was closer to the storage room than we were. At this rate, the two of us would be trapped outside. We quickly ran back. I thrust my spear at a zombie which was trying to get to the storage door. That was a mistake. I managed to pierce the neck of the zombie, but I couldn't pull my weapon out. With my spear still in its body, the zombie reached out to me.

'Uuuuuwaaa!'

Being careful so I wouldn't be bitten, I lifted the spear and threw the zombie off. I had managed to get rid of him, but more zombies had come closer in the meantime.

227

Kanno and I nearly tripped as we fled inside the storage, but just as we were about to close the door behind us, a zombie managed to get its hand in, blocking the door. A second hand and a third hand followed. The door couldn't be closed anymore.

'Upstairs! To the rooftop!' shouted Kanno.

Everyone abandoned their tasks. The women went up first, followed by Shigemoto. Kanno and I, however, were being gradually overpowered by the growing number of arms getting in, and the door flung open.

'Go on ahead!'

Urged on by Kanno, I went up the stairs. Outside, I felt rain drops falling on my face. Kanno was right behind me. We would all make it to the rooftop safely.

'Aaah!'

Kanno, the last in the line, suddenly cried out. A zombie had grabbed his right leg. I turned pale. One bite and it would be all over.

Suddenly a short figure jumped forward and plunged a sword into the zombie's face.

'Mifuyu!'

It was Shizuhara. Her attack had loosened the zombie's hold on Kanno's leg, and he had managed to climb up the last few steps of the stairs, but now she had become the new target herself. She desperately swung her sword around, but she was being attacked from all directions. There was a cry.

'Aaaaaaah!! Get off her!'

A rain of spear attacks fell down on the zombies as Takagi wielded her weapon and we somehow managed to drag Shizuhara out. Everyone was here now.

Next was the rooftop door. We only needed to push back the one zombie that had reached there, and close the door. That was all we had to do.

'No...'

The blood drained out of my face as I faced the zombie which had pursued us up the stairs.

'A—Akechi...'

A male zombie had made its way right in front of me.He was completely covered in blood and bite marks, but nobody could mistake his appearance.

He was my Holmes. The man who had saved me and brought me everywhere. The man I hadn't been able to save.

I had seen many deaths until now. I had learned to cope with disasters humans are powerless against, and with sudden goodbyes. But I couldn't push him back. How could Watson push the returning Holmes back down the waterfall?

Everything moved in slow motion. Our eyes met. He wasn't wearing his rimless glasses anymore. His red eyes didn't recognise me. Akechi's hands grabbed my shoulders and his open mouth moved towards my neck. A jolt went through my body.

A spear had been thrust through Akechi's eye and into his skull. I turned around to find Hiruko standing behind me.

'I won't let you have him.' She spoke determinedly.

'He's my Watson.'

She let the spear go. Akechi started to fall back with the spear in his head. It was like the moment the thread Kandata was climbing snapped in Ryūnosuke Akutagawa's story *The Spider's Thread*. Like Kandata, Akechi too fell back into the underworld, taking the other zombies down with him.

The door was closed.

'No, Mifuyu, Mifuyu!'

Takagi was crying Shizuhara's name out loud. Shizuhara was lying in Takagi's arms. She had a painful-looking bite mark on her shoulder. Everyone knew what this meant.

'I suppose this is karma.'

Shizuhara stood up and gently pushed Takagi away.

'Don't feel sad for me. The devourer becomes the devoured. This, too, is a sign from heaven.'

She held Takagi's spear as she backed off to the edge of the rooftop.

'Mifuyu…'

'I'm sorry for the trouble I caused, Rin, everyone. I am not afraid to die, but it will take too long for me to join Sachi like this, so I will finish it myself.'

Without any hesitation, she thrust the spear into her own eye socket. She fell back and her small body flew through the sky as Takagi screamed. The next second, a loud thud came from below. And then there was silence.

Four hours later, the rain cleared and a rescue helicopter appeared.

EPILOGUE

The summer that had taken so much from us had passed. Robbed from that weighty role I once had, my life returned to normal. Today I was visiting my usual café.

My glass of cream soda had been placed on the short table. The first person who ever treated me to this drink wasn't amongst us anymore.

More than had a month had passed since the incident. The number of deaths caused by the bioterror attack with the new virus is currently reported at 5230 persons. There had been more than 5000 victims. You could also say there had only been 5000 victims. Compared to the earthquake I experienced, the number was small.

Perhaps that is why after two weeks of frantic reporting by the media, the circus was over. Mentions of terrorist attacks and zombies dwindled and, by now, all of us had returned to normal life. I don't know whether there had been machinations behind the speed with which the whole affair died down. But it was not surprising that stories about a bizarre murder case in a boarding house, and the young people who had lost their lives there, soon faded into obscurity.

Takagi left the university at the end of summer. She went out of her way to contact me, to tell me she was going to nursing school next year. She also confessed to me that she had been the one to write the initial threatening note. Her hopes that the trip would be cancelled had not come true. She now wanted to become a person who would be able to save others, she sighed as she left.

Nabari had to take a long rest to recover from the trauma of the incident, but had returned to university a few days ago. Kanno has quit his job at the Villa Violet, but it seems Nabari is still in contact with him. That was one of the few good things to come out of the ordeal.

Shigemoto has disappeared. His case, however, is unusual. According to people who know him, he has not been seen on campus even once after the incident, and nobody has been able to contact him. I remember something that bothered me. After we had been saved from the Villa Violet, we had been put in isolation and quarantine for some time at a facility for a thorough examination and questioning. The police or some investigator had stumbled upon the notebook in

Shigemoto's luggage, and he alone had been led to a different room. I do not know what happened to him after that.

And as for me?After it was all over, Hiruko once again asked me to become her assistant. I confessed my secret to her. After the murder of Tatsunami, when Shizuhara and I looked at each other, Shizuhara had not threatened me. She had pleaded with me.

Please. I swear I won't hurt anyone but Nanamiya, so please let me go.

I had agreed, simply to protect my own image, but even though it had been my mistake which had ultimately cornered Shizuhara, she had kept her end of the promise up to the very last moment.

'I'm sorry. I can't become your assistant.'

I knew how desperate Hiruko had been to solve the murders, but I had deceived her and allowed Nanamiya to be killed. I had no right to be her Watson. I can still see her sad smile in my mind.

The bell rang as the doors of the café opened. The figure walking towards me was silhouetted against the bright sun outside. A mysterious, beautiful woman who appeared simultaneously adult and childlike.

'You're early. Have you been waiting a long time?'

'No, I only just arrived myself.'

I called the waitress over. Akechi was gone, but the Mystery Society still had two members.

'Shall we start then?'

'Yes. I asked an acquaintance to investigate the organisation, and this is his report.'

I will atone for my sins from now on.

THE END